THREE TALES BY THE BAY

THREE TALES BY THE BAY

ADAM C. KELLEY

Quailsong Press

Author's Note

There is no spelled out profanity and there are no descriptions of body parts or graphic descriptions of sexual activity in this book, but this is not juvenile fiction. I tried it out on a 13 year old and he put the book down. I tried it on an 18 year old and she liked it, and prefers it to other things I've written. Your mileage may vary.

There is some material (violence, extreme lifestyles) that people may object to, but mainly what makes it "mature" is the theme explored. Without the prospective of having managed relationships and watched social change over years, it may seem like one cringey thing after another. With that perspective, it should be a better experience.

Front Cover Art
by Amelia Cui

Back Cover Art
by Adam C. Kelley

Poems
"The Panther Woman" by Norah May French.
"The Ashes in the Sea" by George Sterling
"The Second Coming" by William Butler Yeats
"Canción de Jinete" by Federico García Lorca
          English translation by Adam C. Kelley

Published by Quailsong Press.

Three Tales by the Bay
Second Edition - @2023
Copyright @2016 by Adam C. Kelley

Contents

FARALLON 22ND-CENTURY

To those who struggle to be one.

With gratitude to family and friends who spent hours editing and
suggesting changes, especially Alta.

Bohemia 1907

One

I face the tranquil day with tranquil eyes
On high sea-hills my cheeks are cold with mist,
In white foam-fingers quick desire dies.

Dies as a strangled bird the wave has torn--
Ay, drowns and dies this winged desire of mine
In white sea fingers of the tidal morn.

But I would kill the restless silken night
And I would still the wings that beat the dark,
And grasp the little throat of heart-delight,

And drown the savage will that understands
How love would laugh to clasp your bending head,
How love would hold your face in her two hands,

How love would press your angry lips apart,
And leave the willful bruising of her kiss
In the sweet satin flesh above your heart.

Nora stroked her mare and admired it. Jimmy had already dismounted and was walking slowly along the beach. She rubbed the horse's nose, scratched it under the itchy bridle.

Jimmy was a boy. His wild clownish hair set off his face in a way that shouted boy. He loved to swim, and play ball and engage in foot races. He loved to travel. He loved riding horses, and he loved chasing girls, much to his wife's annoyance. Nora understood all of those things instantly and it was that boyishness she chose today.

The sea sparkled under the late autumn sun and on the bare skin of Jimmy's arms as he moved easily along the beach.

She let go of her horse and shoved Jimmy as she ran past him to the breakers. Jimmy chased after her. When he caught up to her she was standing ankle deep in the water, watching it wash over her feet. She looked up at him, smiled, splashed him and ran away again.

Jimmy pursued her but without hurry. They both knew how this would end.

When they were done playing with the breakers they stretched out under a tree overlooking the sea and Nora teased him about politics while they ate lunch. They argued with fervor but no conviction. Jimmy was quick witted, but Nora was quicker. She could tie him up in knots, then let him go just long enough to draw him in further.

That was all it took, Nora thought lazily. These quick witted ones were easy to play with, easier than the common plodding ones. Smile at them, and they thought you liked them. Look in their eyes, and they thought you were interested. Listen to and disagree with them, and they thought you were their brilliant match. Do those things and you could do as you pleased. She suppressed a smirk until the right moment to make him doubt her assessment of him and then let it peek through long enough to make him ardent. When she saw it she laughed out loud and he laughed too, relieved.

After lunch they lay quietly watching the ocean and, at moments, each other. She played with his feet and calf muscle with her toes. He had his shirt off, his eyes closed.

Nora's mind wandered. The horses picked among the weeds at the edge of the dunes. She remembered a photograph of horses lying dead in the street under the brick rubble of a wall after the great earthquake. She thought of the crumbled chimneys and cracked facades she had seen when she first arrived in San Francisco. She thought of Harry.

Harry.

She had arrived from Los Angeles by train with her sister Helen a little after the great earthquake. They picked their way through the shattered streets to the bungalow they would share on Lombard Street. Harry had offered it.

Harry called on her early, seemed eager to see her latest work. "Maybe we could publish something in the Argonaut," he had mentioned. They had enjoyed each other's letters. He was dashing, the opposite of the man lying next to her, but then not the exact opposite. The exact opposite would be Allen and yet not that either.

Harry made her smile. The early days were the best. She would get off work at the telephone exchange and they would go to the Coppa with his friends who quickly became her friends. They would eat, drink, sing, act, and most of all talk. The talk flowed fast. They were all of them shooting stars against a background of dull constellations and duller conversations, finding in each other the companionship they could not find with co-workers, wives, and lovers.

One night when George was with them he had defended something saying, "Surely all sensible people would agree," and Nora struck back, "I have an idea that all sensible people will be damned." The group burst into the laughter of admiration and Porter immediately wrote it on the wall next to their table signing it "Phyllis," Nora's nick-name.

She and Harry would often walk home together after the group broke up for the night. She noticed the way he watched her and felt it. She had missed it. Allen had looked at her that way, and more importantly, at one time that had mattered. She put the thought away.

The spring had been bright and sunny despite the damage to the city, but as the summer wore on the marine layer came in making the mornings gloomy.

The work at the exchange was gloomy too, only the brilliance of the evening company made up for it. When the men went away to the grove for the summer encampment it was even worse.

"Why shouldn't she come?" Gelett had said.

"Because she's a woman. No women at the encampment," Xavier said.

"Phyllis isn't a woman!" Gelett said.

Harry raised an eyebrow.

Nora watched him.

Gelett rose to defend his position. "Do we invite women to our gathering?"

"Occasionally," Xavier said.

"But only as guests," Porter pointed out.

"Except for Phyllis," Harry added obstinately.

"Ah, but we haven't yet determined if Phyllis is a man or a woman," Gelett pronounced.

"I think several of us have in fact determined that she is indeed a woman," said Harry.

"Fair enough," Nora said nodding.

"Well you may have, but I say she is no woman, so hear me out," Gelett commanded. "Why don't we invite women to our gatherings?" he continued.

"Because they would inhibit the conversation," George said.

"Precisely!" Gelett said. "When there are women present we can't speak freely. We have to add a level of decorum to our speech and leave out certain sensitive or technical topics. We can't discuss women, or relationships or all accord would be ruined by the strain the mere conversation puts on those relationships. We dare not discuss the technicalities of our writing for fear of shocking, or worse, boring them."

"We include Mary in our writing conversations," George objected.

"True," Gelett conceded "and yet although she comes to our parties we never invite her here. Why not?"

"Because she's a prude *and* a hypocrite," Herman said bluntly.

Gelett pointed at him, "Because she's a woman! So, I put it to you gentlemen. Does any man here feel like he has to hold anything back because Phyllis is present?"

"Sometimes I wish Phyllis would hold back a few things," Xavier said but while the others laughed they had to admit they didn't.

"Then I move," Gelett continued, "That we declare Phyllis to be not only a Man but a full brother in all our adventures."

"I'll second that," Jack shouted out.

"All in favor say 'aye'."

"Aye!" they all shouted in unison.

Nora laughed then bowed.

Gelett feigned a sudden regret and said, "Phyllis, does this mean no sex?"

Nora looked at him gravely and said, "For you, I'm afraid it does, unless one my brothers would like to take on the job."

Gelett looked to them with mock hope as each shrugged, shook his head, or mouthed "Sorry," then dejectedly left the room only to return to acclaim with a waiter carrying another round of drinks.

In the end it was deemed impractical to try to sneak Nora into the grove, and so began the dullest two weeks and three weekends of her whole stay in San Francisco. She went home each evening to Helen and listened to the radio. Once she went out with some of the girls from work, but the conversation was so weak that after fifteen minutes she said something wry, made an excuse, and went home.

She tried drinking to excess, but found the nausea unwelcome.

When the men came back one Monday evening she was eager to see them, but they seemed very dull from too many days talking together. The party broke up early and she and Harry went off to his house for a quick tryst before she returned home.

The months stretched on. There were days when Harry talked of divorcing his wife. She had been gone over a year, left him to go back east, but there was still the paperwork to do and Harry didn't relish the animosity that would flow from it. Nora only listened. She gave him no encouragement. She seemed to expect nothing.

Once she said to him, "Harry, we both like picking flowers, but have you ever planted any?"

Harry just shook his head and said, "I've never been much of a gardener."

"Maybe we should be gardeners," she said.

"Think of the dirt, and worms and perspiration." he said.

"Think of the fruit!" she responded.

But it was late and he was tired. "Oh, I'll pick some flowers up for you tomorrow if you want," he said.

Nora didn't answer him.

After a while he noticed her silence and said, "What's the matter, Phyllis? Have you become sentimental? Shall I write you a ballad? Shall I sing beneath your window?"

Nora smiled thinly and replied, "If you do, I may have to sue you at law. Not for my sake, mind you, but for the good of the neighborhood."

"That's very public minded of you," he responded.

"I live only to serve," she replied.

Harry smiled, "I knew you were still in there, Nora."

"Who's Nora? I'm Phyllis."

He gave her shove.

With Allen, it had been different. She had been younger, more earnest. She remembered the first time she saw him near the marina in Los Angeles. He was tan, confident and active. They had fallen into conversation easily. They became something of an item whenever he was down from Santa Cruz. When he came by yacht, he would take her sailing. He seldom spoke of his wife, but when he did it was with such pathos, that Nora loved him all the more. "We all need someone," he said one night. "I'm beginning to think it's you." Before she knew it they were engaged. The plan was set. He would divorce his wife and they would be married. He would be fair to his ex-wife, see that she had what she was owed and wouldn't have to worry. It would all be very modern, very enlightened. They could all be happy.

But Allen didn't come back right away. When she wrote to him, he responded obliquely that he wasn't sure exactly when business would bring him back to Los Angeles but that when it did he would be sure to call on her. She wrote again, passionately, but he didn't respond. When he came back by train the following week he explained that she needed to be more discreet. Things weren't settled with his wife yet, and if too much was said he wouldn't be able to settle it amicably. Nora relaxed. Things went back to normal, and then he was gone again. He wasn't gone too long. When he came back he brought the yacht and they sailed to Catalina.

The day at Catalina was perfect. Allen did no business. They lounged on the deck in the afternoon, then swam in the ocean as the sun went down. They lay out under the stars, Nora feeling the cool air blow across her body and then giving herself wholly to him, keeping nothing in reserve.

The next morning they had intended to explore Avalon, but the weather turned cool, and Allen thought it best they head back before any serious storms appeared. Nora stood on the fore-deck and tried to imagine the future in the spray of the ocean around her, but nothing came to her.

When they reached the Marina, there were messages waiting for Allen. He kissed her and said he had to go. She lingered on the yacht, but the marina made everything ugly. The stained ships, the twisted men that tended them for their owners, the ugly utilitarian buildings clustered around it, all made her want to go. When the wind shifted and the smell of rotting fish and shore trash reached her, she made up her mind and left.

At home she maintained a calm expression for her parents then went into the back yard and laid herself down under a tree. She watched its leaves wiggle in the sun and thought of her hiding place behind the old Ranch house before it burned down. It was on a hillside above the garden and she could see out over the fields of orange trees and beyond that catch a glimpse of the sea. It was her hidden fortress with branches reaching to the ground forming cave or pavilion that no adult disturbed. Often she hid there during her parents' garden parties, listening to the adults talk into the night. She imagined herself a spy gathering secrets, but often as not her mind glazed over and she fell asleep to the sound of the murmuring giants that kept her safe.

She remembered riding her horse through the hills, feeling the strong faithful animal move in time with her, feeling the land fall behind them at a gallop, knowing the world was as full of possibility as the sea was full of pearls.

Allen left for Santa Cruz the next afternoon without saying good-bye. He sent a note later that was as empty as all his letters were. "Why can't he write a real letter!" she fumed before deciding it didn't matter.

She attended drawing classes, and published poems in local magazines and newspapers. Her art friends were beginning to notice her, but although she never lacked for anything to say to them, she never knew how to connect, never knew which girls should be trusted and which would sell her for a bit of social advantage. Men were easier to understand.

When she saw Allen again a few weeks later he was in a thoughtful mood. He talked to her about his travels, about people he had known and missed, and about his time in the war. He was talking to her about old friends as if she were one of his old friends. She found herself angry with him. She stiffened a little, but he just rubbed her shoulders and seemed not to notice her mood. She fought off the impulse to scream at him and let the feeling subside. He never noticed.

After that she withdrew from him a little. She reserved a part of herself, for herself. That done, it was easier to see him in a comic light. She enjoyed their outings, but he was no longer the powerful man of business and action in her eyes. He was the sad middle-aged man of regrets, doting on a girl half his age. She grew to secretly despise him at times, but she didn't speak it, and it generally passed. If he knew what she thought, and a few times she thought he did, he didn't seem to care. She was with him and pleasant, and that was what seemed to matter.

In her more reflective moods she thought, "How can that be all that matters?" and her respect for him dimmed in those moments. In the fall she broke off the engagement, but a few months later he persuaded her to be engaged again. She didn't think much of it, not even enough to resent it. Not long after, her pen-pal Harry had offered the bungalow. Helen liked the idea immediately and convinced her father they should go together in the spring...

Jimmy was saying something to her and she was back under the tree with him. When she didn't respond he propped himself up on one elbow and watched her. He seemed to like what he saw because he smiled and watched all the longer. Finally she looked at him.

"You were far away," he said.

"Not so far," she said quietly then changed the mood by stroking his hair for a moment before pushing him face first into the sand and running for the horses. She made it to the edge of the forest above Carmel before he caught up with her, his horse vaguely spooked by all the sudden action. They rode on to the headlands and looked out over the sea, then back through the forest until they got to the stage where George liked to put on plays. The stage was rough-hewn and set in a fairy land of impossibly large trees, an opera house built without hands.

Jimmy started to speak, but Nora silenced him with a finger to her lips and when they had solemnly proceeded to the edge of the grove and stood in the shadows at its edge, she rewarded his obedience with a kiss, then rode off again towards the dunes. They watched the sun go down, then found a secluded spot among the dunes and completed the night naked under a full moon. When they were done he sprawled out looking up at the moon, satisfied. She looked at his clown hair and his silly smirk, and wondered if his wife could really love him, wondered if anyone could.

"I should go," she said.

Jimmy looked at her searching, but said nothing.

She nodded slightly and repeated, "I'm going."

"OK," he said, and watched her put her things back on until she wanted to hit him. She said nothing.

In the morning she got up early. She went out into the morning fog to a bluff above the ocean and watched the sun slowly push back the fog. The gray reminded her of days in San Francisco.

The glory of summer had faded. She had enjoyed her friends without commitment and almost without complication. The telephone strike had given her the break she needed to publish. The story didn't appear under her name, but even if Harry had touched it up a bit, it was hers and it got brief national attention. A few weeks later she realized she was pregnant with Harry's child. It wasn't a problem really. Nothing modern medicine couldn't solve, and George knew a doctor that could help. It was simple really.

Or rather if she ever told the story, it would be simple. The reality wasn't. The doctor's office was cheap and the doctor's big hands did their work without gentleness or pity. When it was over he patted her on the head with that same hand. She fought off the urge to hit him, then doubled over as cramps set in. When she finally made it home she curled up in a ball on her bed and cried silently.

Helen wasn't sure what was wrong. She sat by her, stroked her hair and didn't ask too many questions. After a few days she made herself strong, went back to work, and back to meeting with her friends. The men were a little subdued when she first appeared, watching her.

She shook her head at them and said, "I've been gone a week and you saps are still sitting here just the way I left you. I'm starting to wonder if you're only here because none of you can get a date."

"She's still Phyllis," Gelett said.

Jack got her a chair as the others made room.

Harry didn't say much.

Once it got going the evening was as bright as ever, except that towards the end Nora tired visibly.

"You should rest," George said, "Harry, take her home."

Nora started to say something, but George shook his head, and the others backed him up.

Harry and Nora walked the same streets they always did. Harry had little to say, and Nora let him be. The night was laced with fingers of fog, not thick enough to matter, but lingering. Half way home he reached for her hand and she took it. His hand was cold and hard in hers. She looked at him. He looked back at her, his eyes trying to speak, but he said nothing and looked away. She turned the collar up on her coat with her free hand. When they got to the steps of the bungalow he stood silently, thinking. He looked at her almost solemn, almost noble, something she hadn't seen in him before.

He stood for some time looking at her, then said, "Good night Phyllis. I'll see you tomorrow."

She looked at the ground and nodded, "Good night Apollo. See you tomorrow."

At the next meeting Phyllis was fully herself, in full command of her faculties. She was the bright light none of them could equal, and it went on that way for some time. She became if anything, more adventurous, and even some of her "brothers" benefitted.

After a few weeks, her strength seemed to weaken. She was writing less, and none of it was getting published. She was as witty as ever when she engaged, but she engaged less often. She became a brilliant flame that sometimes pushed back the grey evenings and sometimes died down to be absorbed by them.

She became reckless.

Whatever his feelings had been on other occasions, George turned paternalistic toward her.

"Come down to Carmel and stay with Carrie and me. It will do you good to get out of this broken City," he said.

Nora's mind flickered between that fatherly face, and the ardent focused face she had seen above her in George's studio on cool windy days when there was nothing else to do. Her mind tried to reconcile that they were the same face. It gave up. She smirked and accepted the invitation. That had been weeks ago.

The fog was gone from the sea now. She stood and went back to George and Carrie's house. The day had grown warm. A fly buzzed around the house. A dog with mournful brown eyes lay in the corner, watching. George had gone back to San Francisco the day before, so Nora and Carrie had the house to themselves. Nora was vaguely agitated. Carrie was half-heartedly working on a painting. She took a break and watched Nora idly. Carrie's face was passive with a hint of curiosity, but she said nothing and went back to painting.

In the afternoon, Jimmy came to see them, his clownish hair and freckled face filling the door frame. Nora ignored him, but he sat down anyway in the small kitchen and began a stream of pleasantries and small talk. It was lunch time. Carrie got out bread, meat, mayonnaise, and the rest of the fixings for lunch. Nora, suddenly energetic, was at Carrie's side.

"Let me," Nora said.

Carrie was surprised at the sudden offer, but relented and sat down while Nora made the sandwiches. When they were done, Nora picked up one of the sandwiches and brought it to Jimmy. She stopped a few feet from him at an awkward distance, her face flushed. She held out the sandwich to him, her hand shaking, "Here's your sandwich."

Jimmy hesitated, staring at her.

"Here's your sandwich," she repeated, her voice squeaking. Her hand shook and the sandwich fell on the floor. The dog grabbed it before anyone could stop him and ran outside with it. Nora ran to the back room.

Jimmy stood for a moment unsure what to do. Carrie motioned for him to leave, then went to check on her.

In the afternoon they found the dog dead in a pool of vomit under a tree by the kitchen. When word got back to Jimmy, he packed and left town.

Nora kept to her room and said nothing.

The next day she walked up to the point, sat under her tree and watched the sea change colors till the morning heat came on. She watched the shadow of the tree move, watched the edge of it creep towards her. She watched it carefully until the line between shadow and light reached the bottom of her shoes then pulled a pistol from the folds of her dress, put it to her head and pulled the trigger. A lock of hair fell in her lap as leaves showered from the tree above her. Her hands were still shaking as she put the pistol away, picked up the lock of hair and went to George and Carrie's house.

When she arrived she was light and gay. She showed Carrie the lock of hair, told her the story and laughed. Carrie wrinkled her forehead.

"What's the matter Carrie," Nora said, "Don't you see the humor in it?"

"No," Carrie admitted and Nora laughed again and fixed herself something to eat, saying nothing more about it.

In the morning she was calm. She made breakfast with Carrie and chatted amiably. After breakfast she sat on the front porch, listening to the waves crashing in the distance for an hour, smiling from time to time.

Carrie relaxed a little and went back to painting.

At midmorning Nora went out to her forest and walked through the trees face up to the dappled light filtering through the canopy. She spun like a little girl. She walked through the tall ferns dragging fingers through their fronds feeling each bump under the leaves dance across her fingers as she passed. She walked to the stables, stroked her favorite horse and fed her sugar cubes.

In the afternoon she strolled down to the pharmacy and asked for some powder to polish silver. "I've run out," she said with a shrug and a smile. The pharmacist looked at her for a moment then filled the order.

She hung around in the chairs by the post office, chatting with the authors who came to pick up their rejection letters, commiserating with them. When they wandered off to find dinner, she went to the beach and watched the sun go down. The clouds caught fire. She smiled, memorized the details until it faded to gray, then went back to George and Carrie's house. She sat on the porch again, listening to the distant waves.

Carrie sat down beside her.

"I'm glad you're feeling better," she said.

Nora smiled and hugged her.

When the stars came out, Carrie excused herself and went inside. Nora watched the stars for an hour, then content, went to bed.

In the stillness of 2:00 AM Carrie heard a sound.

"Nora?" she said.

"I'm getting a drink of water," Nora assured from the bathroom.

Carrie drifted back into a half dream but then awoke again to the sound of stillness.

"Nora?" she called.

Nora didn't answer. There was a moan from the direction of Nora's bed. Carrie lit a lamp and found Nora gasping in her bed, a glass of water on the table and an empty glass vial next to it. She called for the doctor and tried to clear the vomit from around Nora's mouth. Minutes passed. Nora stopped breathing. Carrie sat there with her and cried. More minutes passed. The doctor came. He took charge of the situation, gave orders to be obeyed. It didn't matter.

A few days later Allen, Harry, Jimmy, George, and Helen were at the mortuary. Allen picked forget-me-nots from the grave of a girl in the cemetery outside the mortuary and placed them on Nora's breast. The body was slid into the flames. They waited in silence for the fire to do its work.

A week later the whole tribe gathered at Point Lobos. George spoke.

Whither, with blue and pleading eyes,
Whither, with cheeks that held the light
Of winter's dawn in cloudless skies,
　　Evadne, was thy flight?
　Such as a sister's was thy brow;
Thy hair seemed fallen from the moon
　Part of its radiance, as now,
　　Of shifting tide and dune.
Did Autumn's grieving lure thee hence,
　Or silence ultimate beguile?"
Ever our things of consequence
　　Awakened but thy smile.
Is it with thee that ocean takes
　A stranger sorrow to its tone?
With thee the star of evening wakes
　　More beautiful, more lone?
　For wave and hill and sky betray
　A subtle tinge and touch of thee;
Thy shadow lingers in the day,
　　Thy voice in winds to be.
Beauty -- hast thou discovered her
　By deeper seas no moons control?
What stars have magic now to stir
　　Thy swift and willful soul?
　Or may thy heart no more forget
The grievous world that once was home,
That here, where love awaits thee yet,
　　Thou seemest yet to roam?
　For most, far-wandering, I guess
Thy witchery on the haunted mind,
　In valleys of thy loneliness,
　　Made clean with ocean's wind.
And most thy presence here seems told,

> A waif of elemental deeps,
> When, at its vigils unconsoled,
> Some night of winter weeps.

The crowd stood silent, huddled against the Pacific wind that even in November cut through layers of clothing.

Allen stepped forward and reached for the urn. Jimmy stopped him, insisted the right was his. Harry stopped Jimmy. George stepped in. Allen took a swing at Harry and missed. Jimmy tackled him before he could try again. Harry waded back into the fight.

The surprised group watched them struggle on the ground, until finally Carrie took the urn from the seawall and shook the ashes into the wind and sea.

The men stopped fighting.

She put the urn down.

Amazonia
21st-Century

One

Alex smelled star jasmine and then geranium. She focused her thoughts and saw a large moth flirting with a flower. She was still in her bathing suit from a day of playing in the cool tree covered creek behind the cottage, but here there was sun and the sidewalk warm beneath her feet and there were flowers and the moth. Her mother called. She turned to answer and opened her eyes.

She was sitting on the floor against a wall of what had been her fifth grade classroom. It was quiet. Somewhere a seagull called in distress. Somewhere there was a man's voice, but the sharpest sound was the breeze playing with a single piece of paper on the bulletin board. Except for the paper, the room was static chaos, nothing in its place and nothing moving. She did not yet know why she was sitting on the floor, or for how long. She did know the broken glass dusting everything looked like glitter in the afternoon sun and that except for the still forms she did not look at, she was alone.

Four miles away in his classroom Jonathan pushed through the rubble that covered him and stood, staring at nothing. After a moment he stepped around an overturned table, over a broken terrarium, and past a girl's back-pack into the hall. He paused, examining a drop of blood on the floor. It was still red and perfectly round. He saw another, then another forming a trail of small drops he followed to the front of the school, where he sat on the front steps and waited.

In a small theater on Castro Street, at 2:15 PM, on a late summer afternoon, when the haze had finally burned off, the world came to an end for San Francisco Supervisor Angela Steel. The nuclear holocaust she had portrayed in protests, and seen depicted in a hundred movies, with burning and radiation sickness didn't happen. What happened was a gale of supersonic glass followed by tsunami.

Angela, or Nancy Merris, if you prefer the name she was born with, was practicing her final show when the noise hit, the building shook, and the lights went out.

She helped her stage partner Raul, to his feet. Then they felt their way back-stage, changed out of their leathers and into street clothes.

She crossed the street to the firehouse, found the station chief and identified herself.

He looked up, distracted, finally recognized her and nodded, saying "You were just elected last week. What can I do for you?"

"I want to help," she said.

"You could monitor the situation on the radio from my office."

"No. I should be on site."

The chief reflected for a moment, spoke by radio to the incident commander, got her into proper gear, and sent her to the waterfront with one of the men.

As she picked her way through the rubble she thought, "I was supposed to be here."

The whole board of supervisors had been there except for her. It was scheduled as a "fact finding visit" but they were really just making nice before negotiating the city's next bond issuance. It should have been one of her first official duties, if she hadn't had that one last show.

They pulled twenty survivors from the wreckage, but only five survived. She didn't know whether to be surprised that there were so few or so many.

They never found the bodies of her fellow board members.

Five days after the end, the lost children of the City were housed in an older loft on Mission Street. Over the following days a few children were claimed. After the fourth day, no more parents came.

Jonathan lay awake in the dark listening to distant thunder. He could tell by the sound of their breathing that some of the younger children were awake too, and he was sure his new friend Alex, was awake.

He waited, hoping the rumbling would move on, but it grew closer.

Lightning flashed, intense, brilliant, finding its way through every crack in the boards covering the windows.

"No!" a toddler commanded in his sleep, but the thunder came anyway.

Jonathan heard Alex turn towards him.

"I'm awake," he whispered, before she said anything.

"If they get going we'll have to deal with Pinch Face," Alex said sleepily.

She was right of course, she often was.

"I'm on it," Jonathan said, and they got up quickly and smoothly.

Several other older children, as if on command, were also in motion.

They fanned out through the room speaking softly to the little ones. They were all awake now, some shivering. The fire had gone out. They herded them into a circle, huddled close together, and began softly singing funny songs.

The lightning and thunder grew brighter and louder until it finally resolved into heavy rain. The younger ones were soothed by its drumbeat, but Alex, Jonathan and the rest of the older kids exchanged glances and made sure none of the little ones touched the water leaking in around the edges of the windows.

They got the younger kids back to sleep in piles of two and three, in the center of the room. Pinch Face never came out of her office.

When the others were quiet Alex and Jonathan sat close and put their heads together.

"Were you dreaming about it?" Alex whispered.

Jonathan thought for a second and said, "No. Were you?"

Alex nodded, "The same one..."

"You never yell or anything in the night."

Alex shrugged, "I didn't yell when it happened."

Jonathan reflected and said, "I didn't either."

"Do you think it will happen again?" Alex asked.

Jonathan shook his head and said, "I don't know."

They looked at the little kids sleeping peacefully nearby.

"They don't understand." Jonathan said.

"No," Alex said, "I don't think they ever will. All they know is their moms and dads didn't come for them. Someday they'll figure out they never will."

They talked back and forth with long gaps until they slipped into sleep and then Jonathan was back on the steps waiting for his mom to come. He waited all night until he woke up.

In the morning Pinch Face brought them a box full of canned food. The cans had symbols on the labels and no words, but they recognized the pictures. Alex, Jonathan, and the other big kids; Fat Jimmy and the twins - Shawna and Malcom, got the little ones organized, opened the cans and distributed the food.

Jonathan examined the cans. They had gotten wet and been dried out so the labels were faded and wrinkly. That meant they must have come from the flooded area, from the tsunami parts of the City.

"It's Chinese," Fat Jimmy said.

"Oh," Jonathan said.

"They were on a ship heading for China when the bombs went off and the tsunami flipped the ship and a bunch of the containers washed up in the old baseball stadium."

"How do you know?"

"I heard Pinch Face and the Queen Bee talking. They found a lot. We're going to be OK."

Two

Pinch Face, or Peggy Connor, was in Angela's new office complaining.

"How much longer do you want me to watch them?"

"Just until the emergency is passed, then we'll find places for them," Angela said.

Peggy sighed, "I'm not good with kids. I'm really not."

"How are you at moving canned goods and water, or clearing debris out of buildings?" Angela countered.

Peggy sighed again. "They're kind of awful. Do you know what they call you?"

Angela smiled, "Yes, they call me the 'Queen Bee'. Do you know what they call you?"

"No. What?" Peggy asked.

"It doesn't matter. They're just kids. It doesn't matter if they like us," Angela answered.

"I guess not," Peggy said. "Just try to get someone to spell me off as soon as you can spare them."

"I will," Angela lied reassuringly.

"Thanks."

When Peggy left, Angela locked the door and stood at her window. The window was a luxury. There wasn't much unbroken glass in the city, but her new office had some. She looked out over the wreckage.

The financial district was a forest of broken buildings, the shorter ones rubble, the taller ones stripped of their outer envelopes and left naked to the elements.

Weeks passed. They expected help from the outside world every day, but it didn't come. No help. No communications from the outside. After two weeks she had sent teams down each remaining major road out of town. They all came back in less than two days and all of them died within a month, one of injuries he sustained on the road, the rest from radiation sickness.

She looked out her window thinking. The shattered water front and beyond that the blackened waste land of Oakland, gave no answers. She turned back to her desk.

The food distribution was not going well. The first shock of the disaster had worn off, and generosity was turning to long term self-interest, which meant that food was starting to disappear before it made it to the distribution warehouses.

She suspected the fire fighters and police each had a stash, but they were too powerful to challenge directly, and if the collection of cans she had hidden in her own wall was any indication, then almost every-one involved in salvage had spirited some away. Still it had to stop. If people in general realized what was going on, there would be fighting.

She rolled the problem over in her head most of the afternoon and finally decided on something symbolic rather than confrontational. She would hold an election.

The election would be ten days from the announcement. To main-tain continuity during the crisis she would stay in office for another year until the next election and would move to mayor. A new board of supervisors would be elected.

Looking at the map, the old geographies no longer made sense. Half of her own district had been physically destroyed, and far more than half its people. Five other districts no longer existed. In fact even having a Board at all probably wasn't necessary since the total number of survivors was less than what had been in her original district. The more she looked at the map, the less the old seats seemed rational. She considered the map looking for new districts, and then stopped.

Power in the city had never been truly geographic. The old geog-raphies had been drawn and redrawn repeatedly over the years to make them reflect various interests. Now it was no longer necessary to have any pretense of geography. They would simply have seats for each interest. There would be a seat for the Police, a seat for the Fire Department... no, one seat for both, call it "Public Safety;" a seat for what was left of the business community, finance was gone..., one for medical, a seat for lesbians, a seat for gay men, a seat for the transgender, a seat for parents with kids in school, a seat for the arts community, a seat for racial minorities. Each person would choose which interest group they wanted to represent them and vote in that election. It would be simpler, more honest.

The day the election was announced was bright. Something returned that had faded over the previous weeks. There was a lot of discussion. No one objected to the basic format but there was some argument about the specific groups. The Police and the Fire Department each wanted their own groups. The single straights wanted their own group. The gender fluid claimed a group.

"As Mayor I will represent the gender fluid," Angela said and the room quieted, "I'm one of you, and you can still join one of the other groups." It turned out that most of the single straights who were objecting were also athletic, so Angela proposed and they accepted an athletics group.

The Police and Fire were trickier. Angela could count on the grudging support of the Fire Chief, if she didn't push him too far, and there were more firefighters left than Police. The Police Chief, Carol Scott, was another matter. She was ultra butch, and had seemed dismissive if not openly hostile whenever Angela met with her... and she had all the guns.

After a pause, Angela said, "I think it's very important the views of the Police and Fire Departments be fully represented. I think we can do better than creating another seat. I propose that the deputy Mayor be selected from among the members of the Police department. The board of supervisors is more of a legislative body, and the Police properly belong in the executive branch anyway. The Police would still be represented by the public safety supervisor and the deputy Mayor would of course attend and participate in all board discussions as a non-voting member."

"Who would do the selecting?" the Police Chief asked.

Angela spread her arms wide, smiled, and said, "The people, of course."

A murmur of assent rippled through the room. The Police Chief glanced from face to face trying to gauge the mood, something she was not particularly good at, then suddenly brightened and said loudly, "Sounds about right."

Angela smiled, and said, "OK. The seats are Public safety, Business, Medical, Lesbians, Gay men, Transgender, Parents, Arts, Racial Minorities, and Athletics. I will serve as Mayor until the next election, and we will elect a Deputy Mayor from among the members of the Police department. You will have three days to register as a member of an interest group, then candidates will have three days after that to register for election. The election will be in ten days. All in favor say 'Aye'."

"Aye!" the room shouted in unison.

"All opposed say 'Nay'."

"Nay!" said a single old female voice from the back of the room.

Angela faltered, clearly surprised, but continued, "It appears the 'Ayes' have it. The election is set."

The crowd cheered. Raul announced he was opening the bar down the street in celebration. The crowd approved. The owners of the bar had been dead for weeks, so they didn't object.

The crowd thinned quickly, groups splitting off. As Angela came down from her podium and crossed the room the old voice that said "nay" was suddenly standing in her path. Angela looked at her, surprised. The midmorning light was harsh, cold. It darkened the shadows in the old woman's wrinkles, making them stand out, making her seem hideous.

"Why are you doing this?" the old woman said.

Angela looked at her trying to place her, trying to understand, before finally saying. "Doing what?"

"You are setting up a government that will end in misery. Why?"

"I'm just trying to make sure the people have a voice in their new government."

"You are clinging to power and you don't even know it. You're the only one who can undo this. If you don't undo this it will destroy us all. It will destroy you."

Angela stared at the woman. "Who are you?"

"I'm Senator Floriston. I was the Majority leader of the US Senate for three years when you were still too little to walk, let alone pole dance."

Angela placed her then. She was the crazy lady that used to haunt the coffee shop in the lobby of the Board of Supervisors' building. She would try to get supervisors to have coffee with her and if they did she filled their ears with all manner of hate speech. She was an old school bigot. It was a mistake no supervisor made twice, and she had taken a good deal of teasing from the other board members when she fell for it on her second day.

"I was never a pole dancer," Angela said, "and you were never a Senator, ma'am."

"Close enough, and yes, I was a Senator."

Angela checked herself. Arguing with the mentally ill was pointless. "I'm sorry. I'm sure you were an excellent Senator. Is there anything I can do to help you? Do you have adequate housing and food?"

"Don't patronize me! This is important. You are violating the very principles of government that keep large states, let alone small polities from spinning into chaos."

Angela rolled her eyes reflexively. "I have to go," she said and retreated to her office. The old woman continued to yell at her until she was inside, and possibly longer for all Angela knew.

"Maybe it will be good to have a Police officer as Deputy Mayor after all," she thought.

She relaxed into her chair. "I'll have to see if the doctor can do anything for her," she mused aloud, then poured herself a drink and sat back to watch the sun sparkle on the bay.

Three

Pinch Face wasn't in a good mood.

"#$%&* kids," she said right in front of them.

"What's eating her?" Johnathan said.

"Simple," said Fat Jimmy. "She has to be here while the doctor examines us, which means she can't go to the first meeting of the Lesbian District."

"So?" John said, "I wouldn't care if I missed a meeting. I hate meetings."

"You'd care if you wanted them to elect you to their seat," Alex said.

Pinch Face seemed to hear something Alex said and was staring at her, swearing softly. They decided to move back to where the doctor was examining the little kids.

Jonathan was suddenly animated, "How long are they going to keep us here?!"

"None of the families will take us until they know we aren't sick with something that will kill their kids," Fat Jimmy said while punching a new whole in his belt.

Jonathan grunted comprehension.

"You three are next," the doctor said.

The old loft they were in wasn't exactly a doctor's office. Mercifully, the little kids' examinations were over and they had mostly moved into the next room to play. The doctor took their temperatures, examined their throats and noses, looked at their finger nails, took their blood pressure, and asked them a lot of questions. Then one by one he gestured for them to go behind a sheet he'd rigged up and take off their clothes.

Jonathan could hear the others outside of the sheet. They were fidgeting but they weren't saying anything. When the examination was done he got dressed and came out from behind the sheet. He couldn't look at Alex. He glanced at Fat Jimmy who kind of smirked at him until it was his turn to go. Then Jonathan smirked at him until he realized that left him alone with Alex on the bench. They didn't say anything until Fat Jimmy can bounding out from behind the sheet and took a theatrical bow then they both laughed. The doctor looked up from his clipboard, looked at the three of them and at the sheet, then shook his head smiling. "Why don't you boys go in the other room. Alex will join you in a minute." Fat Jimmy lingered until Jonathan hit him and they both left, slightly relieved.

When Alex joined them a few minutes later, she said, "We all passed, so we can get out of here soon."

Dr. Abbott packed up his things, said his goodbyes, and began walking back to his office. The sun on his shoulders felt good and for a moment he relaxed. There were moments he could forget all that had happened, and be almost normal, but then some small detail would bring it all back. On this walk it was company ID badge lying in the road. He looked at it, saw a picture and a name. It was no one he knew. He moved on, and tried to keep his thoughts in the present, but the past came anyway.

He had been on the west side of the hospital when it hit. The whole building rocked and shattered. At first he tried to believe it was an earthquake. In the earie quiet that preceded the shouting and moaning, he turned the corner and surveyed the scene. The building was open to the sky on three sides and both patients and medical staff where down. Without discussion, those able to converged on the east side. At first they pulled out the least injured and most likely to survive, but as they realized the scale of the disaster, they began, as one, to give priority to fellow staff and some of the children.

He wanted to believe it had been a rational decision to save those that had the most life left to live, and those that could help save others, but he didn't remember thinking that, so he didn't know.

They were out of blood in half an hour, out of saline solution in an hour, and out of everything else soon after. Some of the maintenance staff went to the warehouse to see what they get, but hours later they came back and just shook their heads.

Towards the end of the first day he heard that his own family had survived, and only then realized it had been worrying him. After another 30 hours he got sustained sleep. But in his dreams he endlessly stitched and sewed and bandaged, and chose who to save and who to let go, so when he woke to pale morning light real work was a relief.

And now the streets were quiet, and the sun was shining, and at the end of the day he would go home to his family, and no one would pick up the ID lying in the road, and he would forget again for a while.

Four

Raul hadn't started out as a performer. He'd started out as a bartender and at the moment those skills were more useful. The moment the election was announced he knew he had to run for a seat. He didn't particularly care which seat, so it was just a matter of choosing one he could win. He had been surprised when his old stage partner had nixed the most obvious seat for him, a gender fluid seat, but it didn't slow him down. He had no children that he knew of. He wasn't in the medical community, or public safety. He wasn't part of the business community. He wasn't transgender, or a lesbian, despite what some of his gay friends said about him when they wanted to give him a bad time. There was no way the athletes would vote for him.

He was a racial minority, at least partially, but the competition there would be fierce and probably ugly, and the African Americans in particular wouldn't care for some of his other characteristics.

That left the Arts seat, and the Gay Men's seat. He wasn't exactly Gay, though he could be Gay enough if it suited him. Some of the purists wouldn't vote for him. He was an artist, but looking across the crowd after the announcement he was pretty sure the artists he saw wouldn't vote for him. They all took their art very seriously and they quietly resented his kind of art being classified with theirs. Even Angela had the sense not to publicly refer to herself as an artist.

The decision made, he set to work the moment the vote was over and the election was in motion. He called out to his gay friends and invited them to the bar.

The atmosphere at the bar was warm and convivial. He kept the drinks flowing as though another truck load of bottles would arrive tomorrow. He kept the banter going. A group of men fetched their instruments and started playing music. When he judged that the buzz was just right, he down behind the bar, pulled off his shirt, put on a bow tie and jumped up on the bar flexing just enough to make every muscle ripple.

It was a bold move, he knew. It could sink his chances if it went wrong. The men with the instruments were in a good mood and went with it, starting to play an old burlesque stripper song flamboyantly. Suddenly Raul had company on the bar top playing along. A good natured chuckle spread through the crowd, but by the time they'd finished their number and Raul, still shirtless, was back to serving drinks and accepting compliments, the mood had begun to turn wistful, and then, at least for a few of them, into something hungrier. As the evening wore on, Raul politely and affectionately declined a few offers, waiting for the ones he knew would count, and those came eventually but he made sure the understandings were discrete to avoid offending the others.

Five

Fat Jimmy had a problem. Alex and Jonathan were acting weird. Ordinarily he wouldn't have cared, but they needed to get the little kids in line before the potential parents arrived, and before Pinch Face made them cry. Fat Jimmy understood the need, but he didn't have the same touch with the little ones that Alex and Jonathan had. Even if he had, he couldn't handle all of them. The littlest ones were taking their clothes off faster than he could get the others dressed, and breakfast was late. Alex was moody, and Jonathan wouldn't look at her. It had been that way all morning ever since he got up and saw them talking to each other. They were talking about something with kind of an edge in their voices and then they saw that he was awake and stopped talking. Now they wouldn't talk to each other at all and were just sulking.

Jimmy gave up trying to dress a particularly squirmy two year old and walked over to them.

"I don't know what's going on with you, but these kids need to be dressed and fed and run around a little." Jonathan glanced at Alex. Alex kept hers eyes fixed on Fat Jimmy.

"Come on," Jonathan said.

Alex rolled her eyes and said, "OK."

"I'll go find out what happened to breakfast," Fat Jimmy said and left as Alex and Jonathan started moving toward the little ones, making a hissing sound that always got their attention.

He went into the room where Pinch Face hid to see if the food was there. It was. She was picking through it, looking for the good stuff. Fat Jimmy shuffled his feet to make a sound.

"Good, you're finally here," she said, slightly startled. "Get this stuff into the other room and get the kids fed."

"Yes ma'am," Fat Jimmy said with just enough mock seriousness to irritate her but not set her off. By the time he'd moved all of the food, Alex and Jonathan had the kids mostly dressed and lining up singing some annoying song about the food train. The slightly older ones refused to sing, but they got in line.

By the time perspective parents started arriving everyone was fed and the last of the kids were falling down, dizzy from running in circles or spinning. Fat Jimmy got the quieter games out to keep them busy while the parents looked around.

The Queen Bee made an appearance, then went into the office with Pinch Face. The first parents that arrived didn't seem to know what to do. They waited in the front room for a while before starting to wander around the big room. The next set did the same thing, but didn't wait as long. Fat Jimmy watched them fascinated. It was interesting to see them following the same pattern, even though they were all very different. Most of the parents that came were in pairs, although as Jimmy watched the uncertainty between some of them he wondered how long they had been together. There was one group of five women that had banded together. Each group or person hesitated before going in, then they watched the kids, and then they tried to talk to a few.

One woman started to approach a blond one year old, but then sat on the floor and cried. She put her hand over her mouth and muttered, "I'm sorry, I'm sorry, I'm sorry." Her hesitant partner came and put his hand on her shoulder. She grabbed it and held on to it.

All of the kids stopped and looked at her. Some of the little ones started crying. The woman tried to pull herself together, but that just made it worse. Some of the other little kids nearest her came and made a circle around her, touching her softly, patting her. She fell apart again.

The Queen Bee came out of the office with Pinch Face behind her.

Pinch Face started shaking her head and moved towards the woman. The older kids moved towards Pinch Face, slowly, but timed to place themselves between Pinch Face and the woman before she got too close. The woman had mostly quieted by the time Pinch Face reached her.

"Let's try to pull it together, honey," Pinch Face said, "You're upsetting the children."

The woman nodded assent and looked at the ones standing closest and said, "Thank you."

She looked away from them quickly then. Her partner waited, awkwardly. They walked to the front room. Fat Jimmy sat just outside the doorway and listened. He couldn't hear them when they talked low, but he heard enough to piece the conversation together.

She said something about "All of them," in a kind of shrill voice.

He said something with "feed the two we have" in a low tight voice.

"I know, I know..." she trailed off. "Maybe two?" she said hopefully and later more upset she said "I had three of my own," and he muttered something meant to be reassuring. In the end they left with just the little blond girl she had seen first.

At first the little kids didn't seem to notice the other kids leaving but as there were fewer and fewer around they began to watch more closely. When it became obvious the parents were mostly going for the younger kids, the older ones started to get sullen, which didn't help their chances any.

By the time the Queen Bee left, Pinch Face was obviously irritated. There were still ten kids left, including most of the older kids. "Clean this mess up, she shouted at no one in particularly and locked herself in her office.

Angela hit the street. By the next day she had placed three of the boys with the Fire Department, and two girls with the parks and maintenance department. The five remaining kids, Alex, Jonathan, Jimmy, Shawna, and Malcom were old enough to almost take care of themselves. Angela had them moved into the building where her new office was and set them up in a couple of the rooms there.

Pinch Face was finally free, though Angela still owed her a favor.

Six

The day of the election was a golden late fall day in the City. The air was crisp and clear, without a hint of fog. A rain shower the day before had washed the streets clean. The candidates stood just beyond the limit line outside the polling stations and greeted people. The polling was complete by noon and counted by 2:00 PM, then Angela announced the winners.

It was all so much more calm and quick than in the old days. There were speeches until 3:30 PM, and then the part most people had been waiting for began, the parade. Some of the music was not as good as in the old days, but the floats were, if anything, better. People had put a lot of effort into them, and there were plenty of materials to choose from in the washed out parts of the city. Some were even equipped with bicycle generators that lit up the floats and added sparkle as the evening came on. There was a little less naughtiness than usual, a little more joy in being alive. People seemed to exhale and breathe after months holding their collective breath.

At the closing ceremony, under a rising moon Angela spoke with the new board of supervisors standing behind her.

"Citizens of San Francisco, my people, we stand here today at the beginning of a new order of things. We have all lost much, and many that we loved, but within that loss is the opportunity for something new, maybe in time something better. I feel the potential lingering over us. Do you feel that potential?"

The crowd rumbled in the affirmative.

"So, I propose, and tomorrow at our first meeting I'll ask the board to approve a new name, not for the city, but for the new order that we are building. As all of us are different in our own ways but united as one people, I propose that we be known as 'The Rainbow Republic'."

The crowd roared its approval. The members of the board looked at one another trying to gauge each other's thoughts, then looked back at Angela, then seemed to relax.

Angela finished with, "Tomorrow we get down to business, but tonight we have fun."

A band started playing. The partying went late. In the morning there were still a few hold-outs sleeping under blankets around the square.

Mid-morning the new board assembled in the building Angela's office was in.

The Fire Chief was there representing Public Safety.

Dr. Abbot was representing Medical.

Raul was representing Gay Men.

Mia Fong, Carol Scott's on again off again partner was representing the Lesbians.

Don Brannan represented the Business Community.

Virginia Cost was there for the Transgender Community.

Erika Norton had been elected by the Parents.

Sarah Michaels sat for the Racial Minorities.

Wally Andon represented the Arts Community.

Barry Mays represented the Athletic community.

And Carol Scott, the Police Chief, rounded out the group as the Deputy Mayor.

The board spent the first twenty minutes chatting and sizing one another up. They took a few symbolic votes, ratifying the name of the government, appropriating and naming the building they were in as the new City Hall. Then they separated.

The next time they met, they each gave status reports for their communities and discussed priorities. When Dr. Abbot's turn came, he said,

"Our biggest problem is that we don't really have a functioning hospital and we are out of supplies. The generators are still functioning but we don't dare run them for more than a few hours a week because we have no source for new diesel. Similarly, we are out of all consumable medical supplies except some syringes we saved and sterilized, some sutures and bandages we were able to dig out of the rubble of our old supply warehouse, and a motley collection of little used medications.

We also have a limited supply of the antiviral drugs we'd bought in bulk that happened to arrive just before the disaster. With our reduced population the antivirals will last about a year, but there can't be any new cases. Any new cases will cause us to run out sooner.

Other than the electrical power issue, we feel our most pressing need is to develop a process for manufacturing our own saline solution. We should be able to make it out of sea water, and it will be useful in cases where there is blood loss or diarrhea, and we expect those situations will be more common now.

Our next priority will be to develop some sort of antibiotic out of fungus cultures or sulphur compounds, or both. It won't exactly be FDA approved, and there will be some risk in using it, but I think we will be glad to have it.

We think those three initiatives will fully occupy us for the next several months and we would appreciate any support the board can give."

The Fire Chief said, "We still have some diesel but without it our firefighting equipment is useless. Also, we are still using the trucks to clear streets and get into collapsed buildings that hold critical supplies."

Virginia from Transgender said, "Didn't they install solar panels all over the old City Hall? They were installed lots of other places too."

"Yes," Dr. Abbot said. "The hospital has some too, but they don't seem to work when there is no main power."

"Doesn't the hospital have some battery back-up power?" the Fire Chief asked.

"Yes, but we have to run the generators to charge them, so same problem," Dr. Abbot said.

"We can use the panels to charge the batteries, if we use power from the batteries to trick them into turning on," Wally from Arts said.

The Fire Chief nodded agreement.

"Isn't that kind of circular?" the doctor asked.

"Not really," the Fire Chief said. "You can charge up the batteries the first time with the generators, then create what looks like main grid power using the batteries and inverters, and the solar panels will think the grid is back. Then they will come on and keep the batteries topped off. We'll just have to make sure we have a way to shut off the panels if the batteries are full and the voltage climbs too high. I'll get some of the guys from public works to come over and change the wiring."

"Great!" Angela said.

"We may need to pull more panels from other buildings," Wally said.

Next they discussed making saline solution, but Raul interrupted.

"Before we just accept that saline and antibiotics, both worthy projects, are next, there are other medications that might be higher priority," he said.

The board quieted and listened. "Many members of my community need the antiviral drugs or they could die, pretty horribly too. If we can't make a new batch of antivirals before we run out, we will be back to the pre-medication days. I think an actual threat of death needs to be dealt with before a potential threat like a future accident or a future disease outbreak."

The doctor hesitated. "We don't have the technology, or the industrial base to synthesize the types of drugs, and there are several types, in the antiviral cocktail."

"So, what are you proposing? Are you suggesting that we just let a large portion of my community die? Are you sentencing them to death?" Raul said.

"I'm not sentencing anyone to anything. My staff and I are simply unable to come up with any way to make the medication," the doctor said.

"But you can make saline solution. You can make antibiotics."

"We can probably make saline solution and we might be able to make antibiotics."

"Then why can't you make the medications that my community needs?"

"Because saline solution and antibiotics can be made with 1940's technology and that's about all we can recreate. Antivirals require late 20th or early 21st century technology and that's just gone."

"It's not like you have to reinvent it. You still have the old research. You still have the formulas or something."

"Actually we don't. We have what we carry in our heads. We have a few articles we've managed to save. We have the chemical structures written out on the prescription information slips packaged with the drugs but we don't have access to most of the information. Even if we did we would need to set up a fully functional pharmaceutical factory. That's not something we can do right away. I think we need to concentrate on the basics first."

"What is more basic than human life?" Raul asked.

"By basic, I mean we have to focus on small measures that will help lots of people, and that we have a reasonable chance of pulling off. I'd love to have a pharmaceutical factory but I don't believe we could actually build one in time to prevent even one death, and if we try, we doom anyone that we might have saved if we hadn't wasted our time and resources. We simply aren't able to do it."

"I can't accept that," Raul said.

Doctor Abbot sighed, "I don't like it either, but what would you have us do?"

"We could try!" Raul said.

"The sewage treatment system has been off-line for over a month. How long before dysentery breaks out and we watch babies and old people drop like flies when we could have saved them with simple salty water?" the doctor said.

"My constituents aren't going to like this," Raul relented.

"Public works is trying to at least get the sewage to dump into the bay instead of backing up. I'll find out how far they've gotten," the Fire Chief said.

"Shall we move on to the saline solution discussion?" Angela asked.

There was a pause. Erika of the Parents cleared her throat and asked, "Are there any oral contraceptives left?"

The doctor ran his fingers through his hair. "A few... not enough."

"Any chance we could make those?" Erika added a bit sheepishly.

"Don't be ashamed Erika, we'd like to know too," Mia said.

"Us too," said Barry.

"Yeah," said Sarah.

"Don't forget us!" Wally chimed in.

"Maybe," the doctor said, "I don't think we could synthesize it, but we might eventually be able to get the hormones from animal sources. Even then I don't know if we could get it into any sort of convenient delivery system like pills. It's not something we should even discuss for at least a year."

"What do we do in the meantime? This isn't exactly the kind of world we want to bring children into," Erika said.

"I'm sure we can all figure something out," the doctor said. "But eventually we will have to start having children again or we'll die out. I'm not saying today, but none of us are getting any younger and older pregnancies are more likely to be complicated."

"We found a couple of pallets of condoms," Raul offered. "We can share some of them."

Angela spoke up. "I propose we do the saline solution first, then the birth-control, then the anti-biotics, then the antivirals."

The doctor shook his head. "Saline, antibiotics, and then we discuss it again."

"Do you want power for your hospital?" Carol said.

"Of course."

"I'd suggest you do what a clear majority of the board wants."

"It's not going to ..."

Carol looked at him hard.

Angela said, "Let's put it to a vote."

The vote wasn't even close. Public safety and Transgender voted with Medical, but the rest voted with Angela.

Seven

Early fall gave way to the rainy season and the band that played most weekend evenings moved indoors.

Public Works got water restored to part of the Castro, and got the sewer to flow to the bay, which lead to The Great Toilet Flushing Party of December.

The hospital got enough power back to run an operating suite, two exam rooms, a lab, and some computers in records, at least on sunny weeks. Other weeks, they had to prioritize.

Food was becoming a problem. There were still enough canned foods to keep away hunger, but the supplies were disappearing faster than they should have. The scavenger teams were moving farther up and down the shore looking for shipwrecks than before, but a growing realization that the food wouldn't last forever was spreading, and perhaps not coincidently, fewer food finds were reported.

The board met right after Christmas to come to discuss the plan.

The Fire Department and the business community proposed creating a fishing fleet. Several of the old piers were still usable with repairs and there were a handful of pleasure boats and even a couple of real fishing boats that had washed up in the financial district. With help from Public Works and the Fire Department they had already moved one into a make shift dry dock for repairs.

The Arts community had been considering what could be done with Golden Gate Park. Most of the glass on the east side of the green house at the Flower Conservancy had been damaged but they could close off half of it to grow food in the other half.

"We could grow potatoes in the botanical gardens next to the marijuana farm and in the meadow too," the Athletics offered.

A plan began to emerge and by evening it had been accepted.

By early March, vegetables were growing in the green house and soil preparation had started in the botanical garden and meadows.

The canned food supply was shrinking. A small team was sent across the bay in the first repaired boat to scout along the coasts of Oakland, Berkeley, Richmond, San Rafael, Tiburon, and Sausalito. Oakland, Berkeley and Richmond were waste lands, burned in the fire. There appeared to be motion in San Rafael, and a plume of black-smoke rose near the ruins of the bridge.

The water fronts in Tiburon and Sausalito were simply erased. There were buildings still standing somewhere beyond, but no signs of motion. They did not go ashore anywhere, and there did not appear to be anything salvageable along the shorelines.

The first four boats of the new fishing fleet were ready the last week of March. Carol decided to go out with them. They sailed beyond the ruins of the golden gate bridge and went due west , then north a little trying to find fish with as little contamination as possible. They let down their nets and drifted for an hour. When they brought the nets up there were only a few dozen fish, and worse, the homemade nets were torn and failing. They started for home, but the wind failed and they were forced to wait. When the wind picked up again, it was late. They barely made it back to port before dark.

The next day while the nets were reworked, Carol and some of the Police department decided to try collecting shellfish. The doctor had said shellfish were a bad idea, that they would concentrate the radioactive particles in the water. But they had been talking about shellfish in the bay. It occurred to Carol that the shellfish at Ocean Beach on the Pacific side might be OK. They brought a Geiger counter from the emergency cache with them and made a day of it.

They moved down the beach checking different batches of mussels until they found a patch that wasn't too "clicky."

Working together they harvested three gunnysacks full.

They made a big fire and roasted the shellfish as the sun went down. For a moment they forgot. They forgot it all. They were just on the beach. There was laughter, and hunger as the smell of something not from a can began to fill their noses. A thin cat wandered down from the highway and sat watching them.

They began dancing around the fire. They danced and sang until the mussels started popping open and then they gathered around eagerly. Someone bumped the roasting rock and the mussels all fell into the fire except one that the cat snagged and ran off with. The mussels were ruined. The offending officer was given a good razzing, but it came out harsher than anyone intended.

The fire was still hot. They tried again. This time they were more careful. The cat came back, watching them with intense eyes. Carol regarded the cat and thought they should make a few extra for it. Then she looked across the breakers watching the moonlight reflecting unevenly across its choppy surface. After an eternity the new batch of mussels began popping open. Carol reached for one of the larger ones, lifted the shell to her lips and one of her officers slapped it out of her hands. She rounded on her ready for a fight, but the officer pointed at the cat. It was twitching and thrashing.

"Forget radiation, that's shellfish poisoning. These mussels are no good," she said.

Carol relaxed. The others threw their mussels into the fire, then sat around the fire morose for several minutes, occasional glancing at the burlap sacks full of their labor.

"What do you want to do with those?" one of the men asked.

Carol was thoughtful for a moment then said, "Let's bring them back with us. We can clean up the shells and trade them or something."

The group shrugged and walked home, lugging the bags with them.

The next day Carol got up early, careful not to disturb Mia, and began steaming mussels in the kitchen. She watched the little curls of steam leak out of the shells and float around the kitchen. She was fairly certain that not all of the mussels were toxic, but there was only one way to know which ones were, and the cat at the beach had given her the key.

The City was full of feral cats. There were also a few packs of dogs that had taken up residence in certain areas, but the cats were every-where. As they had on other mornings, they began to appear around the balcony she used as a cooking area, waiting for what they could steal. Carol carefully cut each mussel in half and fed half to a different cat, keeping track, then waited. If the cat showed any symptoms the mussel went into one bowl. If it didn't, it went into the other. After a couple of hours Mia came out onto the balcony and hugged Carol from behind.

"What are you up to?"

Carol hesitated then said, "Just trying to figure out if these mussels are any good."

"Ummm!" Mia said reaching for one of the bowls, "Something fresh."

Carol took the bowl away from her.

"Can't I have some?" Mia asked.

"No. I'm still working on it."

Mia went inside disappointed.

Carol looked at the cats in the street below and regarded the seven that were dying. She didn't hate the cats. For the most part they did the city a service, but as was obvious from the five living ones, there were just too many. These seven would serve the City more than most.

<h1 style="text-align:center">Eight</h1>

Angela liked to stop by the kids' apartments on the way to her office most mornings. To keep them out of trouble she was employing them as pages, and now that phones weren't working and people didn't always monitor the radio, pages were actually useful. The kids seemed to be getting something out of it too. They were certainly meeting all the right people.

When she stopped by that morning they were busy enjoying a new heating system they had assembled. Angela observed it warily. There had already been two carbon monoxide deaths since the weather turned cold. The venting was OK, but its chief safety feature was that they were using Raul's seaweed alcohol as the fuel. They had even drilled a hole in the wall and put the storage tank outside to keep it well away from the flame box.

"How do you get the alcohol?" Angela asked.

"We get a percentage of the load from the hospital when we deliver it for Raul," Alex said.

"Smart!" Angela said.

"Fat Jimmy heard there was a problem with delivery. Jonathan figured out how much alcohol we needed and how much Raul would part with. Malcom and Shawna wrote up the contract and found the wagon. All I had to do was make the deal and take my turn hauling the wagon," Alex explained.

"You're a good team," Angela said, and she meant it.

They were gaining all of the skills the next generation of leaders would need, and Angela was beginning to think of them in those terms. Fat Jimmy naturally had a good eye and a good ear, Alex knew what each of them was good at and what they were not good at and how to deploy them, Jonathan was quieter, and at first Angela didn't see much promise in him, but as things settled down, she could see that he was the analyst, he understood the bigger picture better than the rest of them. The other two were more process oriented. The five of them were unstoppable.

"Do you need anything?" Angela asked.

Alex shook her head.

"Come up in an hour and I'll have your assignments ready," Angela said leaving.

She went up to her office. Moisture had condensed on the inside of the window and she thought of the kids' heater and chuckled to herself as she lit a fire in the little burner she'd brought in.

She began going through the business of the day. Twenty minutes later she heard Carol in the hallway but instead of passing by the door and going directly to her office she stuck her head in the door.

"Busy?" Carol asked.

Angela looked up and shook her head, "No, come in."

Carol had a covered plate in her hand.

"Tired of canned food?" Carol asked with a sparkle in her eye.

Angela nodded wearily, "Yes!"

"Mia and I have some left-overs from our meal this morning and I thought of you," Carol said. She put the plate down and pulled the cover off with a flourish.

"Clams!" Angela exclaimed. "I love clams."

"Mussels actually, but after so long they might as well be clams," Carol said and added, "I hope they didn't get cold on the way over."

Angela tried one and closed her eyes in ecstasy. "They're cold, but I almost don't care."

She moved next to her burner, flame roasted each one and popped them into her mouth.

"I'm sorry things have been so tense between us," Carol said. "I can be a bit difficult, and I really thought you weren't up to this job, but you've proved me wrong. You're doing great."

Angela nodded. "I don't blame anyone for doubting me. I was very new at the job. I'm just glad we can work together. You have lot of skills that have helped this city."

When Angela finished eating Carol picked up the plate, flashed her a smile and said, "If you need anything, I'll be in my office." Then she left and closed the door behind her.

Angela went back to her work. She had figured out the questions she needed answers to and now she was lining them up with the people who could answer them. She licked her fingers to separate a couple of papers that were sticking together and couldn't feel the tip of her tongue. Her lips felt funny too. Other than that she felt fine. She smacked her lips together playfully trying to wake them up and went back to work.

Once she had the people lined up she chose the order they should be contacted in and started assembling the page cards. Her toes fell asleep, which wasn't surprising given the cold. She shook her feet and stamped them trying to get the blood flow back.

Her intestines started to loosen and she decided she might have to make a run for the bathroom at the far end of the hall. She started to wonder about the mussels, but she had cooked them thoroughly, and besides, she didn't feel nauseated. She shook it off and went back to work.

"I'm probably just not used to real food," she thought. After another 10 minutes, she felt very tired. When she finally noticed how tired she was long enough to review how much sleep she'd gotten, she realized she wasn't tired, she was short of breath. She tried to relax and breathe but her muscles wouldn't respond. In fact, although she was beginning to be afraid, she wasn't tense at all. Her muscles were actually more relaxed than normal.

She turned on her radio to call the Fire Department, but someone was continuously transmitting music over the channel, a problem they had discussed before. She switched to the back-up channel, but no one was listening. She tried to get up from the desk, but her muscles were responding slowly. She recalibrated and was able to stand, but by the time she got around her desk, her knees were buckling.

She fell to the ground with just enough control to keep from whacking her head on the floor. She laid there and called out feebly. Her sense of hearing grew stronger. She could hear a fluttering sound outside her window, a bird trying to land on the ledge. Somewhere in the distance she could hear music playing. She could hear someone shifting her weight in a chair just outside her door. Angela called out, "Carol, help!" but it came out soft, raspy and slurred. She thought she heard a slight motion, but there was no other reaction. It got harder to breath. She could hear her heart beating. Her mind wandered. She could see her mother as she had been when she was little. They were eating a Sunday afternoon picnic and laughing. She heard a voice in the hall. It was Alex. She cried out, "Alex, help!" but no sound came out of her drooling mouth. She heard Carol's voice saying something, and Alex responding, "but *she* told me to come up now!" and Carol responding firmly saying something with the word "disturb" in it.

"Alex!" Angela tried to say again. She heard Alex turning to go. "Alex!" she gasped and looked around. There was an old top heavy torchier lamp near her foot. She pushed it. It rocked for a moment then toppled with a crash. Then the lights in Angela's mind went out.

Nine

When the lights came back on, her throat hurt. Dr. Abbot was standing over her. There was a bag over her face. A tired looking nurse was squeezing it over and over. Dr. Abbot smiled thinly when her eyes opened. She could hear Alex's voice. The ceiling overhead changed to one with lit lights and the soft hum of machines. They took the bag off and hooked a machine to the tube she now noticed was coming out of her mouth. Someone pricked her arm. She tried to look at her arm, but she couldn't move. They began threading a tube into her nose and it hurt more than her throat. They turned her on her side and then her stomach felt cold. Things went dark again.

When she opened her eyes again, the tubes were gone. She was in a room with no lights on. Gray daylight was coming through the windows. She didn't try to move, afraid it wouldn't be possible. Everything was sore. Her head hurt. When she finally did turn her head, she saw Alex and Jonathan leaning against each other, dozing in a chair.

Fat Jimmy came in with food, looked at Angela and said, "Hey guys, she's awake."

Alex was next to her instantly. "Are you OK now? Everyone helped; the Fire Department, the hospital, everyone."

"What happened to Carol?" Angela said in a soft scratchy voice.

Alex shrugged, "Nothing. She tried to help, but she was going too slowly, so we sent our own runners."

"Where is Carol now?" Angela asked.

Alex shrugged and looked at Jonathan. Fat Jimmy rolled his eyes and said, "She's in her office, or at least she was an hour ago.

Angela nodded. "You did well. When I get back to the office I want you to tell me everyone that helped, I need to thank everyone."

Alex nodded.

"Oh, and don't go back to your apartment tonight. Get the twins and go stay at the firehouse. I'll send for you." Angela said.

"OK?" Alex said mystified.

"I'll explain later. Just do it," Angela said.

In the afternoon she could hear Dr. Abbot in the next room talking to someone. She had grown weary of the hospital and decided to discharge herself. She dressed and went to the next room over.

Dr. Abbot was talking reassuringly to the old crazy woman that had assaulted her on election day. "Don't worry Senator," he said, "We'll take care of everything." The old woman looked at him child-like, almost adoring, and nodded.

When he came out of the room he said, "Going somewhere?"

"Yes. I'm going home."

The doctor nodded, "OK, but no more shellfish."

Angela nodded and said "You can be very sure of that!" She turned to go, but stopped and said, "Why did you call her Senator? It can't be good to feed her delusions."

The doctor laughed a little, "Simple. Because whatever she may have become, Senator is her real title."

Angela was still a little sore. She stopped by her apartment, found her purse, and went to the offices. In the hallway she could hear Carol in her office talking on the radio with some of her officers. Angela waited patiently for her to finish. Her head still hurt. When Carol had finished talking, Angela walked into her office, put her hand in her purse, pulled out a 9mm pistol and shot Carol in the face.

Carol's body jerked back then bounced forward onto the desk. Angela left the office, locking the door behind her. She went down the street to Carol and Mia's house and knocked on the door. Mia opened it. Angela studied her face. There was no shame or fear in it, only compassion.

"I heard you were sick," Mia said.

"Yes. I was, but I'm better now. Is Carol here?" Angela asked.

"No. I think she's at the office."

Angela nodded. "That makes sense. She wanted me to pick up some shellfish. Is it here?"

"Oh. That must be why she wouldn't let me eat any of it yesterday. Sure, come in, the bags are in the kitchen," Mia said waving her in.

Angela looked at the bags. "Where did she find them?"

"I think they were at Ocean Beach. Most of the force went out there night before last and they came home with these."

"There are more of these than I thought," Angela said. "I'll send someone around to get them. Don't eat them. They're what made me sick."

Mia turned pale.

"What's the matter?" Angela asked.

"Carol was cooking some up yesterday morning. You don't think she ate them too, do you?"

Angela smiled and shook her head and said, "I'm sure she didn't."

Angela took her hand out of her purse and left the house. She went to the fire house, told them Carol was dead in her office, then went and sat in Raul's bar and waited.

Forty-five minutes later the entire Police force was standing around her, clearly agitated.

"Did you shoot Carol?" the officer in front of her asked.

"Yes," Angela said.

The candor took them back a little.

"Why?"

"Did you eat the mussels you found on the beach night before last?" Angela asked.

"No. They were no good."

"Why did you bring them back to town?"

"Why does it matter?"

"Tell me why and I'll tell you why I shot Carol."

"Carol said maybe we could clean up the shells and trade them or something. I figured she just didn't want us to feel like we had wasted our effort. She was always looking out for us that way."

"So, Carol knew the mussels were no good."

"Of course she knew that. She almost got poisoned with the rest of us. If it hadn't been for that cat we'd all be dead."

"Carol brought me a plate of those mussels yesterday morning and fed them to me. Then she waited outside my door while I was dying."

"That's why you shot her?"

"No. I shot her because she tried to assassinate the Mayor. If we tolerate that, none of us will be safe."

"You can't just shoot people. There needs to be a trial."

"We just had her trial."

"After you already killed her!"

"What was I going to do, call the Police?"

"Yes."

"How do you think that would have gone?"

One of the other officers spoke up, "She's right, this is the only way, and I say we use it on her. Solve the problem once and for all."

"You could do that. I'm sitting right here. But you need to think about where that leaves you. You all know I'm telling the truth. Carol was power crazed from the beginning. You all saw it. Do you think the rest of the City didn't see it? If you shoot me, you will leave a power vacuum. The citizens will never let you fill it, and you don't know who you'll have to deal with next. I could have killed half of you before you realized what was happening and turned the public against the rest of you but I didn't. The next person may not be as forgiving; besides, I don't think you had anything to do with it."

The officers looked at each other.

"We'll have to discuss this. This isn't over," the lead officer said.

"Discuss it. I'll wait. But this needs to be over today."

The Police gathered in the dining room. There was a low murmur of discussion, some of it heated. When it wound down they approached.

"We're going to talk to Mia about this. If she says it's over, then it's over, and you'd better stay away from her in the meantime."

"I already saw Mia this morning. When you talk to her, don't leave anything out."

After the Police left, the door to the store room behind the bar opened and Raul and his men came out lowering their shot guns and rifles.

"Remind me to never piss you off," Raul said.

Ten

A few days later it really was over. Mia ranted at first, but when she finally thought it through, she told the Police to let it go. In the end they didn't like how Angela had handled it, but there was little doubt she was telling the truth, and that still counted for something. Angela appointed Mia to fill Carol's seat. No one expected her to accept it, how could she? But she did.

In the spring, Mia moved in with Angela, and no one said much about it. There was a sense in the City that they had all gone beyond what anyone would have done in the old days, and there was no room to be judgmental about it.

The change of season helped. The fishing fleet was finally bringing in fish reliably and there was work to expand it. The potatoes were starting to grow in the park, and they'd had a taste of fresh lettuce over the winter.

The hospital had figured out its saline solution process months earlier, and was now fully stocked with the stuff. They had moved on to birth-control but progress was slow. So far all they had managed to do was isolate estrogen and progesterone from the urine of the only pregnant mare in the city, but it was a proof of concept only. It was a long way from a usable tablet, and even further to a production line.

When asked about it, Dr. Abbot shrugged and said he didn't know when it would be ready. "We only have one mare. We'd have to breed a whole herd before we could start real production." Angela suspected he was diverting resources to producing antibiotics, but she wasn't willing to call him on it unless someone else did first.

In the summer a large submarine was spotted in the bay. They tried to signal it. The officer on the conning tower looked at them through binoculars and ignored them. It disappeared up San Pedro bay before any of the fishing boats came back. When it came back the next day, they had a boat and sent it intercept to the sub. A voice warned them off over the loud speaker. The boat hesitated then continued forward which brought a short burst of light machine gun fire across its bow.

The boat turned away then paralleled the sub. The captain of the fishing boat waved his radio mic at the deck officer and began calling to the sub over the radio. Eventually the radio crackled to life.

"Unidentified sailing vessel, unidentified sailing vessel, unidentified sailing vessel, this is the USS New Mexico. Do not approach. Over."

"USS New Mexico, this is the Rainbow Republic fishing vessel Vesper. Permission to come alongside to discuss trade. Over."

"Negative Vesper. Permission denied. Do not approach. Over."

"USS New Mexico, do you have any information about the state of the nation? We've had no outside news in more than a year. Over."

"Vesper there is no nation to speak of. You are on your own. Over."

"USS New Mexico, can you tell us who did this? Over."

There was a pause.

"Vesper, we don't know who fired first, but it was a full nuclear exchange between the United States, Russia, and China. The governments of all three nations have failed. Over."

"USS New Mexico, who's in charge out there?"

"Vesper, there is no single authority in charge. There are regional interests."

"USS New Mexico, what about the other countries?"

"Vesper: Most of Europe, Canada and Australia were included in the nuclear exchange. We have scattered radio reports indicating regional conflicts with heavy use of biological weapons covering most of the southern hemisphere. The government of Mexico has been overthrown and the new government is not communicating with us, but their propaganda transmissions indicate they intend to rid the continent of all people with primarily European ancestry and we have scattered reports of a Mexican Army headed north. Over."

There was a pause.

"USS New Mexico, where will you go? Over."

"Vesper, some place safe. Over."

"USS New Mexico, why won't you trade with us? Over."

"Vesper, we've already resupplied and some of the biologicals used in the southern wars were really nasty. If any of you are sick, we don't want it. Good luck Vesper."

"USS New Mexico, we have no serious illness in San Francisco. You can come ashore if you want. Over."

There was no reply.

The fishing boat followed until an adverse wind made that difficult then broke off and went back to report.

In the fall the potato harvest failed, and for some reason the fleet was bringing back only a few fish. They fell back on their dwindling supply of canned goods. Then one week, a third of the stockpile of canned goods disappeared. They had been there on Monday, guards were outside the warehouse all week, but when it came time for the distribution on Friday, the equivalent of three shipping containers was missing. The guards had seen no one coming or going.

The Police began an investigation. The board of supervisors met in emergency session.

"Mia, how much longer will the remaining food last?" Angela asked.

"Maybe five months," Mia responded.

The Fire Chief nodded.

Brannan said, "If the fish come back soon we should be able to make it to spring."

"We could send the scavenging crews across the bay to Marin and see what they can find, or down into the wreckage south of the city. I doubt we'll find more containers in the wreckage, but there may be canned goods of some kind," Mays suggested.

Angela nodded. "I think we should do all of those things but," she slammed her fist on the table, "This looting has to stop! The hoarding has to stop! The scavenging crews need to bring everything back to the warehouse and not hide anything in their own stashes. It has to stop!" she shouted. She turned away from the table and rubbed her temples. She turned back to the table.

"Chief, how much food do you think has been spirited away over the last year?"

"I don't know Ms. Mayor," he said lamely.

She looked down the table from face to face. "Abbot, Raul, Don, Erika, Sarah, Wally, Barry, Virginia, can any of you give me an idea of how much we've lost?"

They all murmured in the negative or simply didn't answer.

"What about you Mia?"

Mia turned up the palms of her hands and said, "A lot."

"Would it have been enough to get us through the winter?"

"Probably," Mia said.

Angela looked at the board again, very intently. "The looting has to stop! The stolen food has to be found! The Police will search house to house starting tomorrow morning. Any community found hoarding food will be dealt with severely." She looked directly at Mia, then Barry, and the Fire Chief. "Do you understand?"

There were nods all around the table. Angela nodded back and stood up straight. She turned her back to the table and took a drink of water before adding, "Of course any community that returns stolen food this afternoon can do so on a no questions asked basis." Then she left the board room.

The afternoon was tense. There was a flurry of activity and at first Angela hoped it meant food was about to be returned, but by evening none had been returned.

Over dinner Mia asked Angela how the search should proceed.

"That depends," Angela said.

"On what?" Mia asked.

"On which community you want to take the fall for the portion the Police stole."

"What makes you think the Police have stolen anything?" Mia asked.

Angela just laughed. "I'm not blind. Neither is anyone else in the City. EVERY Community has stolen food, and the Police, Fire Department, and Athletics have stolen more than any of the others per capita, because they had the means to do it."

Mia paused a long time before answering, "The Police won't be framing anyone."

"Maybe they should," Angela said. "The looting really has to stop. Everyone is guilty but we can't very well punish everyone, and if we don't punish anyone the looting will continue."

"Who would you suggest we frame?" Mia asked indignantly then continued, "I think we should just conduct the search and see what turns up."

"Do you really think anyone will be fool enough to leave their stash in their houses after my announcement yesterday?" Angela asked.

"Maybe someone will slip up," Mia said.

"What if it's Public Safety that slips up Mia? or the Police?"

"It won't be the Police!" Mia said evasively.

"OK, but what if it's Public Safety? Are you ready to take on the Fire Department and Public Works?" Angela asked.

Mia said nothing.

"I didn't think so," Angela said. "So what are you going to do?"

"We're going to search and see what comes up," Mia said.

Angela exhaled sharply. "You better hope one of the other communities has more courage than you have."

The next morning the search started with the homes of the Police themselves, overseen by the representatives of all the other communities. It turned up nothing significant.

It proceeded to Raul's bar, then to the homes of all the members of the Gay Men's community, which turned up nothing.

The search turned to Public Safety. That search was slower, but not necessarily more thorough. Members of the Fire Department could be seen keying the mic's on their radios behind their backs as the searchers left each house, but their precautions were unnecessary. That community had better places than their homes and offices to hide a stash.

When the Police arrived at Virginia Costs' house, they called her outside to meet them, then detained her during the search. The other members of the Transgender community rallied to her defense gathering around the Police and demanding that she be freed and be present while her premises were searched. After twenty minutes the Police relented and Virginia followed them through the house. In the basement they found a full pallet of stolen food. "That's not my stash of food," Virginia protested, "Do you think I'd be dumb enough to put a stash of food in my basement? Do you think anyone else will be dumb enough to believe that?" she continued. The Police arrested her. Similar stashes were found in the homes of other transgender men and women, principally the ones that had come to Virginia's defense. The Police arrested them all and began transporting the stolen food back to the warehouse.

The rest of the searches yielded nothing.

The next day Public Works set up a crude scaffold with eight nooses daggling from the top.

The day after that Angela made the case against the accused in a dramatic speech that ended with, "We all have things we aren't proud of, but if stealing food goes unpunished, we won't survive the winter. That is the one thing that can't be tolerated. Let justice be executed."

The condemned were marched onto the scaffold. Virginia continued protesting their innocence until the noose was around her neck. Then a strange calm seemed to fill her. She looked at the assembled crowd with something like pity on her face.

"They took us first because it was easy," she said, "how long before they..."

Angela made a gesture, there was a thumping sound, and the floor fell out from under the eight. Afterward, the crowd was quiet enough that those towards the front could hear the ropes creaking.

That night at dinner Angela congratulated Mia on a Job well done. Mia stormed out of the room. Angela called after her, "The stealing will stop now! We've saved the Republic!" and more quietly, "We've saved the people."

Eleven

The next morning the city was quieter than usual. The days were getting shorter. She had scheduled the regular board meeting for an hour earlier than usual. It was important to get everyone focused on the future as quickly as possible.

While she waited in the board room for the others to arrive she considered what should be done with the transgender seat now that Virginia was gone. There were still five members of the Transgender community left in the city. She could appoint one of them to the board; whether they would accept or not was another question. That raised the question of whether five people should have the same number of votes on the board as, for example Public Safety, which represented nearly 120 people. But, absolute numbers had never mattered before. The Police were the next smallest group but they still held the Deputy Mayor position. She would put it to the board to decide.

At five minutes before the meeting was to start, no one had arrived yet. Angela was not very surprised. Mia had already said she wouldn't be coming to today's meeting. Five minutes past the hour Raul and Wally came walking in together and sat down. They waited another ten minutes, and Angela said, "Looks like we'll have to send pages out. Wally, would you get Alex for me?"

Ten minutes later Wally came back with Alex in tow.

"Good morning Alex," Angela said, genuinely pleased to see her.

Alex did not look directly at her.

Angela looked down and softly said, "Yes, it was a tough day yesterday. I think we are all a little affected. Would you send the pages out to the other seven members of the board and ask them to come in?"

"Six," Alex corrected.

"How did you know Mia wasn't coming in?" Angela asked.

"I didn't. So you want me to call the other five members of the board then."

Angela was puzzled for a second, then understood, and nodded. Alex left.

Forty minutes later Alex was back. "No one was home."

"None of the five supervisors were home? Where did they go?"

Alex shrugged.

"Didn't anyone say?"

"No one came to the door at any of the houses."

"Did you check the Fire House?"

"We checked the one closest to the Chief's house and the one across the street. There was no one at either, and the engines are gone."

Angela got out a radio and called for the Fire Department but there was no answer on any channel. After she had finished trying, one of the Police officers responded and asked what was going on.

"Have you seen any of the board members or any of the fire fighters today?"

"No. I just got up when I heard you calling. I'll look around."

After twenty minutes he called back.

"I don't see any fire fighters anywhere. For that matter there's no one at the Wharf, and all of the fishing boats are gone."

Angela called in the rest of the Police. Mia reluctantly came in and started sending for members of her community. Raul and Wally each had teams assembled in about an hour. They spread out a map of the city and divided it up by sections, then sent teams out. Each team either had a radio or a page with them, and by evening it was clear what had happened.

The hospital was empty and its entire staff was gone. Key pieces of equipment were missing. The power had been left on and they found Senator Floriston's body in one of the freezers.

All eight fishing boats in the expanded fleet were gone. Only one boat, still in dry dock, was anywhere close to operational.

What crops there were in the green house and at the Park had been harvested and were gone.

The only working fire boat and all of the Fire Department's diesel were gone.

Except for the Police Department, every member of every community except Gay Men, Lesbians, and the Arts were gone.

A quick review of their houses and apartments showed they had taken all of their food and clothing with them. They had also taken small things; photographs, journals, books.

When they came to the warehouse where the food had been guarded, they found two shipping containers full of food and a note. It read:

Dear Mayor Steel and fellow San Franciscans:

We realize that our departure will be a surprise to you and that the loss of so many supplies will be a blow that you will keenly feel. Please keep in mind that we have taken most of the population with us, and as we see it, have left you more than your share of the supplies. We have tried to make sure we left your infrastructure as intact as possible. We intended to make and leave three new fishing boats to start your new fleet with, but recent events made us certain that we needed to leave sooner than planned. To make up for this, we have left all of the fish we caught last week for you in the freezer of the hotel Kabuki on Post Street. Be assured, fishing is still excellent. The fish combined with the supplies left in this warehouse and the reduction in your population should give you time to finish a new fleet and adapt.

We hope that we part as friends. When we are ready we will make contact with you and perhaps our communities can engage in trade. Until then, make no attempt to find us, and if you should somehow discover our location, do not approach our community. We greatly outnumber you, we are well armed, and we are committed to defending ourselves.

Good Luck.

- Dr. Abbot and the Committee for Emigration.

Good Luck.

- Dr. Abbot and the Committee for Emigration.

Twelve

Angela did not leave her town house for three days.

Raul, Mia, and Wally set up teams to check on the fish, and finish outfitting the one boat that was closest to done.

Alex, Jonathan, Fat Jimmy, and the twins took to wandering the streets admiring the changes. As they wandered, they got a better picture of what the committee had accomplished. Without anyone else noticing, they had cleared a path to a secondary marina south of the old Ball Park. They had harvested dozens and dozens of solar panels from the old Moscone Center and private residences all over the wrecked part of the City. They had been building barges out of old oil drums and lumber from the wreckage, and had abandoned one barge half completed at their new marina.

There were signs of a salvage operation where they had been sorting through the wreckage and putting materials in different piles. All but traces of the copper, glass, and steel piles were gone. Small piles of other materials remained. There were piles of old water heaters, and fuel tanks near the half completed barge.

"How did they hide all this from us?" Fat Jimmy wondered.

"We considered this area a dead zone. They just never gave us any reason to think different, so we never looked here," Jonathan said.

"We were so focused on our own initiatives that as long as enough people from each community showed up for projects, we never wondered what the rest were doing with their time," Alex said.

"Still, it's surprising the Police didn't notice considering how close they had to work with the fire fighters," Fat Jimmy insisted.

"Not really," Alex said. "They were locked in their own ballet with Angela and Mia. Why would they care what the common breeders were doing?"

They continued exploring, and the more they saw the more impressed they were.

When Angela finally emerged, they held a board meeting and discussed the situation.

"They must have gone north," Wally said. "The fleet was usually fishing up North in the middle of the old marine sanctuary. If they had gone south we would have noticed. Besides, I think the Scientologists used to have some sort of doomsday vault up north because they calculated it would have the best chance of surviving a nuclear war. Maybe they were right. Maybe there's good land up there."

"Do you think we should try to find them?" Raul asked.

Mia shook her head. "They seemed pretty adamant about that in their letter."

They looked at Angela.

Angela shook her head. "We can't afford a war right now. We need to get ready for the winter and figure out how to feed ourselves."

They all nodded.

"What have we got left?" Angela asked.

"Two shipping containers of canned food. Three week's worth of fish. The green house plants are starting to grow again. Almost all of the hospital supplies, but they took a lot of the equipment and their saline rig. One fishing boat which we can launch tomorrow and two more we can have ready sometime in the next three weeks," Raul reported.

"Also, the kids tell me the committee was using the wreckage from the Tsunami a lot more than we ever did. I doubt there's much to eat there, but there may be plenty we can use to stay warm and build things," Mia said.

"How long do you think people can last on the food they have cached?" Angela asked.

All three supervisors were quiet.

"Oh come on!" Angela said "We all know Virginia's people weren't the only ones hoarding food."

Raul exhaled. "We can probably make it three weeks, but not comfortably."

"The Police, six weeks, the rest of my community maybe two and a half," Mia said.

"We had about a month's worth, but someone stole the main cache, so we're down to less than a week," Wally said.

Angela rested her chin on her hand and drummed her other fingers on the table.

After a while she said, "Let's throw everything at the fleet. The weather's not good for growing things anyway. Can we get beyond three boats?"

"There are maybe two more we could salvage but they are in bad shape. I think we should take the new boat across the bay and see if we can find any in Sausalito. If that doesn't work then we may have to learn to build them from scratch," Wally said.

"Let's see what Sausalito has. Have the new boat drop you off on its way out to fish tomorrow and pick you up on the way in. Take a Policeman with you. We don't know for sure who might be over there," Angela decided.

They agreed and everyone got to work.

Thirteen

They found five salvageable boats in Sausalito, and the new boat had a good day fishing. That news lifted spirits. Repairs took longer than they'd hoped. It was harder to move equipment and build repair facilities in Marin, and on stormy days the new fleet couldn't go out.

The Marin station found it could mostly feed itself off goods in the wreckage of houses. If the people here survived, they left everything behind.

"That means they're dead," one of them said.

"Or it means they found a better place to go, like the submarine and the breeders," another said.

"No, even if they had a better place they'd take food and clothes with them," the first retorted.

When spring arrived they were gaunt, but they were all still alive. They planted what potatoes they could in the park, and a few volunteer potatoes surprised them by springing up, which seemed like a good omen.

By the end of summer they were putting on weight again.

"Hey Fats," Shawna called out to Fat Jimmy, "Looks like your pants are starting to fit again."

Jimmy shook his butt vigorously and she laughed at him. The other twin, Malcom, had been spending a lot of time with a 24 year old painter named Milly, down in Wally's little kingdom.

The five of them had more time on their hands since the Republic shrank. They had spent some of it on their own garden. They had cleared a space a block from their apartment and had managed to scrape up seeds from dried up kitchen garbage and sealed up refrigerators they found in some of the old hotels. Jonathan barfed the first time they opened one of the refrigerators, because the meat hadn't fared as well as the fruits and vegetables. They also found seeds in unexpected places; little herb gardens growing in abandoned kitchens, and in pots on balconies. They even found some wild plants to try taming.

Angela demanded more of Alex's time than Alex liked. She would call her in for "school" pretty regularly and have her read Machiavelli, and Shakespeare, and Gloria Steinem. Then she would quiz her, or set her to work on various projects. Now that the public works crews were gone, there were more things that needed calculating and managing from the mayor's office, and Alex found herself more interested in the engineering and home repair books Jonathan had scavenged from all over the city.

Once it was clear that they would survive the winter and be in a good position for the following one, new tensions arose at the board meetings. Angela became more mercurial and Mia more sullen.

"Now that things are better, we should have a festival or something," Angela said with great enthusiasm.

Wally got a team working on music and decorations. Raul put the Bar's still into overdrive and organized a storytelling festival. Mia did nothing.

At the next meeting Angela abruptly cancelled the festival, saying, "I got ahead of myself, we can't afford the resources yet."

Mia smirked.

"We've already spent most of the resources that we're going to spend," Raul objected.

"It's cancelled. That's it," Angela said.

Raul looked at Wally. Wally barely perceptibly shook his head and Raul let it go.

That evening the Gay community went ahead with its own party anyway and some of Wally's people stopped by for a drink and some stories.

That night while Raul was cleaning up there was a knock at the back door. Raul peeked through the window. It was Angela.

"Crap!" he muttered to himself and opened the door.

"Yes, we went ahead with the party..." Raul said.

"I don't care," Angela said.

"Then why are you here?" Raul asked annoyed.

"I think we should put on our old show," Angela said.

"What? Why?" Raul said trying to run back-of-the-envelope political calculations while Angela responded.

"Like you said, people need distracting, they need a celebration or something, and our show was pretty good."

"I didn't say that. You said that and I just agreed with you," Raul said.

"The show was good though. Wasn't it?" Angela asked.

"Yeah, it was great. I think it got you elected, but what's that got to do with anything?"

"I just think we should put it on," Angela said.

"That could really complicate things for me..." Raul said.

"Not that much. It would be worth it. We don't have to run for weeks or anything, maybe just a couple of shows one weekend."

"I don't know..."

"Come on, let's go practice, and then we'll see if it's still good enough to perform publicly," Angela said.

"Uh, OK," Raul said as understanding started to seep in.

He grabbed a sweater, checked to make sure no one was watching, and walked with Angela to the old theater. Their stuff was still there. It took a while to change into their old costumes in the dark and make their way to the stage.

Angela remembered the entire show, every line, every action. When they had finished the show Angela didn't immediately get up from their last position. She lay across his chest and he stroked her hair. Quiet filled the theater and she closed her eyes and breathed long and deep. He had never seen her like this. But then she was on her feet.

"What did you think?" she asked.

"I thought it was good," Raul said.

"Yeah it was," she said. "We can talk tomorrow about whether or not we should put the show on."

"Yeah," Raul said.

They never mentioned it again.

At the next board meeting Mia said nothing. She just glared at Raul. Raul asked her what was wrong but she just looked at him. Angela pretended not to notice.

When the meeting was over Wally caught Raul outside the building and said,

"Wow! What was that about?"

Raul shrugged, "I don't know, maybe it's just that time of the month." But on his walk home he started running through the political math again, and decided he'd better cat things up a bit around the community just in case this thing blew up.

Fourteen

In the early fall on a sunny afternoon when the air was still and the bay was uncharacteristically smooth like glass, Wally's friend Lana was sitting on the pier mending a fishing net. Her hands were moving with smooth measured motions and she felt she finally knew what she was doing. Not that she had ever been terrible at it. True, in the begging they used the wrong fibers and the nets didn't last, and they hadn't made them quite tight enough at first, but she had always been able to tie the knots better than most of the group. Today it was all just flowing, and she felt a certain joy in knowing that those simple knots would mean food for all of them. She had just finished the last net when she looked across the bay and saw it.

"Wally!" She called out. "Somebody go get Wally." She said and started trying to prep one of the new little row boats they had made out of wrecked lumber. Somebody went for Wally and one of the men that had been mending nets with her helped her get the boat in the water and the oars in place. When Wally got there he looked over the scene. There was a man on a raft floating slowly by the dock. He wasn't moving.

"Come on, he's drifting away," Lana said.

"Hold on," Wally said checking things more carefully with binoculars.

"What are you worried about? He's obviously in no condition to hurt any of us," Lana said impatiently.

"You can never be too careful," Wally said.

"Come on," Lana said and Wally got in the boat with her.

The rowed out to the raft, tied a rope to it, and towed it back to the dock.

When the raft moved, the man on it opened his eyes. They had let out a little line so he'd have to swim if he meant trouble, but all he did was look at them dully and then close his eyes.

When they got him to the pier, several of the others helped to pull him off the raft. As they did he vomited a little into the water, but he didn't have much to vomit. He was painfully thin.

They got him into a bed and got some water into him and he slept. In the evening he seemed a little better. A group gathered around him, hoping to hear his story.

After a while, Wally asked, "What's your name?"

The man seemed to think a while and then said, "Eric. My name is Eric."

"Where did you come from?"

"San Jose. South San Jose."

"What's wrong with you?"

"I'm not sure. Radiation maybe. Dehydration maybe. I got sick on the raft."

"Why did you come by raft?"

"I couldn't go south, the Mexicans were coming from the south and killing all the white people. They almost caught me. I couldn't go up the peninsula, San Francisco's radioactive from the airport north. I just found this raft and got on it hoping to make Fremont, but I got sick."

"That explains why no one's come before," someone said.

"Which way did the Mexicans go?"

"I don't know."

"Did they see you get on the raft?"

"Am I alive?" Eric said and slumped.

They were satisfied.

"Sleep. We can talk more in the morning," Wally said.

During the night Eric cried out, but then quieted. In the morning he was dead.

Then Lana started vomiting, and Wally, and everyone east of the financial district.

Wally got on the radio and called to Angela.

After he explained what was going on Angela said, "What can we do for you?"

"Check the hospital. If someone could bring us saline to keep us hydrated, we might have a chance."

"I'll check into it," Angela said.

They checked the hospital and found two bio-hazard suits, saline kits, and in a corner of the lab they found Dr. Abbotts' antibiotics project. It wasn't all there. He hadn't finished it. He had created the first cultures and left notes, but there was nothing they could use.

They grabbed the saline kits and the suits and stood in the ground floor door of the hospital debating what they should do.

Angela looked at the suits. "These things were never meant to be worn outside the hospital, let alone walking down debris strewn streets. If the suits get even one hole in them, whoever we send could get sick."

Raul nodded. "The street's mostly cleared. I'm worried about how we decontaminate the suits once the people come back."

"Go by boat," Mia said. "You two can carry the suits and supplies to the breeders' marina, go by boat to the pier, then come back the same way. You can bathe the suits in salt water, then lay in the sun, then strip in one of the abandoned buildings, shower off, go into another room and put on fresh clothes."

"That might work if we had a boat... and a shower," Raul said.

"Breeders' Marina is where they are making the row boats," Angela said, "and we can bring water to shower off with. Who should we send?"

"You two should go," Mia said flatly, "Never send someone else to do what you're not willing to do."

"You're part of the board. Maybe you should go," Raul said.

"Let's all go," Mia said.

"We only have two suits," Raul said.

"Well, sometimes sacrifices have to be made," Mia said.

"Stop it! Both of you. This is a public safety mission. It's a job for the Police," Angela said.

It was evening before the two officers arrived at the fishing pier. By then no one was well enough to greet them. They moved carefully towards the first hut that had been set up near the pier, went inside and found Wally, Lena and the dead man. They set up the first IV, but as soon as they let go, the needle fell out Wally's arm.

"It's dripping too fast," one officer said to the other. They adjusted the flow and this time the needle stayed in. They kept sticking Lena, but they couldn't find the vein. Finally they said,

"We'll come back," and moved on to the next hut.

They ran out of supplies so they didn't go back to Lena.

When they had distributed everything, they rowed back up the waterfront in the moonlight.

They spent the next two days in a ruined store by Breeders' Marina, eating food that had been stashed for them there beforehand. Then they went back to the pier to check on everyone. All but three were dead. Malcom's friend Millie was among the survivors. They gave her all of the supplies they had brought and put her in charge of the survivors.

They spent another two nights in the store until they were sure they weren't sick then reported back.

The officers were sent back one more time ten days later to move the survivors away from the infected area and burn the huts.

Fifteen

For the next week the City was in a foul mood. Not only had the artists died, but they didn't dare use the fishing boats and nets on the pier, and to make matters worse, they'd used up all of the alcohol burning the huts.

The Police felt entitled to the first new batch Raul distilled, and no one argued with them.

A week after that, they went in and moved the boats to Breeder's Marina, scrubbed them with alcohol, and made new nets which weren't as good as the originals. The crews that scrubbed down the boats demanded the first catches in return for their labor, and no one argued with them either.

When no one else got sick, the mood lightened some. The board met again and tried to decide what should be done next. They had missed several weeks of fishing, but they also had fewer mouths to feed, and the boats were bringing in new catches again. The food supply was fine.

"We need to start planning for a better future, not just for survival," Angela said.

"Good luck with that," Mia said.

"Mia, if you don't want to be on the board anymore, just resign and I'll appoint someone else until the next election," Angela said.

"I want to be on the board," Mia said. "If you want me off the board, maybe you should just shoot me, or hang me."

Raul sighed.

"Then why are you constantly so negative?" Angela asked.

"You know why," Mia said.

Angela gave up.

"Maybe this would go better if you weren't here, Angela," Raul suggested.

Mia looked up with interest.

Raul continued, "We aren't exactly a board anymore. It's just the Dykes and the Fags and you, whatever you are."

"He has a point," Mia said.

Angela was speechless for a full twenty seconds. "Is this a coup?" she finally said.

"It's a recognition of reality," Raul said.

Angela seemed to be struggling with something, then finally said, "Let's give it a try for two weeks. I'll leave you alone for the next two weeks and then we'll meet and decide how it's going."

"Works for me," Raul said.

"Yeah," Mia said.

"OK," Angela said and left.

She needed time to think. She was pretty sure Mia couldn't pull it off. Things would fall apart. Mia herself might ask her to take the reins again. But she needed to be sure.

She would have to think of something relatively soon. She would need control if the next generation were to have a chance at a real life, or even exist at all. But the board was too fragile and the people too exhausted for the things she wanted to propose. She smiled at herself ruefully, and placed her hand on her abdomen absent mindedly.

"Ready or not, I'm pretty well committed to my part in the plan," she thought.

While Mia and Raul attempted to govern, Angela did a lot of "fact finding," which is to say campaigning. She spent time with the Police listening to their concerns. She hosted a bitch-a-thon with Pinch Face and her circle of discouraged supporters. She took the leaders of the butch wing drinking at Raul's. She bonded with the femme wing at a dinner she set up at the old hotel where the Breeders had stored the fish, and towards the end of the two weeks she threw an old fashioned ball at that same hotel.

Alex, Jonathan, Fat Jimmy, Shawna and Malcom were as busy as they had ever been in the old days extending invitations and setting up venues.

Mia was invited to the ball. She had the sense to come, but not the sense to be nice.

By the end of the ball, Angela had accomplished what she set out to do. She had fooled no one. No one mistook her for a friend. Most had noticed that she made few promises, but there was at least a consensus that Angela could be worked with, and Mia for all her purity, could not be.

When Angela rejoined the board meetings the third week she said,

"I had a good vacation. How did things go here?"

"Fine. Better than fine. Great!" Mia said.

Raul hesitated, and said, "I think we made great progress. A lot of things that hadn't been getting attention got ironed out."

Angela nodded.

Raul and Mia watched her, waiting for her rejoinder.

"Why are you looking at me?" Angela said.

"We want to hear what you think," Raul said.

"I'm glad that things are working so well," Angela said. "I think you were right. Things have changed. Your constituents are living in one part of the city, Mia's are living in another part. I have no constituents of my own. I still think we would be better off as one people. We could try a rotating presidency of three, where each group elects its own leader and both groups elect a third president that would serve as a tie-breaker. Each president would take turns being the executive, but if that won't work, I'll step down and hopefully we can be friends."

"I don't see that working," Mia said. "We've spent the last few months trying to work together and that hasn't been good."

"I didn't say I had to be the third president," Angela said. "It's possible none of us would be presidents. It would be settled by an election."

"It only works for me if you disqualify yourself from the election," Mia said.

Angela looked at Mia for a while, and said, "I understand how you feel." Mia began to object but Angela talked over her, "Mia, believe it or not, I actually do understand how you feel. I think it's important that one of us be in the presidency, so if we both win, I would step down and appoint my successor."

Mia's face hardened. She shook her head and said, "If? You underestimate me Angela. I'm not making any deals with you," Mia said.

Raul carefully watched the exchange between the two. He shook his head.

"Mia, I think that was a fair offer. I think it might be better if we stuck together in a new form," he said.

"Why? So *you* can find a way to oppress us next?" Mia said. "We are already separate. We were separate before all of this began. You can't possibly understand that. Neither of you can. You're both frauds."

Raul tried to guess how many of her supporters agreed with her. He looked at Angela who just shook her head.

"There it is again!" Mia said, "You two are an abomination. Can either of you think for yourself?"

"Where is this coming from?" Raul asked.

"As if you didn't know..." Mia said, "Look. This is over. I still represent my people and my people say this is over."

"The constitution we wrote says that has to go to the people," Angela objected.

"That constitution isn't worth the toilet paper we wrote it on," Mia said. "What matters is who will follow whom."

"That will lead to chaos," Raul said. "We can't have chaos heading into the winter. People will die."

"People have died!" Mia screamed. "This ends now."

"I'll step down," Angela said, "Effective immediately. We'll declare an end to the Republic, but you will both stand for reelection. No more lives need to be lost."

"Will you challenge me for the leadership?" Mia asked Angela.

"Yes," Angela said.

Mia laughed, "Well, good luck with that. You're on! In a few weeks you won't even be qualified to run!"

"We'll see," Angela said.

"I'll make sure they see!" Mia sneered.

"We'll announce it tomorrow then," Angela said.

"No, we'll wait till the weekend. Every extra day works to my advantage," Mia said.

"OK," Angela said.

Raul shook his head but said, "OK then."

Mia looked at them for a second, calmed down, and said, "You know... I really hate both of you," and left.

Raul and Angela left a minute later, and walked down the street together.

Raul was thoughtful. "Are you going to tell me what's going on?"

Angela responded, "The republic is unraveling. Mia is removing herself from power, and you and I will go on."

"You know what I mean. What has Mia got on you? Why is she so angry at us? I'm guessing she knows about our little rehearsal, but everyone knows we had a show together. I can't figure why she would care, or how she could use that."

"Mia had issues long before she knew either of us. Why do you think she was with Carol or with me of all people for that matter," Angela said. "What she has on me is that I'm pregnant."

Raul took that in for a few seconds and then said casually, "I kind of forgot that was the usual outcome."

Angela laughed lightly, "Yeah, I get that."

"I'm assuming it's us we're talking about here?" Raul added.

"Yeah," Angela said.

"Are you keeping it?"

"Yeah. I don't exactly trust Mia with a hanger, and anyway its time this town moved on. What do we intend to do, die out as a bunch of sterile old fruits?"

"Are you scared?"

"Yes. We have no medical personnel, and I would be scared anyway, but I'm only 28. I should be fine. Besides what is leadership if not going first when things are scary?"

"So, your suggesting others should do this?"

"What choice do we really have?"

"It's not like we are the last people on Earth, Angela. We can just all get old together and fade away."

"That's not very inspiring."

"It's not that horrible either. I think it's kind of peaceful," Raul said.

"What if you feel differently in ten years?" Angela asked.

"Then it will be too late, and I'll just have to live with it, or at least I would if you weren't having a baby. Will you need any help from me?"

"I'll need our people to be at peace with each other, that's all. That's why I need you to win your election."

"Your news will make that harder. We have some Mia's among my people, and our record isn't so perfect as to avoid all criticism. Honestly, I was expecting to be opposed in the next election anyway. Having the election early and under these circumstances will only make that more serious."

"Will you win?"

Raul grinned. "Yes. It will cost me, but I'll win."

"So will I! After we've won, let's attempt some sort of union. I was serious about a rotating presidency."

"We can try, but it will have to be soft peddled. There were already some grumblings among my people before Mia ever raised a stink. They'll need to be shown there's a benefit to union before they'll agree to it again."

"Then we'll wait, and show them the benefit," Angela said.

Sixteen

The elections went as expected.

Afterward, Raul's people took the name of the Rainbow Republic, and Angela's continued to fly the same flag, but had no real name.

Angela and Raul agreed they would meet only monthly to discuss any mutual aid and address any points of friction between their communities.

The Police split up, the women stayed with Angela, and the men went with Raul. They got together on some Friday's at Raul's place to drink and play cards, and occasionally the straight ones would disappear upstairs, but no one begrudged that.

The general public was less supportive of Angela and Raul's situation, but as long as it wasn't ongoing, and as long as they did the people's business, who was to judge?

In fact, there were some, particularly on the Femme side who were beginning to defend her position and even consider it.

A month after the election, Angela was beginning to show. Mia had moved out right after their last board meeting, and Angela enjoyed the quiet of having the townhouse to herself. She found herself feeling rather maternalistic. Alex started coming over to the townhouse unbidden. She brought a knitting book Jonathan had found and they taught themselves to knit. Soon balls of yarn started appearing out of different women's personal stashes.

Mia was by no means quiet. Though everyone had assumed she was

"

a Femme, in fact had been, now that the Femme's were warming to Angela, Mia was constantly seen with the butch arm.

One day at the sushi restaurant Malcom and Millie had started, Angela watched Mia working a group of obviously uninterested women and had to suppress a laugh. As Lindon, one of the butchest women in the group told her later, "Just because I'm butch doesn't mean I hate kids."

In the end, most of the butch crowd ended up asking Mia to leave them alone. She ended up stuck with Pinch Face and her gang. They had planned to start a bar to compete with Raul's, but their alcohol still was assembled poorly. It didn't produce much and the bar devolved into sort of a drinking club for their own little group.

Two months after the election, two couples came and asked Angela if she could broker a deal with the Republic so they could have children.

At the second request Angela said, "Sure, but what do you need me for? You could just make your own contracts."

"Have you been over there lately?" one of the women asked.

Angela thought about it. "No, I guess I haven't," she admitted.

"You should go. Things are getting a bit strange. We're just not sure what might happen if the whole community isn't backing us."

Angela nodded. "I'll see what I can figure out and get back to you."

Angela decided to join the Police on one of their Friday nights. When they got to Raul's the atmosphere was noticeably darker.

Raul greeted Angela and got her some water to drink. The Police settled into their card game.

"People are saying things are getting weird over here," Angela said. "What's going on?"

Raul raised an eyebrow, looked around casually, and acknowledged it. "Yeah, there's a bit of a funk going on, and some of the guys are getting a bit surly."

"Why?"

"We're running out of medication. Not everybody is sharing. People are starting to get sick."

"I thought only about 15 percent of your community was positive."

"Angela, that's still a lot of people. If it was only one person it would be hard to watch. There's not much I can do but give out free booze to the folks who are suffering, but even that's causing some problems. We had three fist fights and a double suicide last week."

"Is there anything we can do to help?"

Raul sighed and sat back thinking. "Look, if you explain things to your folks and ask them to keep all of the happy talk to themselves for a while, that would probably help. You folks are over there talking about new beginnings and over here it feels like the end and that stirs people up. I don't know. Maybe if you could make some gesture of solidarity it might help, but it'd better be good. If it's going to be weak just don't do anything."

"We'll think of something," Angela said. "Is there anything I can do for you? You tell me what I can do for you."

Raul thought. "I heard you have some sushi over there."

"Sort of..." Angela said.

"Send some of that over."

"Done."

Angela waited for the Police for an hour and finally decided they were staying up later than she was, so she started for home on her own. Three blocks into her walk she decided it was a mistake.

It wasn't so much that people were staring at her, or that it was dark, it was more a feeling that there were other eyes she couldn't see watching her. When she got back to her townhouse she double bolted the door.

Seventeen

Angela assembled a committee the next day. Understanding quickly spread and everyone was anxious to help. The sushi restaurant not only agreed to send something over for Raul, but the equivalent of a whole week's worth of sushi, assuming the fleet was willing to donate the fish, which they were. The new arts council had the idea of doing couples' pictures, especially since so many people were losing loved ones, and they had found some working color printers and cameras. Alex had studied her history and suggested that they sponsor a solemn procession with everyone dressed in black with red ribbons.

When Angela ran the plans by Raul he wasn't sure it was a good idea. "Let me run it by a few people and I'll get back to you."

A week later he came to Angela's office and said some of his people were actually touched and that they should go ahead.

They sent the sushi over three days later, and the following week they held the procession and a sort of living wake at Raul's. By the end of the evening there were a few tears and a surprising number of songs. Not everyone was touched. A particularly sour looking older man sat in a corner, so drunk he could barely sit up straight. He glared at everyone, but said nothing. Others simply didn't attend.

Angela heard little from Raul over the next three months. The Police started meeting down the street from Angela's office instead of at Raul's place. She knew that things were getting worse because of the fires she saw glowing in the night. At first there were a few, then many.

She was getting large enough to be uncomfortable. Alex came by and rubbed her feet and back on some of the colder evenings.

As if by some contagion, Mia and her group began to get stranger as well. At first it was just shouting in the streets late at night after an evening of drinking. The Police had to talk to them a couple of times, which was met with a lot of profanity, and a grudging compliance. But it escalated from there.   Every member of the group started greeting Angela every time they saw her, almost like they were her long lost friends except for the clear hatred in their eyes.

Angela had the pages clear out Carol's old office and create a sort of Police Station. The police moved in gratefully since it was more central than their old location.

Things calmed down a bit. Angela kept things low key out of respect for the tragedy unfolding across town.

One night Angela worked late trying to sort out a nasty logistical problem. She was feeling rather satisfied with herself as the bolt clicked in place on her office door. She walked down the street towards her townhouse. The stars were brilliant, one of the few things that were actually better than in the old days. Her breath made clouds of steam as she lumbered along the street. She had a sense that soon enough they would get through this difficult patch. Soon enough there would be a renewal. She was almost home when Mia appeared from out of nowhere, smiling smugly.

"Hello Angela! She said gaily. How's our baby tonight?"

"Hi Mia. Are you drunk?"

"As a matter of fact, I have been drinking."

"You should go home. It's getting cold out."

"Aren't you going to invite me in for old time's sake?"

"Mia, go home."

"No, I guess not," Mia said.

Angela felt three of Mia's friends move in behind her. She glanced at her door twenty feet away, then turned to see who was behind her.

"Hello Angela!" Pinch Face said. "How are you feeling?"

"Yeah, how are you holding up?" another said, "It's a long walk home. You should be careful."

The fourth woman just smiled at her, leering, and nodding.

When the moment actually came, no one seemed quite sure how it was supposed to go. In the end, Mia just ran at her, knocked her to the ground, then they circled her and kicked her over and over. Angela curled into a ball as best she could. They kicked her until they were out of breath, then rested, leaning forward with their hands on their knees. In the distance someone was laughing, nearer cats in an alley were fighting, but the closest sound was the breathing. When that quieted, they kicked her more until Angela let out a low moaning that seemed to surprise them. They regarded her for a minute, then each kicked her again, and went home.

Had they been sober, they would have finished the job with a brick or a well aimed blow to the head, but as it was they warmed themselves with the thought of her laying out in the cold dying slowly.

She didn't die.

When she woke up the following afternoon she was in bed in her townhouse. She was bruised everywhere so it hurt to turn. Her sheets were ruined. She had a fever. Alex and Jonathan were there. Raul was there. She knew by their anguished expressions the situation was bad. She drank some water and let go, drifting into the delirium of fevered sleep. She woke up shivering some time the next day, aching. She was in the old hospital. The lights were on. Raul saw her open her eyes. He was speaking to her. She listened. "It died," he said, "It's making you sick, you have an infection," he said.

Angela didn't understand the relevance of what he was saying, but she continued watching him. In the anguish of his face she realized, that despite everything, in his own way he loved her. She tried to hold onto the thought, but he was speaking again. "We looked it up in the books. The hospital has the machine we need so, we're going to get it out. OK?"

She looked at him, trying to bring back the other thought, but the aching came back. She put her hand on her hard hot belly. Raul was speaking. She nodded. They tried to get her drunk, but she passed out again after the first sip.

Eighteen

Mia, Pinch Face and the others kept quiet when they heard Angela was alive. She was in bad shape, and apparently not talking, so there was hope. Even if people knew what they had done it might be OK. No one really liked Angela. Still, they gathered a few materials just in case they had to run for it. The Police did not knock on their doors. No investigation started. They began to relax.

Mia ventured out late on the third day to get supplies. She felt eyes on her, but never saw anyone look at her. "Paranoia," she concluded, closed her eyes, and willed herself to move more confidently. The sun was getting low in the sky and reflected off shop windows. A chill set in and she sunk her hands into her jacket pockets. As she got closer to the market there were more people on the street. Swirls and eddies of people swimming like sharks. She felt uneasy, trapped. She turned to go home, but as she did the crowd tightened. She turned again, looking for another way, but the circle closed around her. She tried to force her way through but multiple hands grabbed her and lifted her off her feet.

She struggled, kicking, until somebody hit her in the head and she froze, stunned. They passed Pinch Face's house.

Pinch Face was being pulled out of her door, but she wasn't going quietly. She was cursing and kicking people while holding onto the door frame. After a couple of tries they succeeded in pulling her out. She got off two wild punches before submerging below a swell of roughened faces and hunched shoulders.

The crowd surged towards the marina. The other conspirators were similarly swept along until all four were deposited on the pier.

An early winter dusk settled in. Pinch Face continued swearing softly but the crowd didn't make a sound. Mia and the others were also quiet. They hung Pinch Face upside down on the net drying rack. She thrashed all the more, and then a member of the crowd stepped forward and hit her with a baseball bat as hard as she could in the stomach. Pinch face groaned and stopped struggling. Mia and the others waited to see what would happen next. The crowd shifted their attention to them.

Mia cleared her throat, tried to find some words that would help, but when she said nothing they lifted her, and tied her to the rack the same way but they didn't hit her and she didn't resist.

When they were all hung up, their leader took the bat and hit pinch face in the leg. It made a sickening sound and Pinch Face swore again. She broke the other leg, and Pinch Face whimpered but said nothing more. Then she hit her over and over until she was unrecognizable, spit on what was left of her face, and handed the bat to the next person in line. She held it, shifted it in her hands feeling the weight and balance.

There was a pause. In that silence Mia finally cried out, "Please say something!"

Water lapped at the pier, but there was there was no reply.

"Say something! Say anything!" Mia pleaded.

The woman holding the bat swallowed then hit her as hard as she could and passed the bat on to the next person.

Feet shuffled and scrapped on the heavy boards of the pier as they took turns slowly beating her and the others for 45 minutes. When it was fully dark, they went home in silence.

The moon rose and made little points of light on the breeze roughened surface of the bay. Mia watched it, felt it seep into her and felt the pain go.

In the morning the Police cut the bodies down and threw them into the bay, in time for the tide to carry them away.

Nineteen

Angela did not try to recover. They had to make her eat, drink and shower. By spring she had recovered somewhat. Some spring nights she would sit on the roof of her office building, dangling her legs off the ledge and watching the fires burn in Raul's part of the city. They were not so many now, but they were still regular.

Raul came to see her sometimes, but they did not discuss business. They discussed foods they missed. They discussed birds Angela had seen coming back to the City. They discussed anything but business and feelings. Raul was starting to age. She knew he was no more than 29 or 30, but his hair was turning gray at the temples. She knew this would be a liability for him, but she said nothing about it.

Some mornings she wondered about where the City's other inhabitants had settled. They had heard nothing from them. She thought about leaving the city. Maybe Raul would leave with her. Maybe Alex would come too, and they could find something better.

But as the weather warmed people began asking her opinion on things. The Police had been holding things together and serving as go-betweens for the two communities. No one wanted to take her place. She realized that somehow she had become the hope for her community. If she left, she would take that hope with her. She started going in to the office. She started taking reports from the Police. Eventually she went to see Raul at his place. It looked sad. Raul seemed guarded in his responses. The sour looking man she had seen the night of the wake seemed to be paying attention to their conversation, and Raul never looked in that direction.

"Things have been a little rough," Raul conceded. "As a result there had to be some adjustments made to our governance structure, and everyone is still getting used to their new roles," he said obliquely.

"I see," Angela said crisply with just the slightest glint in her eyes that let Raul know she understood what he was not saying. "Has the epidemic subsided at all?"

The sour man shifted in his seat.

"The holocaust is not over," Raul said carefully. "Even when people stop dying, it will never really be over. We will always carry it with us."

The sour man seemed to relax.

Angela nodded, "Of course."

It was more than a week before Raul found an excuse to visit Angela.

"I'm not going to be able to visit here much anymore," he said.

"Got you on a short leash do they?"

"Yeah, you could say that. I probably spent too much time here when you were sick. I ended up getting forced into a power sharing situation, and they are a little paranoid that we might form an alliance and force them out."

"Maybe we should," Angela suggested.

Raul toyed with the idea and then shook his head. "That would get pretty ugly, and everyone's been through enough. This should settle down in time."

"I'm sorry if helping me put you in a bad situation," Angela said, "and in case you weren't sure, it did help me."

"There was some criticism that I cared more about your people than my own, and given our history I was pretty open to attack on that count. On the other hand what happened to you brought me a fair amount of sympathy. After all, no matter how jaded someone is, everyone had a mother and everyone has had a lover. What happened to Mia also served as a warning. So, I don't know if coming here got me in trouble, or saved me, and any more I don't care."

"So is old sourpuss at the end of the bar there your partner?"

"One of the minor ones... He's actually more of a minder. The real power brokers have better things to do than watch me all day."

"I thought that old guy was dying... I thought he was one of the positives," Angela said.

Raul winced, "Angela you can't talk like that, not even here. They're serious about this holocaust stuff. You can't be calling people 'positives,' or say anything that might sound trivializing in any way. For some of the guys, it's almost like a death cult or something."

"Sorry. I imagine it really has been pretty tough to watch so many people you know die."

"It has. And to answer your question, he was. When some of the men ran out of medication they just didn't get sick. We don't know why. A lot of them had been on the medication a long time, but not all of them. Maybe they had a natural immunity. Anyway they've formed their own sort of sub-community and they are pretty serious and a pretty powerful group, and there isn't much they aren't willing to do."

"Well, if we can't meet like we usually do, maybe it's time for us girls to throw our weight around a little and insist on the old monthly coordination meetings."

"We won't really be able to discuss things openly," Raul said.

"I know, but the communities really do need to coordinate, and at least once every other month you'll be on our territory and you'll have a chance to defect if you need to."

"I don't think it will come to that. I don't think I'm in any actual danger."

"Neither did I."

Raul conceded the point.

"I'll come up in a week or two and start insisting."

"OK, I'll play along."

They got some sushi and then Raul went home.

Twenty

While Angela was sick, they split the fishing fleet so that each community was now operating independently except for the projects in the park.

Angela walked along the water front and saw the new pier going up on the pylons of one that had been destroyed in the disaster. It was good to see construction happening, still Angela couldn't help but think of how the labor and materials could have been spent on something more productive. The existing pier was already a chore to maintain and had more than enough space for the combined fleet.

As planned she went to Raul's a week after their meeting and proposed a monthly coordination meeting. There was less resistance than she had expected and the meetings became regular.

By the end of summer deaths had dropped to only one every eight weeks or so and some of the tension was lifting. By November Angela had gained enough good will with the new coalition to begin proposing substantive areas of cooperation.

"Each of our communities has faced tragedy this year, yours more than mine," Angela said graciously. "We must never forget the events of the last year, or the people we've lost. For that memory to persist we, as a people, must persist. We must go on."

A sour expression passed over the face of one of the representatives, Randolph. Another, Norm, who was generally more patient said, "What are you proposing Angela?"

"Most of us were raised in hetero-sexual families and here in the City we've generally been content to let the next generation come from the same place. That's worked well in the past, but there just aren't enough couples like that left in the City. We can't rely on that system any more. I've been approached by more than one couple and a few individuals, to see if we could put a system in place that would allow them to have children with the support of the communities. I'm proposing that we put such a system in place."

The leadership of the Gay Men looked at each other.

"I have no use for it," Randolph, said.

"Do you have an objection if others want to be a part of it?" Norm asked.

The first pulled a face, and finally said, "I suppose if people like Raul or others want to do that sort of thing it's none of my business."

Raul was surprised to find he was embarrassed. Randolph noticed it and cracked a tiny smile.

"The thing is," Norm said, "We're starting from a false premise. Just because we have children doesn't mean they'll join our communities."

"In what sense?" asked Raul. "Do you mean they might not be LGB, or do you mean we'd have to set up a whole other community just for straight people?"

"I guess I meant they might not be LGB," the man said, "In fact, the research says most of them won't be."

"Does it matter?" Raul asked.

"I guess not," Norm said. "But it would mean that every year there would be more straight people, and fewer LGB. Our communities would eventually become straight with just a small minority of LGB people. It seems like everything we've built would be lost in a few generations."

"That would happen anyway if we die off," Angela pointed out.

"Not everything would be lost," Raul said. "Surely love for their parents and grandparents would create and maintain a very loving equal society."

"Not if they feel the way I do about my parents," Randolph said laughing. "But seriously, we could set up traditions and institutions that would at least partially maintain the character of our communities. I mean, look at the Spartans. Almost all of the men were Gay, or at the very least bisexual or gender fluid. That wasn't a result of nature alone. It was the result of proper schools and proper training."

Raul looked a bit stricken, but he didn't say anything.

"Is something the matter, Raul?" Norm asked.

"No. I just think Sparta is a bit of an extreme example. That was a very rigid militaristic society."

"I only meant that we could influence the nature of our future society," Randolph said.

"Yeah, I don't think we mean that as a model or anything. We'll have to work that out as a community. The question right now is do we want to have our communities cooperate in having children?" said Norm.

They looked at each other, then both Raul and Norm looked at Randolph.

"It's all voluntary, right?" Randolph asked.

"Of course," the other two said in unison.

"Then I think it's fine. Maybe even better than fine," Randolph said.

"Then we are agreed?" Angela said.

"Yes," Raul and Norm said.

"In principle," Randolph said. "We still need to work out the details."

"True," Angela said. "For example, this is likely to knock down the productivity of my community. I'll have more mouths to feed and fewer worker-hours to produce that food with. Is there something that your community can do to ease that extra burden until the children are grown?"

"Seriously Angela?" Raul said.

"So now we're buying babies?" Norm said.

Randolph held his hand up, "She has a point. Not only that, these kids should know their birth fathers too. Our community should step up and host half of the children as soon as they are weaned."

Norm objected. "What you are proposing goes against a century of feminist progress. Angela, is your community going to be OK with that?"

"I don't know," she said. "I suppose it allows both communities to have both the burdens and benefits of raising children right away. There is a fairness to it. My people would have to be able to visit their children."

"Of course," Randolph said, "and the biological fathers and their partners should be able to visit their children before they are weaned and visit the ones who stay behind later."

"Yes," Angela said.

"Hold on," Raul said. "I think we're getting ahead of ourselves. We agree there should be a voluntary program for people to get together and have children, but that doesn't mean the community should dictate every facet of that. I think we should let people make their own agreements."

"What if people don't keep those agreements?" Norm said.

"Then the communities would enforce them," Raul said.

"How would we even know what those agreements were?" Norm objected.

"We'd have to create a registry where agreements would be recorded," Raul said.

"How would the communities enforce the agreements?" Norm said.

"If someone from my community violates the agreement, then we would enforce it. If someone from your community violates it, your community would enforce it," Angela suggested.

"Who decides what a violation is?" Norm objected.

"This coordination council," Raul said.

"There are only two votes on this council," Norm pointed out. "What if we can't agree?"

"There's a bigger problem," Randolph said. "Suppose a lot of people agree that the kids will be raised until they are 18 with Angela's people and suppose our people agree to partially support them until they are 18 and then when the boys are 18 they don't want to join us, they want to stay with Angela's people. Then we'll have been bled dry for decades and wither away anyway."

"That's a lot of "supposes" in one scenario," Norm said.

"Yeah, but they're all likely. If the people I'm representing are going to support this, I think we need assurances that the boys will be joining us at a specific date."

"So, before we were talking about half the children, now you're saying just the boys?" Angela asked.

"Half the children will be boys, and the whole point is to keep the communities going, so boys would make sense for us, and girls would make sense for your community," Randolph said.

"There's still a chance that at 18 or 21 or whatever the kids will decide they don't want to join our communities," Norm said.

"That's fine. We're not running a prison here," Randolph said.

"Not all of my people will be OK with giving up their boys so young," Angela said.

"Then they don't have to participate," Randolph said. "This is a voluntary program. If they don't like the terms, they can negotiate their own thing with someone privately."

"I liked the idea of the registry better," Angela said.

"I can respect that, but I can't sell that to the people I represent, and we rule by consensus," Randolph said. "Raul, are you on board with a simple division?"

Raul shook his head slightly and said, "I guess as long as it's voluntary and people can make their own agreements if they don't like the pre-negotiated one, then I can't really oppose it. But I want a registry set up for those that make their own agreements, and a commitment that each side will enforce those agreements."

Randolph looked at Norm. He shrugged.

"OK, you've got a deal." Randolph said, "Angela?"

"OK. I agree to it provisionally. I want my community to ratify it before it goes into effect," Angela said.

"Yeah, that's a good idea. I think we'll do the same," Norm said.

Twenty-One

The measure passed easily in Angela's community, but only after a lot of discussion.

It passed by a closer vote in Raul's and with a surprise provision.

"I can't agree to this," Angela said when the provision was announced at the next meeting.

"Why not? They're orphans. Who will object?" Randolph said.

"I will," Angela said and then added, "and they will. They've already started forming bonds of their own with each other."

"That sounds a little incestuous," Randolph said, "I mean they're practically siblings... in fact I think two of them are siblings. But leaving that aside, the real point is my people need a gesture of goodwill. We need to know that in two years you won't just back-out and keep all of the kids. If I go back and tell them you won't give us our half of the orphan's now, why would they believe you will give them their half of their own children in two years?"

"Surely you're not going to put your own feelings above the good of both communities are you?" Norm added.

"Raul, do you have anything to say about this?" Angela asked.

Raul spread his hands out on the table. "I don't agree with the provision. I think it's wrong, but all I can do is kill the whole deal. It's take it or leave it. All I can say is that I'll personally keep an eye on them. They've agreed to let them stay at my place."

"I can't just agree to this without talking to them. The oldest one is 15, they have to have some say in this," Angela said.

"We'll come back tomorrow. I just hope you won't let a 15 year old decide the fate of both our communities."

After they left, Angela spent the afternoon avoiding the thought.

In the evening, instead of going home, Angela went to their apartments and knocked hesitantly. They all gathered in the girls' apartment.

Angela told them about the provision.

"You told them no! Right?" Alex said hotly.

"I told them I had to talk to you first."

"And now you have, and now you go tell them no," Alex said.

"If I tell them no, then the deal is off. No new babies."

"No. It doesn't mean no babies. It means this deal is dead and they'll have to agree to a better one," Alex corrected.

"I don't think it would turn out that way."

"Look, they need this deal as badly as we do. You know that. That means they'll deal. They're not going to blow the whole deal to make good on a favor promised by one leader to his group. They already agreed to the basic deal. They're just seeing if they can get a little sweetener on top. Tell them no," Alex said.

"I think they will sink the deal. The power structure over there is a little odd. It only takes one leader to veto anything, and the leader behind this and the group he represents isn't all that interested in children. I doubt they'll even participate after it passes."

"Then why do they want us?!" Alex shouted.

"Not you. Just the boys."

"The boys ARE part of us!" Alex insisted.

"All right then, just half of you."

"You haven't answered the question!" Alex said.

Angela dropped her head.

"Which of their leaders is demanding this? It isn't Randolph is it?" Alex interrogated.

"Yes, it is Randolph."

"Are you crazy, Angela?"

"Raul says they will live with him. He says he'll keep an eye on them."

"And you believe him?"

"Raul has never lied to me."

"Raul can't even maintain leadership of his own community, Angela."

"That may be partially my fault."

"That doesn't matter. Look, you have to walk away from a bad deal. Maybe you'll get a better deal later, but even if you don't it's still better than having a bad deal. You taught me that, Angela."

"This isn't a bad deal, and it isn't your decision," Angela said.

Angela turned to Jonathan, Fat Jimmy, and Malcom.

"Will you go over to Raul's community, to the Republic?"

"Are you sure you can't get a better deal, now or later?" Jonathan asked.

Angela sighed. "I'm pretty sure."

"Then I have to go, or we are doomed. I'll go," Jonathan said.

"Are you an idiot? Did you hear anything I just said? Do you have any idea who you are dealing with?" Alex said.

"There are decent people over there, too. They'll help us, and if it gets too bad, we'll just come back. It's not like we won't see each other. The republic is only four blocks north of here," Jonathan said.

"You are an idiot," Alex said.

Jonathan didn't say anymore.

"I don't like it," Fat Jimmy said. "Those guys are perverts."

"Will you go if I send you?"

Fat Jimmy looked at Jonathan, "Yeah, if I have to."

"What about you, Malcom?"

"Does it matter what I say? You're sending us anyway."

"I want to know what you think about it," Angela said.

"I don't want to go."

"Will you go if I send you?"

"No. So, what are you going to do?"

Angela stood up. "I have a meeting with them tomorrow. I'll let you know what happens."

She left the apartment and started for the door of the building.

Alex followed her out. She got in front of Angela and pushed her against the wall.

"Listen to me Angela. Those are my boys. If you send them over there, I will never speak to you again, I will challenge you for the leadership, and I will take this community to war if necessary to get them back. Do you hear me?"

"What if the people choose me instead?" Angela asked.

"Then I will kill you and do it anyway," Alex said.

Angela smiled and shook her head slightly. "I wondered what it would take for you to stand up to me. I'm proud of you. I honestly am. You made a couple of mistakes. The first is, if you're going to kill someone, never warn them."

"I'll do it," Alex said.

"Maybe," Angela said.

Angela left. She chuckled a little to herself on the way home. Not because she was sure Alex wouldn't try to kill her, but because something good had come out of this obscene provision after all. Alex had found her gonads.

Twenty-Two

When Angela met with the representatives of the Republic, she agreed to the provision.

"So we are in agreement," Randolph said.

"In principle," Angela returned.

Randolph scowled a rueful grin.

Angela continued, "They have to stay at Raul's until they are 18."

"Done," Randolph said.

"You have to guarantee that no one will touch them until they are 18."

"Sometimes a fellow likes to hug someone," Randolph said.

"You know what I mean."

"Done," he said.

"We can visit them whenever we want."

"Done," he said, "Is that it?"

"No. I have to hold one of them back."

"Let me guess, the youngest," Randolph said.

"No. Actually the oldest."

"Look, the provision calls for all of them, that's the deal," Randolph said.

"I've got a situation. One of my rivals is opposing the whole deal. She has her own designs on the oldest. If I give him to you it may be my last act in office, and believe me, you don't want to deal with her," Angela said.

"So you are scared of someone after all," Norm said. "I think I just won a bet."

"You can sell this, Randolph. We both know that. Take the deal."
Randolph looked at the others, and said "OK, you've got a deal."

Twenty-Three

Fat Jimmy and Malcom moved to Raul's right after Thanksgiving. Raul did his best to make them comfortable. He gave them jobs running materials for the bar, and they were good at it. He also began using them as pages, as Angela had, but not to everyone. There were some houses he didn't send them to, and the boys figured out the pattern quickly and managed to disappear whenever those people came into the bar.

Alex didn't forgive Angela, and she didn't speak to her either, but she didn't oppose her, didn't threaten to kill her anymore. Shawna wouldn't look at Angela, and she couldn't look at Alex or Jonathan. She moved out of the apartment and went to live with Millie.

With the others gone, and Angela excommunicated, Alex and Jonathan spent all day together and they stopped caring about going to their own apartments at night. They just stayed wherever they were when it was time to sleep.

In time Angela started sending down assignments via intermediaries, and they did them, but they still didn't speak to her.

As the gloom lifted in the Republic, the Police started having their combined poker night at Raul's again. The booze was better. Alex, Jonathan, and Shawna went with them to visit the boys.

Jonathan didn't say much. Alex asked them a few times through the evening if EVERYTHING was OK.

"Really, we're OK," Malcom said the third time it came up.

Fat Jimmy didn't join in on that assessment.

"Fats, is Malcom right?" Alex asked.

Jimmy shrugged, "So far. Raul is good to us."

"But..." Alex prompted.

"But nothing," Fat Jimmy said looking around the room casually.

Alex stopped questioning him.

They came back on Christmas and brought presents, which embarrassed the boys because they hadn't made anything for them.

By January, Alex started reporting in to Angela for work. She still hadn't forgiven her, but she would communicate with her enough for work. Angela assigned her to set up the registry for private arrangements and to monitoring arrangements made through the new accord.

There were surprisingly few, to be precise, none. At first they speculated it was the weather. Alex keenly wished for Fat Jimmy's ears on the street. After a few more weeks Angela contacted some of the people that had asked her to broker a deal.

When she returned from her visit, she plopped into her chair and exhaled.

Alex watched her but asked nothing.

Angela waited a while and finally said, "I know you want to know, so I'm just going to tell you. They're trying to make private deals."

Alex nodded but said nothing.

"... And they're not getting any. Everyone they approach over there refers them to the publicly arranged deal."

"Everyone?" Alex said despite herself.

"Everyone!" Angela said raising an eyebrow.

Alex resolved to ask Fat Jimmy about it.

A few nights later Alex said, "Jonathan, don't come with me tonight to see the boys."

"Why not?"

"I have to flirt with Fat Jimmy and that won't work with you there," Alex explained helpfully.

"What?! You've never been into him before," Jonathan said.

Alex laughed a little stronger than she'd meant to, and said, "I need information from him. He can't speak freely. If I try passing notes or something he's going to get nailed as a spy or something. If I'm flirting with him then it will seem perfectly natural if I whisper things to him and he whispers back, especially if he gets embarrassed after a few of the whispers."

Jonathan nodded sagely. "Fat Jimmy isn't likely to get embarrassed."

"I guarantee that he will," Alex said confidently.

It didn't take long for Fat Jimmy to figure out the game. Malcom never figured out the game, got a bit disgusted with the whole thing, and wandered off after 10 minutes, which only made the whole thing look better.

The sour man was on his barstool monitoring, but all he seemed to see was a disgusting young couple.

When she got home she filled Jonathan in.

"It's no accident there are no private deals happening," Alex said. "The holocaust faction has let it be known that it won't tolerate any side deals. I guess they beat a couple of guys up pretty good a few weeks ago as a convincer."

"Does Raul know?"

"He has to know they got beat up, but if he knows why he hasn't said so out loud. Actually even if he does know, what's he going to do?" Alex asked.

Alex wrote a report and put in on Angela's desk leaving her name and Fat Jimmy's off it. Angela knew whose report it was, and knew there was no point in keeping the report around. She burned it.

In February women started knocking on Jonathan's door at night. The first night he just didn't answer the door. He stayed at Alex's for the next few days. They could hear the knocking next door. Once two couples passed each other in the hall, seemed embarrassed and kept walking.

Alex broke her protocol of silence long enough to ask Angela about it. Angela told, to lock the outer door of the building at night, and she would take care of it. A couple of nights later it all stopped.

In early March ten couples decided to take the plunge and signed up. A few weeks later ten men from the Republic came across the border. Angela hosted an odd dinner and ceremony, where everyone drank too much, which was followed by several more dinners over the whole month of April, and then the men went home.

Things started to improve. The green house was producing enough vegetables to be significant. The potatoes were looking good. Even the fishing fleet improved its already excellent results.

One poker night the end of May, the Police from the Republic met Angela's Police, and Alex, Jonathan, and Shawna at the border instead of at the bar. They had been waiting for them.

"Bar's closed tonight," the most senior one said.

"You can come back to our place," one of Angela's officers said.

"No, we had a long day today," we'll come over to your place next week.

"The bar will still be closed next week?"

The Republic cops seemed uneasy. Their leader just looked straight at her and shook his head slightly.

"Alright, we'll see you next week."

"Yeah. Next week."

Angela's cops turned back. Alex, Jonathan, and Shawna kept walking towards the bar.

"Hey, the bar's closed!" the Republic cop shouted at them.

Angela's cops stopped and watched.

"We're not going to the bar," Alex said. "We're going to see our friends that live at the bar. They'll let us in even if we can't use the bar."

"No, they won't. You need to go home," a Republic cop said.

Alex stared at him, waiting for an explanation.

"Just go home," was all he would say.

They didn't move. Angela's cops closed in behind Alex, Jonathan, and Shawna.

"What's going on?" one of them said to the Republic cop.

The Republic cops seemed nervous. "The bar's off limits tonight."

"You remember who these kids are right?" one of Angela's cops said. "These are Angela's pets. You sure you want to turn them back?"

"I know who they are," the Republic cop said, standing defiant

"Does your council know you're doing this? 'Cause they will."

"Yeah, they know. Get those kids home. They can't come into the Republic tonight."

Alex stared at him then turned and they went back the way they had come.

Alex went straight to Angela's house. She wasn't there. She had the cops call her.

Once Angela understood what had happened, she paused.

"This is tricky," she said softly to Alex, then turned to her Police. "Get out the SWAT gear, be ready to go in fifteen minutes, and stay off the radios."

"Ma'am, are we going to war with the Republic?" one of the cops asked.

"I hope not," Angela said, "but they know you just called me, and we'd better be ready in case they decide to go to war."

She turned to Jonathan and Shawna. "Have everyone start gathering in front of City Hall."

She turned to Alex, "You're with me."

She keyed her radio. "Republic Council, this is Angela Steel. Over." There was silence.

"Republic Council, this is Angela Steel. Over."

"How can I help you, Angela," Randolph said.

"I have a report you've closed your border with us. Is that correct?"

"That's a little dramatic. We asked some of your people not to party over here tonight. We've been getting some noise complaints."

"Good. I'm glad we cleared that up. Listen, I was planning to come see Raul tonight about a business proposition. Would that generate any noise complaints?" Angela asked.

There was a pause.

"No. I'm sure that wouldn't be a problem, but Raul's not home tonight."

"Well, maybe I could just give the details to Jimmy or Malcom and they could relay it when he gets home. I've been meaning to come see them anyway."

"I think they went with him," Randolph said.

"You wouldn't mind if I dropped by to check would you?"

"No of course not, but I'm certain it would be a wasted trip. No one is home."

"Can you get a message to him?"

"No, I don't know where they went."

"Well, could you have some of your men look around the City for them?"

"Sure thing, and if they find him, I'll have him give you a call."

"OK. Thanks."

Angela weighed her options.

"He's lying," Alex said.

Angela gave her a patronizing look, "No kidding."

"What are we going to do about it?"

"Like I said, this one is tricky. We don't know what's going on and we could make things a lot worse if we go marching in, or we could make things a lot worse if we wait too long, and we can't know which one is the mistake."

Angela got quiet again and Alex let her think.

They went to the offices where the crowd was. She mingled, pulled a few people out and talked to them individually, then stood in front of the crowd.

"People: I'm sorry to interrupt your evening. We seem to have some kind of a situation with the other half of the Republic. At this point we aren't sure if they are having some kind of crisis they don't want to discuss, or if the situation might be more dangerous. All we know for sure is that they closed their border a few hours ago, and they aren't being forth coming about the reasons. I'm taking a team over to investigate, but I want you to stand ready to render aid, and ready for any other contingency."

The Police left the weapons wagon behind City Hall, and Angela talked to them. Two officers stayed with the weapons and were joined by three of the people from the crowd. Angela took the other three officers with her and three more people from the crowd. She stuck a gun in a holster and put her jacket on over it. Then they walked down the street toward Raul's place.

No one met them at the border, but they saw shadows on the roof of one of the buildings. When they got to Raul's all the lights were out. They knocked. No one answered. They went around back. One of the windows was broken. There was blood on one piece of glass, but not much blood. They knocked on the back door. No one answered. They waited.

"Should we go in?" the lead officer asked.

Angela nodded. They tried the door. It was locked. They kicked near the latch, but it had been barred from the inside. They were about to try again, when two republic cops suddenly appeared.

"What are you doing?" they demanded.

"I've got broken glass. I've got blood. Someone could be hurt in there," one of Angela's cops said.

"There's no one hurt in there. That happened hours ago. The building is empty."

"Then it won't hurt to take a look."

"Go home. Believe me, you want to go home," the Republic cop said.

"Seems like this is a bit more than a normal Police matter," Angela said.

The Republic cop hesitated, then said, "This is a Republic matter, ma'am."

"Look, if you've got some sort of instability going on over here, and you don't want to be a part of it, you don't have to be. We'll give you a place to lie low until this blows over."

The cop glanced at his partner, then said, "We're OK. You need to go back to your side of the city."

"We'll go as soon as we know that our boys and our friends are OK," Angela said.

"Begging your pardon Ma'am, but they aren't your boys anymore, and your friends can take care of themselves. Now you should go before the council finds out you're here."

Angela scanned the roof tops in a leisurely fashion before looking back at the cops. "I'm quite sure they know we are here. I told them I was coming myself. Now are you going show us into the bar so we can see that no one is in there and we can all go home, or are you going to get in our way and cause an incident?

The cop glanced at his partner. He licked his upper lip reflexively, then took his hand off his gun. "Look. If you go in there, people are going to get hurt," he said in a low voice.

"Which people?"

"You six for starters, and Raul."

"Is Raul in there?"

The cop nodded.

"How many guards?"

"I don't know. There were just two earlier, but there might be others."

"Where are they holding him?"

"They had him in the store room; one guy inside with him and one guy outside the door."

"Give me your gun," Angela said.

The cop stared at her.

"Give me your gun, and get across the border. If this goes bad, you don't want to be here," Angela said.

The cop glanced at his partner, and said "We're going with you."

Angela looked at one of her cops, she nodded, and Angela said, "OK."

Angela stood back and looked at the building, imagining its insides, then pointed at a window. One of her cops smashed it with a baton and another threw a stun grenade inside. They were through the door and inside in 30 seconds. Angela shot the guard lying next to the store room door, and called to the man inside.

"The situation has changed," Angela said. "You can come out now, hand over your weapons and walk away, or we can come in there and kill you like we did your friend here."

There was silence.

"OK, I guess we're killing you," Angela said.

"Hold on," a voice said. "If you come in here, I'll kill your friend."

"Well I guess you might, but we'll still kill you. The real question is, how committed are you to your cause? We're pretty committed at this point."

"OK. I'm coming out," the man said.

"Nice and easy," one of the cops instructed.

The man came out, gave them his weapons, and Angela shot him anyway.

They freed Raul and he said, "Give me a gun, quick! That guy got on the radio as soon as he heard the explosion."

"We didn't hear him. "

"They've switched channels."

They gave him a gun and they all started moving for the back door. They had just reached it when they saw Randolph standing in it. He had a small lightly armed group of cops and civilians standing in the alley behind him.

He shook his head. "Angela, this is an internal affair. You should have stayed home. Leave Raul with me and you can still go home."

Angela turned to Raul and asked, "Raul, do you want to stay here with Randolph?"

Raul shook his head and shot Randolph.

"Anyone else want Raul to stay with him tonight?" Angela asked.

The whole thing had happened so quickly the crowd didn't know how to respond.

One by one, they put their guns down and walked away, until there was only one man left. He was red faced, sputtering. He raised his gun and three bullets hit him simultaneously.

Angela turned to Raul, "Do you need an army?"

Raul shook his head, "No. I need a radio."

Angela handed him one. Raul changed the channel, keyed the mike and said, "Condition 2. Condition 2. This is not a drill. Condition 2 by the numbers. Execute."

"Station 1 executing."

"Station 2 executing."

"Station 3 executing."

"Station 4 executing."

"Station 5 executing."

"Station 6 executing."

"Come on," Raul said.

"Where are we going?" Angela asked.

"To get Jimmy."

They followed Raul down a series of side streets to Randolph's house. There was a candle burning in a shed behind the house. They went to the door. There was a handmade sign over the door that said "School" on it. Raul pointed, then sent one of the Republic cops to the door, while the rest of the group took up positions. The cop knocked on the door. "Sir, it's Officer Curtis. There's a potential situation and your husband has asked me to move you and your student to a safe location. The door opened. An older sickly looking man came out, somewhat bewildered, with a gun in his hand. He realized what was happening too late and found himself lying face first on the ground with a broken arm behind his back. He was squealing and kicking. Raul kicked him in the head hard a couple of times and he stopped moving.

"What are you doing?" the cop said, "I had him."

"Go look in that shed and tell me you think I shouldn't have done that," Raul said.

The cop went in. He came back out pale, looked at Raul, put his gun on the ground, sat against the wall and put his head against his knees.

Twenty-Four

By morning it was over.

That night, the fires lit the sky one last time. After that, Raul came to the coordination meetings alone.

Malcom turned up at Millie's house the following day. He was cold and wet, and had a nasty gash on his arm, but was otherwise physically unharmed.

Nobody but Angela and Raul saw Jimmy for a week. Alex knew they had taken him to the hospital and done some work on him, but no one would say what. When they finally brought him back to the apartments, Jonathan moved his stuff into Alex's apartment so Jimmy could have the place to himself. At first he slept a lot. He barely looked at them when they brought him food.

A week after he arrived, Shawna came to see him but he said, "Get out," so forcefully that she knew he meant it. Malcom never did come by.

On the tenth night they heard him weeping and screaming through the wall. The next morning he wasn't in his room when they brought food.

They looked for him. After a couple of hours they found him, sitting on the headlands where the Golden Gate used to connect to the peninsula, staring into the water.

He didn't look up when they sat down next to him.

After half an hour he looked at Alex and said, "Why did you save Jonathan instead of me?"

"I tried to save all of you," Alex said. "I don't know why Angela saved Jonathan instead of you. You'll have to ask her."

"I didn't ask why you didn't try to save all of us. I didn't ask why Angela saved Jonathan instead of me. I asked why YOU saved Jonathan instead of me."

Alex furrowed her brow.

Jonathan said, "You were there, Jimmy. That's not fair. She argued for all of us, and even after Angela left Alex went after her, and knowing Alex, that's when the real threats started."

Alex put her hand on Jonathan's arm, and he stopped talking.

"That's not what he's saying," Alex said.

"Jimmy, I put it all on the line to save all of you, but you're right. I only saved Jonathan. That's because Angela knew if she saved Jonathan, I wouldn't kill her, but if she didn't I might. She knew that if she didn't save you, I wouldn't kill her, and she was right. I didn't. I didn't know that, but she did. So, the answer to your question is that I saved Jonathan and not you because even though I care about both of you, I care about Jonathan more. That's not your fault. It's just the way things happened; the ages we were, the order we were found in, the way we were housed, my personality. It had nothing to do with one of you being better than the other or one of you being less. It's just the way it was."

Jimmy nodded. "It's just the way it is," he echoed. He looked at the water swirling below them as the tide shifted. He looked at it for a long time. Then he got up. He looked at Jonathan, and said, "I don't blame you." He looked at Alex and said, "Thank you for being honest with me, and for trying." Then he looked at both of them, and said "Goodbye."

Twenty-Five

Three years passed.

Alex was nearly 19 and Jonathan was only a few months behind her. They were still a team. They were lovers, and as long as Alex was generous with others, and as long as Angela saw Jonathan as Alex's toy, her distraction, that was fine.

Malcom and Millie got married, or as close to it as the law would allow, and they lived quietly so no one would bother them.

Shawna never fully got over Jimmy. She moved on, took her place in society, but she was never quite the same.

Fat Jimmy was now Raul's fierce lieutenant. He never spoke to Angela, Alex, Jonathan, Malcom, or Shawna, unless official business required it, and out of deference to his feelings, Raul rarely required it.

Instead Raul put him in charge of the restructured defense forces, and that had paid dividends. The forces were actually an effective fighting team.

In the same year they were formed, they saved the Sausalito colony from the San Quentin gangs that had been drawn south by the light of their funeral pyres. After that they abandoned the Sausalito colony, and the practice of funeral pyres, and put a watch on the bay.

Their success had put a friendly pressure on Angela to match it, and she did. At first she tried to get Alex to lead it, but she refused, which worried Angela. Eventual she assigned it to one of the police officers, and the force was in some ways even better than Raul's.

In the fall the first batch of babies turned two, were weaned, and the boys were sent to the Republic. They were taken in by, for the most part, loving families. The plan was for them to remain in their homes until they were ten and old enough to go to boarding school with each other under the care of Raul, and Jimmy's hand selected teachers.

In April the rights of spring under the agreement between the two peoples was repeated as it had been each April.

Life began following a natural sequence. Both communities began to grow again.

One day in early summer, Alex caught Angela musing, looking out her window at the flapping rainbow colored flag that both communities flew. Angela turned to her and said, "We aren't really the Rainbow Republic anymore are we?"

"No, I guess not," Alex said. "Whenever people say 'the Republic' they mean Raul's people."

Angela seemed to chew on that thought for a while. Alex had caught her doing this occasionally the past year. She was still as sharp as ever, but now sometimes she liked to just sit and think. After a while she said, "Well, I guess we better get a new name, and a new flag then. Why don't you see if you can come up with something?"

"OK," Alex said, and largely forgot about it until one day she was in the library of the museum and came across an excerpt from Strabo's Geography. She took it to Angela and showed it to her.

"Oh, the Amazons, I remember them," Angela said reading with more interest. "We used to discuss them in school. Scholars said they weren't really like that. Even the ancient historians' stories about them varied from each other."

"They were real? I thought they were just a myth," Alex said.

"They are a myth, AND they were real, and I think they are real again, which is kind of amazing," Angela said. Then she got in one of her thoughtful moods, and Alex left her alone.

A few days later there was a new flag flying in front of the offices. It was really the old flag with the word "Amazonia" stitched diagonally across it. Soon enough it caught on, and Angela didn't even have a referendum about it. People just started calling Angela's community Amazonia.

In the fall they brought in a good harvest. The rainbow communities, the Republic and Amazonia celebrated with food, music, dancing and poetry readings. In the evening by fire light Alex took her turn in front of the combined communities and read Yeats.

Turning and turning in the widening gyre
The falcon cannot hear the falconer;
Things fall apart; the centre cannot hold;
Mere anarchy is loosed upon the world,
The blood-dimmed tide is loosed, and everywhere
The ceremony of innocence is drowned;
The best lack all conviction, while the worst
Are full of passionate intensity.

Surely some revelation is at hand;
Surely the Second Coming is at hand.
The Second Coming! Hardly are those words out
When a vast image out of Spiritus Mundi
Troubles my sight: somewhere in sands of the desert
A shape with lion body and the head of a man,
A gaze blank and pitiless as the sun,
Is moving its slow thighs, while all about it
Reel shadows of the indignant desert birds.
The darkness drops again; but now I know
That twenty centuries of stony sleep
Were vexed to nightmare by a rocking cradle,
And what rough beast, its hour come round at last,
Slouches towards Bethlehem to be born?

The previously raucous crowd greeted it with intense silence.

Applause seemed intolerable. An appreciative murmur spread through the crowd and Alex stepped back into the shadows.

Two days later they all turned out to the water front to see the fleet off for fishing. There was nothing special about that particular day of fishing except that they'd had the previous day off, they were all together, and the sky was deep blue with little puffy white clouds being played with by a changeable wind. The fleets were experienced now, their beige sails snapped in the wind and they stood off like so many birds of a flock. The crowd cheered and held toddlers up on their shoulders to see them better. When all the ships had disappeared, the people returned home, and to their duties.

At mid-day a freak storm kicked up. The wind tore up debris and threw it into the air. People moved their work inside and lit candles. The waves pounded the pier and took little chunks from it. The water swirled, changing colors with the texture of its surface, the angle of the sun, and temperatures of the currents beneath. Sea spray flew from the rocks as the waves pounded even inside the bay.

In the evening the fleet did not come back. About midnight the storm ceased. At dawn people started to assemble along the water front, waiting. An hour later a single boat moored at the pier, the crew cold and exhausted. Raul got a quick report from them while they drank hot tea and were covered in dry blankets by the crowd.

He pulled Angela aside and shared the information with her. "They were at their usual fishing grounds when they got hit. There was a split in the fleet. Your fleet tried to head for a cove. My fleet went out to sea to ride it out, but my boats got separated. This crew hasn't seen any of the others since then. I'm ordering the boat repaired as fast as possible, and I'd like to send it out by noon. Do you want to contribute to the crew?"

"Of course, and the repairs if it will help," Angela said.

The boat went back out with a crew of five, two fresh crewmen from Raul, two from Angela, and the original captain as an advisor. They also carried a row boat. The breeze was so light that it was slow going until they got out of the bay. After two hours of searching there was no sign of the Republic fleet, so they turned their attention to the Amazonian fleet. They looped back towards the coast a little north of where the captain had last seen them and glided south down the coast. When they rounded the tip of Point Reyes they saw the remains of several ships on the rocks around the headlands.

"How many do you count?" One of the men asked a woman with binoculars.

"There are at least four, but there's enough wreckage that it could be all six of them," she said.

They spent half an hour looking for signs of survivors and trying to make out which boats were lost. They finally decided to swing deeper into Drake's Bay, set anchor, and investigate with the row boat. When the light started to fail, they called off the search.

They'd found only one body, stuck in wreckage below the water line. It swayed with the waves, flowing blond hair obscuring the bloated face below it. They couldn't reach it and left it there. They identified three boats with certainty and two or three more tentatively.

The sun had already set and they had missed the tide when they got to the golden gate. They battled the sea for 45 minutes before they managed to enter the bay and tie up.

The crew made their report.

The next day another search was made, but nothing more was discovered.

After three days they gave up.

Raul found Angela on Coit Tower, looking out over the bay.

He joined her and said nothing.

Eventually Angela said, "One boat won't be enough. We've already used up all of the repairable boats. We can try to scale up the row boats we've been playing with, but the timber left in the wreckage is starting to get soft, and it's mostly the wrong kind of lumber for boats, anyway."

Raul nodded. He'd already been through the whole inventory twice.

"We're going to have to get creative," he said with a sigh.

"We can't catch enough food. We can't grow enough food. We've already scavenged everything in the city," Angela ticked off.

They looked across the bay. The blackened landscape of Oakland and Berkley had turned green years ago, but it was still slightly hot and, more importantly, there was nothing to scavenge. "Not much there," Raul said.

They turned their gaze to Marin. They'd had some limited success there, but they had already grabbed the easiest stuff, the San Quentin gangs might still be in the area, and most importantly they only had one boat, and that was needed for fishing.

"If we land our troops there, they would be cut off without support and would have no retreat," Angela said.

"What about the South Bay?" Raul suggested.

Angela wrinkled her brow, "There was a lot there in the beginning, but there were probably a fair number of survivors, too. Between them and the Mexican army who knows what's left."

"The epidemic is probably over, but who knows if it makes carriers or not? The way that ripped through Wally's community I don't think we want to mess with it. Besides, if what the traveler said is true, the area from the airport to Palo Alto is probably still hot. Who knows how many rad's we'd take?" Raul said.

Angela laughed a short dark laugh, "It would be funny if the very thing that saved us, starved us in the end."

Raul was lost in thought for a while, and then said, "What about highway 1? There was some good farmland south of Half Moon Bay. There's a chance the Army didn't bother with it. There might be food there. They also probably have their fishing boats intact, although we've never run into them."

Angela considered this. "The road's destroyed just past Daly City, and it's still slightly hot there. I imagine the road is out in a dozen places beyond Pacifica, but we could get past all of that. The real question is whether or not the food stores and the boat will last until we can replace them, and are the people there too strong for us to take what we need."

Raul frowned. "Let's hope we can enter into some kind of trade with them instead. We have workshops and tools; we may be able to trade."

Angela looked at him, but said nothing. When she spoke she said, "Whatever we do, we need more information. We should send scouts south and get a report."

"Yes," Raul said, "but I don't think it should be our military leaders, we may need them if some of our neighbors to the north decide to pay another visit. I think we need spies."

Angela smiled. "I have just the woman in mind, if you agree."

Raul laughed, "That would be great. Let her take Jonathan with her. He can represent the Men for me, and you know that's what she'll demand anyway."

Angela laughed, "Yes."

It was settled. The fishing boat was put back to fishing. Crews began attempting to construct new ships with parts of less salvageable ships and debris, work was started to upgrade the greenhouse, and Alex and Jonathan began their preparations.

Twenty-Six

The day they left was clear, bright and cool. They were sent away without fanfare. The less that people noticed their absence the better. They were nervous, but neither wanted to show it so they spoke little. The first part of the journey was familiar. The ghost town of the Sunset District affected them. They rested for the night in West Lake at a place where the Geiger counter said it was OK, rested and ate. They ate almost reverently because they understood more than most how valuable the food they carried was now. They cuddled together in the cool ocean air that was all they had ever known, and each in the arms of the only person they could remember ever really mattering.

In the morning they braced themselves for the sprint across the hot wasteland of Daly City to potentially enemy territory in Pacifica. The walk was brutal. The road was reasonably flat but chocked with debris that slowed their progress. Where the road was gone, was worse. Waste high grass made it impossible to see much of the hidden debris, and their arms and legs were bloodied by the time they got to where the road began again. They exhausted their water, but preferred to hike thirsty rather than spend time looking for and carefully filtering water in a place that was both physically dangerous and disturbing.

Debris gave way to ghostly neighborhoods again, and they felt they were being watched but saw no one. Despite exhaustion they hurried their pace. Well after dark, they crashed in a house on the outskirts of Pacifica, filtered water from the water heater and went to bed without bothering to eat. It was a real bed too, though they carefully stripped it of all its coverings and put their sleeping bags on it.

In the morning a bird was singing. Alex listened to it. It spoke of simple things, of finding a mate, of finding food, of making and defending a home, and something more. It was not the only bird singing. Each knew its place in the song, and when the birds' turn was over, other animals took over the song. Each was careful to avoid stepping on the others' song, and then when the sun was fully up, they quieted and returned to simple signaling.

Jonathan was up now, packing quietly and watching her. He packed her things for her. They went into the kitchen and explored the cabinets. They still had food.

"They must have evacuated to somewhere," Jonathan mused.

They hunted through the canned goods looking for anything not too swollen.

"I remember these," Alex said holding up a can of 'Spaghetti O's.' She shook it gingerly wondering if the tomato sauce had eaten through the lining of the can yet, then opened it.

"They're OK!" she cheered and ate two thirds of the can before she remembered to offer some to Jonathan.

"It's OK. I never really liked those anyway," he said.

He was loading up his bag with cans of Spam when he started laughing.

"What?" Alex said.

"I just remembered my Dad used to joke about this stuff. He used to tell my Mom that he wouldn't eat Spam because it wasn't real food and he said it was so indigestible that it would survive a nuclear war." They both smirked but Jonathan grew quiet. "I haven't thought of them in years. Do you think of your parents?"

Alex shook her head, but then apparently she did because she began to silently cry, just for a second. "This is silly," she said, and turned away.

When they were resupplied, they planned their trip. Linda Mar was next. They were both wary of Linda Mar. It was the first really viable town on their path, which meant it might be guarded. If they were caught, they were both clear their cover story was they were explorers from the South Bay. Hopefully there wouldn't be too many follow up questions.

By noon they were entering it. They moved slowly, watchfully, but it was empty. More than empty, it had been stripped of everything edible, and even most of the equipment. They determined not to camp out, but to stay in one of the buildings. They explored the town at a leisurely pace, keeping an eye out for good spots, food, and clues as to what had happened. They settled on a house across the corner from a McDonald's, because the roof looked good but mostly because Alex liked the wild flowers growing in the tall grass around it. They checked the kitchen, but it was empty like the rest. They checked several other houses nearby with the same results.

Jonathan pointed at the door jams.

"What about them?" Alex asked.

"Most of them aren't broken," Jonathan said. "That means the doors were unlocked when the food was taken. Also, there are no bodies. I think this town survived and moved on."

They went back to their chosen house and set up beds. Then Jonathan said, "We have time. Let's go fishing."

Alex agreed. They walked to the beach, found a promising spot and dropped a couple of lines in. They watched the sun go down together then cooked the one little fish they'd caught on the beach over a fire.

They went back to their house, ate some of the Spam from their previous house and went to sleep.

In the morning they got an early start. As they left town, Alex asked, "Do you want to take the long spooky tunnel, or get sand blasted by the wind on a cliff?"

"Who knows what condition those tunnels are in or what's living in them? I'd take the ocean."

Alex agreed.

They passed the turn out to the tunnel and followed the coast road. The warm sunlight made everything seem cheerful and when they got within site of the ocean again it sparkled the way it should. Alex smiled and began to relax for real. She began singing in a low voice and demanding that Jonathan join in. They sang that way for a quarter mile until the road disappeared. They surveyed the situation, then Jonathan back tracked fifty feet and beckoned for Alex. He got a footing, reached his hand out and pulled her up behind him. They continued scrambling up the embankment until they were high enough to get around the blockage. Once they were up there they stayed up there, paralleling the road until they saw no more washouts ahead. Then they worked their way back down to the road.

They came down near the exit of the tunnels and took a side trip to look at them. The mouths of both tunnels were collapsed. They puzzled over how both could have collapsed, then moved on.

A few steps further, they found a food wrapper that had not been exposed to rain. They didn't know whether to be excited or afraid.

"The direction we are coming from is a problem," Jonathan said.

Alex nodded, "Everything from this direction is either abandoned, or, as far as they know, hot."

They got off the road and looked at their map.

"We're less than two miles from Montara, and they had farms. If they still do, I don't see how we can pass through without being seen," Jonathan said.

"For our story to make sense, we have to be seen as coming in on highway 92," Alex added.

"There's a trail a half mile ahead that goes over Scarpet Peak and then down towards the backside of Half Moon Bay. We could cut off cross country for a mile at the end and hit highway 92. Looks like maybe 15 miles, and the only food will be what we are carrying," Jonathan said. "... or we could just travel at night on the main road and hope for the best."

Alex imagined sneaking through towns at night and shook her head. "Let's take the Peak Trail. I don't want to deal with people just yet anyway."

Jonathan nodded, and twenty minutes later they were on the trail.

The marine influence weakened and for the first time on the trip Jonathan began to feel too warm. After three hours they reached Scarpet Peak and stopped. They could see Half Moon Bay below them, and there was motion in it. They lay on their bellies and looked at the town through binoculars, passing them back and forth.

To their right they saw an active marina with at least 200 small slips, and boats coming and going. Next to it was a wide road that went nowhere connected to an access road at three points with crops growing in the space in between.

"Well, they've got fish," Alex said.

Jonathan stared at the no-where road trying to figure out what it was until he finally spotted a small airplane next to it. "Oh, it's an airport," Jonathan said."

"Where?" Alex asked grabbing the binoculars.

"That wide road next to the Marina," Jonathan said.

"No way!" Alex said, impressed.

They watched it for a while, but the airport was still.

Straight in front of them there was a small triangle shaped field with crops growing in it, and houses. To the left were more houses and a few larger fields, and far to the left in the hazy distance they could see what looked like even more fields.

There were people moving in the streets and fields too, most walking, some on horseback. They watched for over an hour and counted five loaded wagons moving down the street.

"Let's stay up here tonight and see if they have electricity," Alex suggested.

Jonathan ran a quick mental inventory of supplies and agreed. They set up camp behind some rocks and ate a cold meal, then went back to watching the town.

A little before sunset the boats started coming back and wagons lined up at the Marina. They counted ten decent sized boats and over 50 smaller boats passing into the harbor. They counted five wagons again.

"I wonder if they only have five?" Alex said.

"Nope," Alex said pointing to four more arriving from the other end of town. Each wagon left after it was filled. The first five returned after dropping off their loads and got filled up again, but the other four didn't come back.

The whole process took a couple of hours, and then the sailors started walking slowly home. Some were met at the edge of the marina by little groups of people that walked with them. The groups were mixed. Usually there was a woman and some children. Alex noticed that almost all of the fishers were men. After a moment, it dawned on them what they were watching.

They were silent for a long time, and then Alex said, "We used to do that. My mom would come for me and sometimes my dad would get off early and come with her and we would walk home."

"Us too," Jonathan said.

They continued to watch, reluctantly passing the binoculars back and forth.

Alex was breathing harder than she should have been. Jonathan was quiet. They watched until they couldn't see them anymore, then they rolled onto their backs and watched the stars come out. After a long time they propped themselves up again and watched for lights in the town. There were lots of little flickering yellow lights, but only two steady blueish lights, one next to the Marina and one far to the left.

"The one next to the Marina is where some of the wagons went," Jonathan said.

After a while, the yellow lights all went out and the moon and stars over the ocean dominated everything. The breeze subsided.

"People used to get married a lot," Alex mused.

"They needed to," Jonathan said. "It was necessary in the old days to pool resources to be able to provide for a family."

"Angela says it was historically a way to enslave women. That there was no way for a woman to make an independent living because only men could work, except for prostitutes."

Jonathan snorted, "That from a woman who was on the Board of Supervisors in the old days."

"Not those old days, the really old days."

Jonathan just shook his head. "People were still getting married right up until the end, maybe not as many as in the really old days, but plenty of them. Both our Moms were married. Were they slaves?"

Alex thought for a moment and said, "I think Angela just meant in the really old days before feminism."

"If Angela meant only in the distant past, why did she still care enough about it to constantly reinforce it?"

"I guess so it couldn't happen again."

"I read an article once where scientists were debating how and when Man domesticated the cat. Then I happened to find another article in the same magazine from twenty years later and they had concluded that man never did domesticate the cat. The cat just found men useful and learned how make them like them."

"So you're saying women weren't slaves."

"No. Women were slaves, and so were men, and sometimes children. That's my point. They already had a word for slave. If a woman was just a slave, they wouldn't have needed the word wife."

"Why do hate Angela so much?"

"I don't hate Angela, much," Jonathan said. "Just a little."

That made Alex laugh.

"Seriously though, why do you think she's a liar?"

"For one, she is a liar."

"OK, good point. But why do you think she's lying about this?"

"I don't know if she's intentionally lying about this. I think I've just read better books than she has. She never reads anything that doesn't support her view, and even then she only reads excerpts of books or newer books that are nothing but selected quotes from old books. If you read the real books, the old books, you see something different. You see people trying to survive and maybe even do well. You see women knowing that it's almost impossible to run a farm or a ranch when they are nine months pregnant, and that it's almost impossible to fight off a horde of raiding men without your own horde of men, and that if a man is sure a child is his own, he's more likely to take care of it. You see men knowing that they eat and dress a lot better with a woman in their lives, and that their children aren't so ignorant when there is a woman around, and that if they treat her well they are much more likely to be sure the children they are raising are actually their own. That's what I see in the books, a mutually beneficial arrangement, where everybody carried their weight by doing the things they did most efficiently. I don't know why Angela tries so hard to believe that all women before 1964 were miserable."

Alex didn't say anything for a while. Jonathan waited for her rage to pass, but when he looked at her more closely, he realized she was calm. She was looking out at the sea, not really seeing it, the breeze playing with her hair. She sat that way for a long time, thinking, and then she did a strange thing.

She stood up, faced him, carefully removed all of her clothing, and stood shivering in the cold night air. He had of course seen her naked before, but he had never seen her naked in this way. He stared at her waiting for her to speak. She said nothing, just shivered until he couldn't stand to see her shiver anymore. He took his coat off and wrapped her in it and held her close. She continued to shiver. He pushed put her into one of the sleeping bags, covered himself with another and wrapped himself around her bag and held on until finally the shivering stopped.

When he let go of her and looked at her face she was looking at him wide eyed. He returned the gaze and noticed the small details that had always been there, but he had never seen; the delicate eyelashes, the fineness of the bones around her eyes and in her cheeks, and the depth of the eyes themselves.

When she finally spoke she said, "It looks like some people do still get married."

"Maybe..." he said tentatively, "we will get married someday."

"Maybe we will," she said weakly.

Jonathan rearranged the sleeping bags so they could lie next to each other, slipped his hand inside her sleeping bag, and held her hand as they went to sleep.

Twenty-Seven

In the morning his arm was stiff at the shoulder, and numb everywhere else. He quietly removed it from her bag and tried to rub some feeling back into it without waking her.

This brought a laugh from Alex, who was not asleep.

"Who are you laughing at?" he asked.

"You," she said.

"Why are you laughing at me?" he asked; knowing he shouldn't.

"Because, you love me."

"So..."

"So I have a power over you that Angela will never know."

"That only works if I really love you."

"You really do," she said.

"That only works for long if you love me too," he said, growing serious.

"I do," she said a little more solemnly.

"Then that means I have the same power over you."

She considered this and sobered, "I hadn't thought of that."

Then it was Jonathan's turn to laugh.

Alex looked at him, not certain she liked the direction this was going.

"It's not that," he said. "It's just that you've lost nothing. You've loved me a long time, you just didn't know it." Then he added more earnestly, "That's why you fought for me."

"So, now what do we do?" Alex said, uncharacteristically uncertain of herself.

"The same as always. I love you. You love me. We have equal power over each other, so we'll have to negotiate, same as before."

Alex grew quiet.

They watched the morning routine of the town. The boats went out to sea early as expected, and as they expected, the fishermen weren't alone when they walked to the Marina. Seeing that, Alex hooked feet with Jonathan, and they kicked in time together without comment.

After a while Jonathan said, "I think we should get married."

"OK," Alex said, "How do we do it?"

Jonathan thought for a minute. "I think we're supposed to go in front of Judge or a religious person or something and tell them we are going to take care of each other, and that we won't be with anyone else, and then he's supposed to write it down, so everyone can look it up and know we did."

"What if I want to be with someone else?" Alex said, only half joking.

"Then you're not supposed to get married."

Alex frowned, "That could cause us problems when we get back."

"Maybe we shouldn't go back, Alex," Jonathan said. "There's life here. They might let us stay. If not, maybe we could go back to Linda Mar and start over."

Alex was quiet a long time. Finally she shook it off and said, "Well, whatever we do, I think maybe I do want to marry you. The promise goes both ways, right?"

"Of course."

"Then it's equal and I don't think I need anyone else that way, and if I can't find a way to be a good politician for the two of us, what's it all for anyway? Let's do it. Let's get married."

Jonathan hugged her. By mid-morning they had seen all they thought mattered of the city from a distance. They ate. Jonathan packed Alex's things and his own, and they set off down the mountain.

As they walked there was a comfortable quiet between them. This was not a new love, only newly realized. After half an hour Alex noticed Jonathan looking pensive.

"What's the matter?" she asked.

"I don't know who we can get to marry us? Assuming we go back, no one will do it for us. If we stay here they must have someone who will do it, but they might not let us stay. In fact we may have to make a run for it. If we end up in Linda Vista there won't be anyone to do it."

"What if we were the last two people on Earth? Would that mean we couldn't get married?" Alex asked.

"I guess not, but we aren't."

"The way you've described it we might as well be," Alex said.

"Well, I guess if we were the last ones, then we would be the judges, the whole government really. Then we could write it down ourselves and put it where all our children could look it up after us."

"Then let's do that?" Alex said. "I'm sort of the Princess of Amazonia anyway. That should be close enough."

Jonathan thought about it. "Maybe we should wait and see if this town's folk will marry us."

"Maybe we should wait and see if the town's folk don't kill us," Alex said. "Besides, if they will, we can do it again."

Jonathan cheered up, "OK, let's do it."

"You put the words together and then show them to me," Alex said.

As they walked, Jonathan tried to remember the words he had read in books. Snatches like "forsaking all others," and "richer and poorer, in sickness and health" tumbled around in his mind. They watched for a good spot to stop. They came to a curve in the road in a sheltered valley. Just beyond the curve was a Cypress grove, and in it a clearing.

"I think this is the place," Alex said in a whisper.

Jonathan pulled out a printed map of the area beyond Half Moon Bay and wrote words on the back of it. When he had finished he handed it to Alex, saying, "They used fancier words in the books I've read, but I think this is more us."

Alex read it silently. "I promise that I will always take care of you no matter what, that I will always make you more important than anything else I am trying to do, and that I will not be with anyone else in my body or mind or heart."

Alex gestured for the pencil and rewrote a part of it, then handed it back to him.

He read it silently. "I promise that I will always take care of you no matter what, that I will always make you more important than anything else I am trying to do, that I will not be with anyone else in my body or mind or heart, and that I will trust you no matter what, even when it seems like I shouldn't."

Jonathan looked at her quizzically.

"I know that before this is over, I'll need you to trust me," she said evenly.

Jonathan smiled and said, "I always have."

Jonathan made two clean copies of the words and put lines below that for them to sign and the date.

Alex found the perfect spot on one end of the grove. They cleaned themselves up and stood formally across from each other, holding both hands. Jonathan recited the words first. The Alex recited the words. Then they both signed both copies. Then Alex said, "I declare you my husband, and myself your wife." Then they hugged for a long time, carefully folded up their copies and stored them in their packs, and returned to the trail.

"Do you feel any different?" Jonathan asked after a few minutes.

Alex thought about it. "Yes and no," she said. "I still feel like me, and I still feel the same about you, but the future looks different to me, and I feel different about it. Do you feel different?"

"Well, I've never owned a slave before," Jonathan said straight faced, "so that's new."

Alex shook her head meaning to play it off, but when she looked at him there were tears in her eyes. "Jonathan, I trusted you with my real feelings, and I'll keep trusting you, but please don't make fun of them."

"I am sorry," he said. "I just wanted to see you laugh."

"I think you just wanted to tell me that you were right and I was wrong," Alex said.

Jonathan considered that for a minute and said, "I didn't realize that's what I was doing, but I think you're right. I didn't intend to be mean about it. I'll try not to do that again. How can I make it up to you?"

Alex slowed her pace, then stopped and said, "Just be my husband, a real husband." She took his hand and lead him off the trail into the shade of a Cypress tree. They made love there. It was not the fumbling gratification they had dabbled at in the City. It was not the grasping sort of thing they sometimes saw at the end of parties, or the calculated affairs of state. They simply gave themselves to each other under the clear blue sky on a crisp day in the fall. They did not worry about the time. They did not worry about their supplies. For an afternoon that day, they simply were and were one. When they were hungry they ate, and when they were tired they slept and each knew that whatever came they would fight it together, so it wouldn't really matter.

When the night came they watched the stars come out one by one, as if they had never seen them before, and in a way it was true. They had each seen the stars. On several occasions they had even seen them together, but the new thing called THEY had never seen them before. When the Milky Way was fully visible, the thought slowly seeped into their minds that whatever wastelands they had seen in the last few days, the universe was full of life, and however strange or familiar that life might be it would have at least one thing in common with them, it would know love, because only love could have built those stars and only love could have peopled their worlds and the imprint of that must somehow be in all of them to some degree. They did not think those exact words, but they each knew that truth, and though the memory would dim over time that truth would never leave them.

They lay awake, silent, holding hands until deep in the night, each listening to the other breathe until they were sensible of nothing else and they slept.

Twenty-Eight

In the morning they hit the trail early. Within five minutes they saw a large area of disturbed earth to their left. The walked closer, got down low and watched people going to work through the binoculars.

"Be careful not to let the sunlight reflect off those lenses," Jonathan said, handing them to Alex.

"Looks like they are digging something up. Maybe it's a mine," Alex suggested.

"If it's a mine, then why did they fill it in only to dig it back up again?"

"You've got me." Alex said.

Jonathan suppressed something.

Alex looked at him and shook her head, "Go ahead and say it. Just because you teased me yesterday and I got upset doesn't mean you can never tease me."

Jonathan shook his head, "I'm not going to tease you about that sort of thing anymore. It's hard for me to tell when it's going to hurt you and when it isn't."

Alex had never thought of herself as fragile. She wasn't. She was about as tough as they came, but she resisted the temptation to think of it as an insult. "He loves me," she thought. "And he's trying not to hurt me." She looked at him slyly and then said, "OK. If you won't say it, I will. You have got me! And I have got you."

Jonathan nodded.

They left the mystery of the digging and continued down the trail...

road actually. A couple of houses came into view in the valley between them and the diggings, with a sweet little farm between them and a creek running alongside it. A minute later a site they both immediately recognized appeared on the right.

"Greenhouses!" they said in unison. They could see ten or eleven of them arranged on the edge of a road in a valley below them. They were much smaller than their one large greenhouse, but still good sized.

"What would you say they are? 125... 150 feet long by 15 or 20 feet wide each?" Jonathan guessed.

Alex nodded.

As they came further down the trail they realized that what they had seen earlier was only the beginning. There were nearly 40 of them; all counted.

Jonathan looked positively hungry staring at them.

"It looks like they are doing it right. We have all kinds of wasted heat in our tall greenhouse. Theirs all have low ceilings. I need to see how they are doing it," he said, looking for a way down.

"I think we better keep going. More and more people are moving around. If they see us poking around, they might conclude we are spies, which we are," Alex reminded him.

Jonathan checked himself, "You're right, but somehow we need to get a look at those if we can."

They continued down and came to a Y in the road with one branch heading to the greenhouses and the other continuing towards highway 92. Jonathan looked at it longingly, then looked at Alex. "Come on," she said, and lead the way.

Five minutes later the road ended above an irregularly shaped field. There was no one in sight, so they scrambled down to the field and hiked on the road beside it. When they rounded the corner of the field and joined the main road, twenty more greenhouses came into view in the valley on the left.

This time Jonathan didn't seem as interested in them. "Come on," he said softly. He grabbed her hand and led her to the right side of the road and below the ridge line.

"What was that?" Alex asked.

"People," Jonathan said. "If we had planned this better we would have traveled this stretch during the night.

Alex rolled that thought over and said, "Thieves come in the night. Walk confidently," she instructed.

Jonathan relaxed, but three minutes later they both froze. There was a small pond to the right of the road, and several grungy looking buildings on the left. It looked like there might be people just beyond them.

"Let's sit down," Alex said.

Jonathan obeyed, but protested softly, "What are we doing?"

"We're not doing anything," Alex said. "We are a couple sitting on the hill looking at the view and having breakfast," she said, getting food from her pack.

"We're clearly travelers," he said.

"True, but we're not moving so no one has to react to us quickly if they see us."

They casually scanned their surroundings. They knew the valley to the left had farms and greenhouses.

"We could go right," Jonathan said. "It looks clear."

Alex agreed, but said, "We don't know what we will run into next. The buildings are more and more frequent and they are probably shoulder to shoulder when we hit the highway. The last thing we want to do is get caught walking through someone's property. This at least is a road."

"If they see us they'll know we came from the north and not the east," Jacob objected.

"We can just say that we got here early and went exploring."

Jonathan thought for a second and then agreed. They walked towards the buildings but 200 feet before the first building, they found a road going left and followed it instead. The road came out behind a building. They skirted it towards the south and east, then hit a paved road and followed it south. They passed some fields then came to some more green houses. There were definitely people inside the greenhouses. They could hear them talking. They kept walking. No one had seen them yet. They came around the corner and saw people standing in front of the building. Beyond that was highway 92. They kept walking; a few people were watching them idly. They reached the highway and hesitated, until Alex gave a slight nod of her head to the left and they went east along the highway.

When they were clear of the parking lot and the people looking at them, Jonathan asked, "Why are we going east?"

"People are less worried about strangers leaving than about strangers coming. Besides, if we're supposed to be coming from the east I'd like to know something about the road," Alex said.

Jonathan nodded and they walked at a reasonable pace.

They passed more greenhouses on the right, and then there were open fields, then more greenhouses.

"This place is amazing," Jonathan muttered once they were clear of the latest set of greenhouses.

A road to the left had a sign with an arrow on it that said, "Land Fill."

"What's a land fill?" Alex asked.

"I think it's that disturbed earth we saw from the trail," Jonathan said.

"Why would anyone fill in some valley with land?" Alex wondered.

Jonathan shrugged.

The road grew steeper.

After twenty minutes they passed yet another small group of greenhouses and Alex and Jonathan looked at each other in amazement.

Five minutes later the road became a mountain road. Twenty minutes beyond that the road was closed by a rock slide, with a cliff rising up on one side of the road and a steep drop off to the valley below on the other.

Jonathan poked at the unstable rock pile. It was shorter on the valley side, but then the likelihood of sliding off the cliff was a lot higher. He chose the cliff side and Alex followed him, but then they froze. There were human skeletons, picked clean and bleached by the sun, scattered on the top of the pile. They picked their way through them and on the other side of the pile were more of them, and cars parked as far they could see to the next curve in the highway.

"Do you want to keep going?" Jonathan asked.

Alex shook her head.

They turned and walked back towards town.

When the road widened Alex said, "Let's stop for tonight," and pointed towards a creek. They jumped the guard rail to the right of the road, slid down an embankment, crossed a field, and found a place by the creek to set up camp. They filtered water, ate the last of their supplies and soaked their feet in the creek. They leaned back in the shade of the trees and listened to the living water of the creek burble. A breeze caught the tree branches and sang a different song. When evening came they went to bed hungry and slept.

Twenty-Nine

In the morning the air was still. Alex kept her eyes closed and snuggled deeper into Jonathan. Then she heard a sound and froze. She nudged Jonathan and felt him come alert. There was a rustling sound fairly close, but it stopped. As if on a signal they both turned at once pulling back and separating as they moved. An Hispanic man in a grey green uniform stood looking at them. The stuff from their packs was spread out on the ground. Jonathan grabbed a rock. Alex grabbed a tree branch and they both started maneuvering for position.

The man rested one hand on his side arm, raised the other hand slightly and said, "Slow down. I'm the sheriff here."

Alex and Jonathan glanced at each other and repositioned their grips on their improvised weapons.

The Sheriff looked slightly puzzled, then said, "I'm not going to hurt you. I'm an American like you." He moved has hand away from his gun slightly. Jonathan and Alex lowered their weapons and the three of them stood there stupidly looking at each other.

Finally Alex dropped her tree branch. Jonathan stood closer to her, still clutching the rock.

"We don't want any trouble," Alex said.

"Then there won't be any," the sheriff said, "assuming your friend there doesn't do something stupid with that rock."

"It's just a precaution," Jonathan said.

"I could have shot you in your sleep," the sheriff pointed out.

Jonathan set the rock down, but within easy reach.

The sheriff relaxed a little. "What brings you to our town?"

"We're just looking for food and safe place to sleep," Alex said.

"Where'd you come from?"

"Menlo Park," Alex said.

"Is that right?" the sheriff asked, looking at Jonathan. "What about you. Did you come from Menlo Park too?"

"Yeah, of course, that's my wife," Jonathan said.

"Folks say there have been some strangers walking back and forth on the highway. That wouldn't have been you, would it?" the sheriff asked, looking at Jonathan.

"It was us. There are more people here than we expected. We weren't too sure we'd be welcome so we decided to come back this way and figure out what to do in the morning. Looks like we were right."

"Maybe," the sheriff said. "Either of you been sick?"

They both shook their heads.

"If we'd had that, we wouldn't have made it far enough for you to be talking to us," Alex said.

"You'd be surprised," the sheriff said with a hint of regret. "How are things in Menlo Park?" he asked, changing the subject.

"Dead," Alex said.

"How did you survive it?"

"We had supplies, but they're gone now," Alex said.

"So you aren't from Menlo Park?"

"No one's from Menlo Park anymore. We were just passing through, like always."

"Where are you from?"

"Nowhere," Jonathan said with finality.

The sheriff chuckled a little, "Yeah, I guess everyone's from nowhere now."

"What happened to the people at the rock slide?" Jonathan asked.

"Well..." the sheriff said, "That was a bad week for everyone," he finished vaguely.

"What now?" Jonathan said.

The sheriff looked at them appraisingly. "Well, what do you want to do? Are you passing through again, or do you want to stay?"

Alex and Jonathan looked at each other.

"What are the conditions of staying?" Alex asked.

"If you stay you have to work for a living. There are no hand-outs. All of the arable land is already in production so you won't be homesteading, and there are too many of us for anyone to try being a hunter gatherer."

"Who chooses where we work and the wages?" Jonathan said.

"That's between you and your employer."

"What if we can't find work?" Alex asked.

"You'll find work."

"What if we want to leave?" Jonathan said.

"You are free to go, but you can't take more than you can carry, and you can't go back the way you came. You have to go south along Highway One."

"What's south?" Jonathan asked.

"Everything is south. The new capital of California is in Monterey, but you don't have to go there. In fact you probably shouldn't. But there are a lot of nice towns between here and there, and you can go over to the Central Valley if you prefer working with cattle or in orchards. Heck, you could catch a train all the way to Deseret if you're feeling religious."

"What's north?" Alex ventured.

"Only death," the sheriff said, then abruptly asked, "So what's it going to be?"

Alex and Jonathan looked at each other and Alex said, "We'll stay, for a while."

"What about you?" the sheriff asked looking at Jonathan.

"I go where she goes," Jonathan said.

The sheriff looked at Alex for a moment, then looked back at Jonathan and said, "You're a smart man."

The sheriff made them stay at the home of an old couple in the mountains just off 92 for ten days. "They're rough old birds," he told

Alex and Jonathan, "They actually got sick in the beginning, but they got better, I don't think there will be a problem. No one sick has come through in a year. The doctor thinks maybe its mutated into something less deadly."

Alex and Jonathan worked for the old couple while they stayed with them, fixing machinery, fences, and ditches; weeding crops and doing whatever was asked. Alex tried to pump them for information about the community, but they wouldn't say much about it. They learned other things, though.

They found themselves watching the old couple whenever they interacted with each other. Noticed him help her cut green beans, noticed her fuss over him, noticed the things he said to her, and on and on. They watched enough that the old man said, "Jessica, have we got something growing out of our heads or something?" She hushed him and said, "Let them be."

When the sheriff came back for them ten days later, they learned that acceptance wasn't as automatic as it had seemed.

"Looks like you're in," he said, handing each one of them a piece of paper with the seal of the city council on it. "Keep those safe. You'll need them to get work, and since you're new in town you may get challenged a few times."

They got temporary work at one of the greenhouses, and Jonathan learned everything they had been doing wrong at the greenhouse in the park.

A girl they worked with showed them an empty house in a neighborhood about a mile from the greenhouses. The house smelled musty, but with their second paycheck Jonathan bought some wood and baked the smell out of the house with a roaring fire in the stove.

All of the houses around them had children in them. On their way to work Alex noticed them walking in packs towards either work or school depending on which shift they had. She asked a girl from work and found out that school was compulsory 3 hours a day during the winter through the sixth grade. There were even classes at the high school for people who wanted to go on.

"Could I go?" Alex said without thinking.

"Can you read?" the girl said.

"Yes," Alex said, "We both can."

"Then you can go, but you have to pay."

"How much?"

"I don't know."

Jonathan watched her and smiled.

On the way home, Alex was in a good mood. She was more animated than he could ever remember her being. They enjoyed a late dinner and sat on the sofa in the living room. She laid her head in his lap and he stroked her hair.

"Does this mean we are staying?" Jonathan asked.

"Do you want to?" Alex said.

"Yes," Jonathan said.

"People back home are depending on us," Alex said, thinking.

"Is San Francisco home? From now on whenever I say home, I'll mean here. Anyway, people back in San Francisco are free to leave just like we did," Jonathan said.

"We didn't exactly leave. We were sent to see what's possible," Alex said.

"We were sent to gather intelligence for an invasion," Jonathan corrected.

"And the intelligence is that they shouldn't invade, but back to my point. How will they know there is someplace for them to go if we don't report back?" Alex asked.

"They'll send another set of spies," Jonathan said, "Do you doubt that?"

"No. I don't, and that's part of what worries me. Angela has been different lately," Alex said.

"She seems more thoughtful," Jonathan said.

"It's more than that. She's less grounded. If she has any indication that she can successfully take this city she'll believe it and try. The next spies might stop at the site of the boats in Miramar and never realize just how strong the city is or that it isn't completely alone. Even if the spies did tell her she might not believe them. I think I have to be the one to tell her."

"I think you're taking too much responsibility. Both the Republic and Amazonia have their own leadership. They can make their own decisions," Jonathan said.

Neither slept well. Alex changed positions in bed every few minutes. Jonathan lay awake dreading the morning.

At breakfast Alex said, "We have to go back."

"Then we'll go back," Jonathan said pale but firmly.

Alex held him.

"We'll need to stay until the end of the pay period and buy supplies. We can tell the neighbors we're going scavenging in Linda Mar for things to fix up the house and ask them to keep an eye on it for a couple of weeks," Jonathan said.

They started out early and made it to the Marina by mid-morning. The boats were out to sea. They looked at the nearly empty Marina, then held hands leaning against the rail for no particular reason before moving on. They made it to Montara by noon and bought lunch. The order took longer than it should have, but they didn't care. It was nice being inside and watching the sea through the windows.

Leaving Montara, they passed through fields growing winter crops and paused at Martini creek to check their water supply, then moved on. Ahead they saw a man walking in the same direction they were but slower. They both noticed him. He was maybe a year older than they were. He wore a wide brimmed cowboy hat, durable traveling clothes, a jacket made of some kind of fabric neither of them had seen before, and a small internal frame pack. He was apparently lost in thought, because he didn't notice them until they were almost within range to do him harm, then he suddenly looked back at them, took their measure, and smiled. It was a nice smile under blue eyes, bushy black eyebrows and a black mop of hair that was two weeks overdue for a hair-cut.

"Where are you headed?" he asked amiably.

"Linda Mar," Jonathan lied.

Alex had noticed that since they'd arrived in Half Moon Bay,

Jonathan had started answering questions whenever men spoke to them. She let him do it, but at first it bothered her. "Why does he assume they're talking to him?" she accused in her mind. After watching a while she realized he answered, and she let him, because they *were* talking to him. They were always aware of her presence, sometimes uncomfortably so, but they always directed their questions to him. Only after she was sure of that point did it occur to her to wonder why she had always been the one to answer questions in Amazonia and the Republic, and having wondered that she concluded it was for the same reason, because the questions were never for him there.

"Where are you going?" Jonathan asked the stranger.

He hesitated and said, "North for now. We could travel together as far as Linda Mar."

Jonathan looked at Alex, but she could see he had already made up his mind, and she didn't disagree. There was safety in numbers, and this guy seemed to be someone they could trust. She nodded and he agreed to the plan. The stranger introduced himself as Sam and Jonathan and Alex introduced themselves.

While Sam and Jonathan got to know each other, and Jonathan revealed too much knowledge about the road ahead, Alex's thoughts turned back to the question of why one or the other of them should be addressed and the other ignored.

She pictured the two of them back in Amazonia and replayed various times they had met someone there before they left. She watched it from different angles and concluded that the reason she was addressed and he was ignored in Amazonia was that she mattered and he did not, or at least if he did matter it was only because of his connection with her, or what he could provide at a particular moment, never for what he was; which was a shame because he actually was a number of really amazing things.

She replayed the same sorts of scenes from the Republic, again carefully reviewing them from different perspectives and concluded that in the Republic the response varied a little more than in Amazonia. If they were there on business together, then it was the same as Amazonia, unless they were talking to Raul who knew Jonathan slightly and knew the other members of their group. But although Raul saw Jonathan as a person, he still only really had use for Alex. With others in the Republic, there was sometimes another element in play that caused Alex to unconsciously step slightly between the person and Jonathan, shielding him from the wrong kind of attention.

She played back scenes in Half Moon Bay and realized there was something of that last scenario in Jonathan's actions there. He was in some ways protecting her, though usually only from potential situations rather than actual immediate dangers. But there was another element to it as well. The men who spoke to Jonathan in Half Moon Bay were always courteous to her. They always, or almost always, acknowledged her with a word or a nod before continuing to talk to Jonathan. They often moderated their speech out of respect for her feelings. None of that had been done for Jonathan in Amazonia. As she turned the matter over in her head she came to the conclusion that these men were in their own way honoring not only Jonathan, but her, and their relationship with their actions. In a way they were acknowledging that they had no right to address her directly without being invited by her, or by her protector, to do so.

Her thoughts were interrupted by a reference to her coming from Sam.

"Have you known Alex long?" he was asking Jonathan.

Jonathan's eyes danced as he understated it, "A while."

It was enough to have told Sam what he needed to know. Sam nodded defeat, but there was a hint of amusement in it.

This was something else Alex had noticed. Jonathan had gotten rather good at the invisible man speech that had always annoyed her when she visited the Republic. At home, Jonathan had shown no interest in it, but here, he was becoming a master of it, which both annoyed and oddly gratified her.

"Well, you make a cute couple," Sam said, but there was something genuine in how he said it, like he was grateful to see it. Somehow noticing that, made Alex feel grateful too, and Jonathan must have felt something because at that moment he took her hand and held it as they walked.

Sam watched them and ventured, "How long have you been married?"

Jonathan looked at him surprised and said, "Almost five weeks."

They were passing the trail-head to Scarpet Peak. Alex, forgetting to disguise their previous journey, pointed to it and said, "We took that trail to the top of the mountain. That's where we decided to get married. If we hadn't taken that trail, everything might have been different."

Sam smiled at her, "Looking at you two, I imagine you would have come to that decision one way or another."

"Maybe," Alex said glancing at Jonathan.

"Where did you get married?" Sam asked.

"On the other side of the mountain," Jonathan said.

"We married ourselves," Alex admitted.

They stopped and showed him the papers.

"That's beautiful," Sam said, "I think you got that just right."

Alex smiled despite herself. That was another thing she had noticed. She was in some ways more tired than she had ever been in Amazonia. She was working longer hours and doing physically harder work. But she found herself foolishly smiling, and the best part was it didn't matter. It didn't put her in a worse negotiating position. It didn't cause people to take her less seriously. It wasn't a threat to her position. If anything, it just made people happy to see her happy when she smiled.

Jonathan squeezed her hand slightly.

"Would you like your marriage recognized by the government?" Sam asked.

"Sure, I guess," Jonathan said, "But we'd have to find a judge or a church person or something for that to happen."

"I think our government will recognize our marriage, don't you Jonathan?" Alex asked.

Jonathan hesitated, and Alex realized her mistake.

"I don't know what the rules are on that in Half Moon Bay," Jonathan said.

Sam saw all of this, but said nothing about it. Instead he said, "Well, if you want it recognized, I can do the recognizing for you because I am both a type of 'Judge' and an authorized 'Church Person or something'."

Jonathan laughed at him.

"Why does everybody do that?" Sam said, "Look I really am," he said, "and I can prove it." He stopped, set down his pack and pulled a leather messenger bag out of the top of it. He opened that and held out a badge for them to examine.

The badge was like nothing either of them had ever seen. It was thick and covered in some sort of clear plastic. In the upper left corner there was a small US flag, but instead of fifty stars it had 12 in a circle and one in the middle of the circle. Below that it said, "The Great State of Deseret" over a holographic symbol of an old fashioned beehive. Beneath the beehive hologram it said "Ambassador at Large" and it had Sam's name and picture on it, only in the picture he was wearing a suit, was less tan, and had a better haircut. Beneath that it said in small print that Sam had full authority to act on behalf of the state, that he should be offered every courtesy, and that any action taken on his behalf or against his person would be considered an act on the State of Deseret.

When they were done reading the front he flipped the badge over. On the back there was a letter from his church saying that he was an authorized minister. Alex looked closely and saw that they were really two separate badges that had been bound together in the plastic-stuff.

"Hmmm!" Jonathan said, duly impressed.

Having completely failed to cover their tracks anyway Alex asked, "What is Deseret?"

Sam looked at them to see if they were playing with him, then decided they weren't.

"Well," he said, "it's the old name for bunch of states in the Great Basin... in the western desert. When things fell apart those states united as a regional government and took on the old name."

"Why is there a messed up US flag on your badge?" Alex asked.

"Because we have adopted the US constitution as our governing document, and when the United States is formed again, we will join it," Sam said.

"Didn't your cities get nuked?" Jonathan asked.

"Las Vegas, Colorado Springs, Tucson, Edwards, Cheyenne, all got it. Mountain Home got hit with a little one. Phoenix got double lucky, their warhead missed and blew up a square mile of desert on the downwind side of the city. Ogden got lucky, their warhead failed to detonate so they just had a weeks' worth of heavy cleanup to do. We don't know why more cities didn't get hit. Looking at the attack pattern elsewhere they should have targeted any city with a large airport or military base. Their arsenal was pretty old. We speculate some missiles may have just failed during the boost-phase, or maybe we were just later in the attack sequence and some of the US cruise missiles got to their silos."

"What about the sickness?" Alex asked.

"It never came. We even had a few sick people wander in but it didn't spread. Maybe the air was too dry, or the soil too alkaline or maybe it had already started mutating."

"What about the Mexicans?" Jonathan said.

"They came. Though to be fair it wasn't just the Mexicans. There were Central and South American volunteers with them. We came to terms with them," Sam said.

"So you're working with the Mexicans?" Alex accused.

"Yes. We couldn't stop them, but we could get better terms not just for ourselves, but for people beyond our borders that would lay down their weapons, acknowledge the Pan American Government, and agree to support a code of behavior. Basically, the Mexicans agreed to spare municipalities that no longer represented a threat to them. In return they've granted us provisional citizenship, and they have agreed not to object to our self-government. They're even considering the U.S. constitution themselves. They kind of admire it."

They walked for a while in silence.

Jonathan tried to feel anger, but couldn't. Alex ran the political numbers and couldn't find fault.

They came to the blown up tunnels and skirted them towards the ocean. When they arrived at the far end of the tunnels and could see Linda Vista, Sam said, "I'm sorry that my government's choice is painful to you."

"I think what's painful is that it all came to this," Alex said diplomatically, and she believed it too.

"I appreciate that," Sam said, and they believed him.

Linda Vista was the same ghost town they had seen before. When they arrived in the center of it Sam said, "Well I guess this is where we part ways. I'm glad to have known you."

"Where are you headed next?" Jonathan asked.

Sam smiled thinly, "To the North, like I said."

Alex and Jonathan looked at each other and seemed to decide something.

"If you're headed any farther north you should spend the night here or in Pacifica," Jonathan said.

"Why?" Sam asked.

"There's a hot spot ahead," Jonathan said.

"I know. That's why I didn't bring my horse."

"What you don't know is that there is debris hidden in what should be the road that will slow your progress. You'll want to be fresh and you'll want plenty of daylight when you start that journey," Jonathan said.

Sam looked at them. "So you know the road ahead?"

"Clearly," Alex sighed.

Sam laughed a little.

"Then you might as well know I'm going to San Francisco," he said.

"So are we," Alex said.

Thirty

They went fishing together and watched the sun go down but caught nothing. Then they shared a meal from their pooled resources. They sat up late and told stories. Alex and Jonathan dropped all pretenses. It felt good to just be three young people on a trip together, and yet there was a weight on Sam that he did not discuss. He told them about his journeys, about the things he had seen and the people he had met. He told them about life in the core of Deseret and it reminded Alex and Jonathan of more things they had forgotten from their childhoods. They told him about how they had come to Half Moon Bay and their hopes for returning, and about when they were little and the day that everything changed and where they had been and then all three stopped talking.

"How did you know about the radiation?" Alex finally asked.

"That's something I can't tell you directly, but if you remember the capabilities of the old days, and if you remember that Deseret retains many of those capabilities, far more than just helicopters and cars, and movies, then I think you can figure it out," he said with a smile. He left a pause and then answered more seriously, "I think you can also figure out that I am not going to San Francisco by chance. Your people will have to make some choices soon. You two give me hope, but I'm far from certain that your people will choose wisely," he said and the weight of communities he had not mentioned in his stories dimmed his mood.

Alex and Jonathan felt it to.

"There are good people there," Alex said.

Sam nodded. "There usually are," he said, his voice tightening. He waited a while before he trusted himself to speak again, "But are there enough? What will the leadership be like and how strong is it? I'm sorry to be so bold, but I'm guessing you two weren't sent on a super-secret mission to open trade."

Alex and Jonathan looked at the ground, guilty. Sam raised their chins with his finger, looked into their eyes and shook his head. "You two are not guilty," he said.

"Because Deseret says so?" Alex challenged.

"Because God says so, and he never lies to me," Sam said with such conviction that they couldn't respond.

They slept then, and despite sadness they slept well and in his dreams Jonathan's parents finally came and walked him home from school, and in her dreams Alex was five and dancing in a circle in her living room with her mother, and in Sam's dreams he was sitting under a tree holding his girlfriend's hand and innocent of all he had seen since, and when they awoke in the morning they packed and walked on together in silence all the way to Pacifica. In Pacifica Sam lead them off the highway toward the Beach.

"Where are we going?" Alex asked.

"Here," Sam announced as they cleared the parking lot and the full ocean came into view. "Now that we've left that stripped dead town behind, I want to give you a present."

Alex and Jonathan looked confused.

"I want to give you that recorded wedding we talked about. Do you want that?"

Alex and Jonathan looked at each other and nodded.

Sam said, "Repeat the vows you made to each other before."

They did, and neither had to refer to the paper. Then Sam asked them if they would keep their promises and asked them if they accepted each other and they said they would and they did. Then Sam pronounced them "Man and Wife." Then he opened his backpack, pulled out the courier bag with the beehive logo embossed on it. He opened that and pulled out a velvety pouch. From the pouch he pulled a charcoal colored piece of glass that sparkled and came to life at his touch.

He took their full names and birthdays and places of birth and tapped it all into the glass. He took down where they were born and the names of their mothers and fathers as far back as they could remember and tapped that in. He took down their addresses in Half Moon Bay and San Francisco.

Then he put the glass away as carefully as he had taken it out and said, "I can't give you a certificate now, but one will be sent to your address in Half Moon Bay and you can always go to the Mayor's office and get a copy."

"How long will it take?" Jonathan asked.

"It will probably be there before you get back. If not, you can get it the same day you get back."

"Doesn't it have to be recorded in your capital first?" Alex asked.

"I just recorded it in the capital," Sam said with a smile.

They were about to start moving toward the road, when he stopped and surprised even himself by telling them of things which could be that they had never imagined and when he had finished Alex and Jonathan kissed each other and hugged Sam. Then they put on their backpacks, walked to the highway and walked north.

As they walked, Sam absently picked long pieces of grass and wove them into two intricate ribbons. When they paused for lunch just before the hotspot, he pulled out his sewing kit, trimmed the ribbons, sewed the ends together to make rings, and handed one to each of them.

Thirty-One

Angela was restless. Alex was late. She had been gone for five weeks and they had agreed that the most she should be gone was four. The situation had not improved. Their little fishing boat had been pushed to its limit, but they had still been dipping into storage regularly. Unless something changed they wouldn't make it to spring, let alone to harvest.

They had pieced together another boat, but it was not strong enough to trust outside the bay, and they did not trust the fish in the bay, so Raul used it for lighting strikes into Marin to find what food they could. They did not find much.

Angela sent Shawna to Westlake with a radio to watch for Alex and report back. Shawna set up camp at the base of a tall eucalyptus tree next to Highway 35, did a radio check, and climbed the tree. She watched most of the day, then climbed down and spent the night.

In the morning she radioed a report to Angela and climbed back up in the tree.

Angela met with Raul.

"We just need to wait a little longer," Raul said. "They'll be back."

"How much longer do we wait?" Angela said.

"A little longer," Raul said.

"Then what?"

"Then we take a task force south and only send the scouts ahead a few hours," Raul said.

Angela paced, and finally agreed.

"In the meantime I'm sending a squad to the south bay to see what they can find," he added.

After he left, Angela looked out her window. The Oakland hills were lovely, covered in their winter green with ruins poking up through it like medieval castles. Her head hurt. It often hurt. She briefly toyed with sending a group across to colonize, but the resources there were just as scarce.

She looked around her office. The furniture seemed worn and dated. Winter sunlight lit the motes of dust that moved with the air currents. She would have to send a team to find better furniture somewhere. Her mood soured.

In the afternoon Raul's men came back, but had been unsuccessful. The South Bay had been largely burned and was returning to wilderness.

When the fishing boat came back in the evening, they reported having sighted whales and discussions started about trying to hunt them. But the next day there were no more sightings.

In the middle of the afternoon the radio squawked. For a moment it didn't register in Angela's mind what was being said. She focused. It was Shawna calling. Angela answered.

"There's movement on the road," she said.

"Is it Alex?" Angela asked.

"I can't see faces yet. One of them could be, but there are three people," Shawna said.

A tingle crept up Angela's skin. Raul was on the radio now. He had been monitoring. "Angela, I'll get my team together, you get yours together, and we'll rendezvous at the rally point in the Sunset District," he said.

Angela forgot to respond.

"Angela?" Raul said.

"Got it. Meet you there," Angela said.

She rang the new fire bell they had pulled down from the old church and saw her teams converging on the street in front of City Hall.

She charged Team A with being ready to leave in ten minutes and excused the rest. She put together her own kit.

They were half way to the Sunset District when Shawna updated them.

"It's Alex alright and Jonathan, but they've got a dark-haired young man with them. I don't see any weapons. They don't appear to be in a hurry," Shawna said.

"Does it look like Alex is a prisoner?" Angela said.

"No," Shawna said, "looks like they are just traveling together."

Relief began to spread over Angela, but then fear was replaced by a sort of resentment.

They were at the rendezvous with Raul when Shawna called again, "It's OK. They're here with me and they are OK," she said.

"We'll meet you at the golf course," Angela instructed.

When they met, Angela's troops surrounded Sam, took his pack from him, searched him, and tied him up.

"What are you doing?" Alex demanded. "Let him go. He's no threat. He's my guest." Angela's troops paused long enough to look at Angela who shook her head slightly and they continued.

Jonathan moved in and tried to push them away from Sam who was sitting passively on the ground. Angela looked at Raul who sent in a couple of men to pull Jonathan away.

Angela took Alex by the arm and led her away from the others. Jonathan struggled to get loose to no avail.

"What are you doing Angela? You're putting the whole community in jeopardy. He's an ambassador and you don't want to mess with his nation!"

Angela shook her head at her. "I'm the one asking the questions here, and you'll answer them."

Alex quieted long enough for Angela to gather her thoughts.

"Your mission was to find out what resources were available, the strength and deployment of troops and to identify the best routes and targets. Not to make contact. You know the general belief that we are nothing but a glowing cinder is what has kept our communities safe."

"May I point out that under your plan the minute we attack another community that belief will be shattered," Alex said.

"No, you may not," Angela said.

"Angela, they already know we are here!"

"Who did you tell?"

"No one. Just Sam and he already knew."

"How do you know he knew? It's one of the oldest tricks in the book to pretend you know something to get someone to tell you what you want to know. Where did you meet him?"

"On the trail here, just outside of Montara."

"And you told no one else?"

"No. But that doesn't mean they don't know we are here."

"Who knows? Half Moon Bay?"

"No. I don't think so. At least if they do know it's not general knowledge. If people ask what's up north they just say "Death.""

Angela exhaled in relief.

"It's not Half Moon Bay you have to worry about, Angela. It's the Mexican Army and Deseret."

"The Mexican army must have moved on years ago, and there is no such thing as Deseret," Angela said dismissively.

Raul joined the conversation. "Angela, you better see what they found on that guy."

Alex looked at Raul with an expression of gratitude. Raul ignored it.

Angela spoke to the leader of team A. She showed her Sam's credentials, and the curious piece of charcoal colored glass.

Angela had them stand Sam up.

"Who are you?"

"I am Ambassador Harrison of the great state of Deseret. Who are you?" Sam asked calmly.

"I am Angela Steel, the president of Amazonia and I am asking the questions here."

She examined his credentials. They had the desired effect on her, but she pressed on.

"There never has been a country named Deseret," Angela said dismissively.

"That depends on who you ask, but whatever the case, there is one now," Sam said.

"Why are you here?"

"I am here to offer provisional citizenship in Deseret, but I should say I'm reconsidering that," Sam said evenly.

"How did you know to come here?" Angela asked.

"We don't disclose our methods, but we regularly check cities and regions that have been out of contact for a long time. In fact, that is my primary role."

"Who knows you are here?"

"My government is aware of my location at all times," Sam said.

"What does your government hope to gain by offering provisional citizenship?" Angela asked.

"Not much. Currently there is a 2% tax on banking transactions, but that barely covers the costs of the services. We believe that a unified vibrant country is in everyone's best interest," Sam said.

Angela scoffed. "There would have to be a banking system and a currency for that to work."

"Ask your own people if it exists. They were in Half Moon Bay for several weeks. I'm sure they encountered it."

Angela went to Alex, "Did you see a banking system in Half Moon Bay?"

"Yes," Alex said.

"What is the currency?"

"The accounts are in U.S. dollars. There isn't a lot of actual paper money or coins, but almost everyone accepts checks. The world out there is a lot bigger than you thought it was. That's why we had to be gone so long. We had to figure out how it worked."

Angela seemed to shake a little. Alex could not tell for sure if she was angry or nervous or something else.

Angela turned on Sam, "Where are you really from? Who really sent you?" What do they really want?"

"I've told you the truth," Sam said. "If that doesn't satisfy you, I have nothing else for you."

Angela pulled her pistol out, pointed it at Sam's head, and pulled the trigger. The old round in the pistol's chamber failed to go off.

"Angela!" Raul roared before she could pull the trigger again. She re-holstered the gun and went to speak with him.

"What you do in Amazonia is your business," Raul said, "But this affects the Republic as well. Do we understand each other?"

They returned to Sam.

"Look, Mr. Harrison. Angela needs some straight answers. If you tell us the truth, we'll guarantee your safety. We can't let you go back the way you came, but we could take you further north and let you continue your journey," Raul said.

"Who are you?" Sam asked.

"I am Raul Dominguez, president of the Rainbow Republic," Raul said.

"Mr. Dominguez, Ms. Steel, before I say anything more, you need to understand that if you harm me in any way, you will be sealing the fate of the people in this city, yourselves included."

"I don't think you are in any position to be making threats," Angela said.

"Ma'am, if you harm me, you will be abandoned. Your supplies will dwindle. Disease, hunger and warfare will destroy all of you. I am not pleading for my life. I am pleading for yours, and for the lives of the innocent people among you," Sam said.

"What makes you think we need you? What makes you think we want your interference? We have survived for eight years with no help from anyone but each other," Angela said, "and we have created something amazing."

Sam nodded. "If that's the case, then just say so. We will leave you alone, except to contact you once a year to see if you still feel that way. But I have seen this all before. Before you decide what to do, I'd like to ask you each one question."

Raul gestured for him to continue. Angela said nothing.

"Mr. Dominguez, what was the population of San Francisco six months after the disaster, and what is it now?"

Raul considered the implications of what Sam had said without actually responding.

"Well," Sam said, "I think it's safe to say, its less than it was."

Raul nodded slightly, involuntarily before stopping himself.

Sam turned to Angela and hesitated before saying, "And you Ms. Steel. How much blood is on your hands, and how much more do you want there?"

Angela turned white with rage, and shot him before anyone could react.

Raul closed his eyes. He rubbed his forehead for a moment before opening them again.

"That wasn't your decision to make," he said.

"Well, I made it," Angela said. "Now you have to decide what you're going to do."

Raul considered his options, then instructed his men to help clean up the mess.

Alex sat down on the grass. Angela was standing over her saying something. Alex didn't answer her. Angela kicked her slightly to get her attention. She looked up and saw that she was holding the charcoal colored piece of glass.

"What is this thing?" Angela repeated herself.

"A computer, I think," Alex said absently.

Angela scoffed. "I remember computers. This is not a computer."

"He tapped information into it," Alex said.

"So the magic man from 'Deseret' taps on a piece of glass, and you think he's got a computer?" Angela said.

Alex didn't argue.

Angela turned to the group, "Anyone want a working computer?"

Everyone was careful not to reply.

"I didn't think so," Angela said and smashed it against a tree trunk.

Alex closed her eyes.

Angela rummaged through Sam's things while the troops dug a

hole. She found nothing interesting, but a newish water pump that she threw to Raul as a peace offering.

Next she went through Alex's pack, pausing slightly when she found several printed checks, but only really stopping when she found the map with promises written on the back. She lifted Alex's left hand and looked at the new grass band on her finger. She turned to Raul, and said, "Does he have one?"

Raul looked to see what she meant, looked at Jonathan, and nodded.

Angela pulled it off Alex's finger, wadded it up in the map and threw the bundle into the hole where they'd thrown Sam's body. Angela threw the rest of Sam's things on top of him and left with Alex in tow.

Raul watched his men shoveling dirt into the hole philosophically, then leaned forward and pulled out the leather courier bag. It was good quality and he liked the tooling on it. When they were done, Raul took Jonathan home with him.

Thirty-Two

Alex did not speak to Angela on the way home. She did not speak to her when Angela locked her in her old room. She did linger over Jonathan's possessions, touching them. Alex expected that Angela would give her space as she had when Jimmy and Malcom had gone over to the Republic, but the next morning Angela yanked her out of bed by her hair and marched her to the little museum on the second floor.

Alex remembered when the museum had opened. It had been a gift from the arts community, a museum with the likenesses and stories of all of Angela's heroes. Angela pushed open the doors and pushed her inside, then fumbled with the curtains until there was light enough to see. The room was dusty.

Angela pushed her slowly past the names and pictures she had heard and seen so many times during her education.

Marylyn Fryes
Margaret Sanger
Elana Dykeswoman
Julia Penelope
Zsuzsana Budapest
Valerie Solanas
Jill Jonston
Janice Raymond
Sheila Jeffreys
Gloria Steinam
Ti-Grace Atkinson

Angela pushed her slowly down the aisle letting each heroe accuse her in turn, until they came to a new display in the very back of the museum. It was not as professionally assembled as the rest, not as slick, and it was much newer. Alex suspected that Angela had made it herself, imitating the style of the artists before her, with less skill but perhaps more purity, more interest, more diligence.

The new display had the picture of a seated woman in expensive Victorian clothing, wearing a white veil on her head and looking directly at the camera. The title said, "Mary Ellen Pleasant."

Angela let Alex look at the picture as long as she wanted. When she looked away, Angela said in a low voice, "Don't look away."

Alex shifted to a more comfortable position and waited.

"Look hard at that face Alex. Do you know who that is?"

Alex gave no reply.

"That is the first queen of San Francisco," Angela said reverently. "She was born a slave and after she was freed she became a member of the Underground Railroad personally conducting hundreds of people to freedom. She was the mother of civil rights in San Francisco. She employed or set up in business hundreds of black people at a time when the city was set against employing any. She singlehandedly forced the coaches in San Francisco to carry black people. She personally financed John Brown's attempt to start a slave insurrection and bought land in Canada for the slaves that were supposed to be freed by it. Even more than that she personally rode ahead of Brown throughout the south, disguised as a jockey, to alert the slaves and prepare them for Brown's attempt. Before Brown's attempt she was risking her freedom to do it, but after the attempt started early she was risking her life. She became one of the San Francisco's first millionaires and twenty years after arriving with no contacts and little money, she was essentially above the law, untouchable."

Alex said nothing.

"Are you listening?" Angela said.

Alex was silent.

Angela grabbed Alex by the hair and pulled her head back forcing her to look at her. "Are you listening? You need to listen! If you don't listen, then I'll have no hope for you. We will be finished, and I will treat you as an enemy of the state, a traitor. Do you understand me."

Alex looked into Angela's eyes and said, "I understand you?"

"Good," Angela said. "Are you listening?"

"I hear you," Alex said.

Angela smiled at Alex's attempt at redefinition and said, "Good enough. I'm sure you're bored with my little history. You've certainly heard enough histories like it through the years. But that history is not the one that matters today. There is another history you need to hear and understand if there is any chance for you."

Alex watched Angela. Angela took that as interest, and began to hope. She continued.

"There is another truth that too few have the courage to see, and without seeing that truth, her accomplishments can't be understood, let alone replicated. She never could have accomplished the things she did if she had not become the queen of San Francisco. If she had not amassed the wealth and influence she did, she could not have helped her fellow former slaves, she could not have tempered racism in the city, and she could not have helped start the Civil War that ended slavery. All of that depended on her amassing a personal fortune and a power base that allowed her to operate with impunity. The truth of how she accomplished that is what you need to understand."

Alex nodded.

Angela smiled and continued, "The seeds of her greatness can be seen when she was a little girl, still a slave. When her mother was dying she told her that although her father was the son of a plantation owner, her grandmother was something more, a voodoo queen. After her mother's death, even as a little girl, even though she was untrained and knew little of those arts, she used that heritage to be a leader among her fellow slaves. She innately understood their superstitions, their fears, and their hopes enough to have influence.

Once free, she put everything second to her goals of liberation for her people, even sending her only child away as an infant to be adopted by another family. But her brilliance really shines in San Francisco. She correctly understood from the moment she got off the ship the two realities that mattered then. First that there was money, and second, that there were too many men and not enough women. She also knew that without women, men quickly run out of uses for money, and she provided them with uses for it.

First she provided them with food, for a fee. Then she provided them with better food. Then she provided them with women, which in time she made sure became their wives. Then she provided them with interesting conversation and the excitement of the occult. In time she provided some of them with children that they thought were their own. She covered up crimes and used her growing network of friends to help her do it. She made sure she got paid for all of this either in cash or information, and of the two the latter was the more powerful.

In time she knew the real origins of the wives of the most important men in town, the real origins of their children; the nature, time and victims of their crimes and where the evidence of those crimes was hidden.

Just as importantly, through her network of servants in important households, secret listening posts in her home and high class bordellos, and the ability to blackmail the wives of all the most important men in the city, she had a better picture of the business dealings of the city than its businessmen, and she passed that inside information to her partner and lover who used it to advantage in investing. She took on the role of his steward which gave her full access to the money being made by his trades.

She also returned to her roots. She never forgot the influence she'd had over her fellow slaves, so she spent the time and money to learn voodoo properly from an expert. That knowledge, combined with real gratitude for assistance; assistance with legal problems, escaping slavery, debts, employment, inconvenient children, and business, made her the true government of San Francisco as far as most members of the black community were concerned.

At her peak she could quite literally get away with murder. When her lover and partner grew ill and called for attorneys to amend his will, he fell down the stairs and died before they arrived. It was ruled an accident. Do you understand why I am telling you this?" Angela asked, and waited patiently.

"I think so," Alex said. "You want me to sell my sisters into prostitution and then the slavery of marriage, cuckold men, use blackmail and subterfuge to obtain actionable information, use superstition and patronage to control my friends, murder those who get in my way, and to sacrifice every normal human relationship at the precise moment when it will gain me the most power."

Angela clapped slowly. "Bravo Alex! But I did not say I wanted you to do any of that. I want you to be able to do that whenever it is necessary, and to do it without hesitation, and to do worse if necessary."

Alex locked eyes with Angela, held her gaze with an icy resolve. Angela did not look away, but the edges of her eyelids trembled slightly.

Then Alex said, "I have thought of you as a sort of mother for a long time, Angela. So, I sincerely hope that what I will say next will make you proud of me."

"As do I," Angela said.

"I have already begun to do as you have instructed me today, but until this moment I was uncertain if you would approve, uncertain if perhaps I had gone too far."

Angela watched her carefully, a mild smile of surprise and expectation playing across her face, but she said nothing.

"You're right. I went off mission; because once I saw the facts on the ground the mission was stupid. I've made my own contacts inside Half Moon Bay. I've got Jonathan wrapped around my finger tighter than ever, which provides me with my own personal guard, at least when I'm not here. I had a contact with a larger ally until you killed him, and now that you have killed him, I have a wedge between you and Raul that I can use at will. I have my own plan to save San Francisco, Angela, because yours simply won't work, and I fully intend to execute that plan whether you like it or not."

Angela smiled, amused. "Is that all you've got?" she asked.

"Of course not," Alex said smiling back, "but that's all you're getting."

Angela paused, thinking.

"Let's hear your plan," Angela said.

"Simple. You let me go back to Half Moon Bay and negotiate a trade agreement, or at the very minimum set up introductions between you, Raul, and the leadership of Half Moon Bay so that you can negotiate. Once the agreement is in place we can use it to get the materials we need to rebuild the fleet. Plus, since currently most of what we have to trade is labor, we will gain experience that will improve our greenhouse operations, farming operations and who knows what else. Once we are back on our feet, there will be more opportunities because Half Moon Bay is part of a wider economy. We may be able to get specialized parts from other regions to fix our infrastructure. It's time to stop hiding behind the myth of our death, which clearly not everyone believes anyway, and rejoin the human race."

Angela shook her head. "If we do that, we lose everything. We lose our self-rule, we lose our identity and our unique heritage, and that's if they don't outright kill us."

"You can't beat them Angela. If you invade, they can probably handle us themselves and if they can't they will call for help and get it."

"Then maybe we don't invade," Angela said, "Maybe we just take what we need and go north and start over."

"There are two abandoned communities between here and Half Moon Bay. We can get things from there and not steal from our neighbors."

"Is there a fishing fleet in those communities?"

"No. Half Moon Bay, or Miramar, has the closest boats."

"That's what we need. If we can get nine or ten boats, then we can feed ourselves, and we will have a way to relocate before they can retaliate."

"Just buy the boats, or buy the pieces we need to make the boats," Alex said calmly.

Angela thought for minute and said, "No. We will take what we need, and you will be our guide."

"How can you be so sure I'll do that?"

"Because you came back," Angela said.

Alex seemed to think for moment, then said, "I'll help on three conditions. One, you will give me command of team A for the operation."

"Agreed."

"Two, you will give me unfettered access to both the Republic and Amazonian planning teams and free movement in both communities."

"Agreed."

"Three, if this thing falls apart: you will resign and appoint me in your place."

Angela smiled and shook her head. "If this thing falls apart, you will be dead."

Thirty-Three

Angela met Raul at his bar.

"Alex found us a fleet," Angela said.

Raul was less than enthusiastic. "I thought you didn't trust her any-more, too sentimental..."

Angela made sure not to look at Jonathan, who was cleaning glasses at the other end of the bar, laughed cynically and said, "Oh, that was just part of her plan. She needed to make sure he would do exactly as she said."

Raul nodded sagely.

The planning started immediately. The DeJong fortuitously had a display of medieval weapons. Since the ammunition was starting to fail, they made crossbows, bolts, bows and arrows based on the medieval examples.

Angela placed Alex in command of Team A but gave overall control of the Amazonian forces to the former leader of Team A. Alex described the location and habits of the fishing fleet. After long discussion it was agreed that the best option was to slip into the Marina at 2:00 AM, take the ten best boats, and be gone before anyone could determine who had done it.

Alex made frequent trips back and forth between the Republic and Amazonia. Often there seemed to be almost no purpose to her trips. Sometimes she would make the trips to get the answer to a very simple question. The minders Angela had trailing her grew weary.

On one of her trips, when the minders weren't in sight she detoured a few steps to where Jonathan was on her way to see Jimmy.

"If you hate me now, I understand. When this job is done, I hope we can come back *home*, and you can always trust me again."

Jonathan nodded almost imperceptibly, said "I understand," and turned away.

Jimmy was less welcoming. "So you finally threw him to the wolves too, huh?"

"Looks like it," Alex admitted.

However Fat Jimmy, Jimmy, was not fully committed to his anger. He had enough weed in his system to be able to let go of almost anything.

"So, what have you gotten us into?"

"What's more important is what I've gotten you out of. I've gotten you out of a full scale invasion. This situation you can survive. In fact, I'm depending on you to survive."

Jimmy's movements didn't change but his eyes focused slightly more. He casually looked out the window noting the position of Angela's minders and then focusing on a passing flock of birds before slowly turning back to Alex. "So, there are things about this operation that Angela isn't aware of?"

"No one can know everything," Alex said, her eyes sparkling.

"What will you need?"

"I need Raul to stay home."

Jimmy laughed, "That won't be a problem. What else?"

"I need Jonathan's guards to be a bit sloppy."

Jimmy cocked his head and shrugged, "OK."

"I need you not to take the lead on this trip. Never send your troops into any place first. Always let Amazonia take the lead, and don't draw attention to the fact you're doing it. If you're assigned to go first, don't refuse, just go so slowly that it's annoying. "

"That was kind of my plan anyway," Jimmy said.

"Stick to that plan."

"Anything else?"

"Yes, but I don't know what it is yet," Alex said.

"I should tell Raul and Angela all about this," Jimmy said.

"Do you want to?"

Jimmy twisted his office chair a few times and said, "No. I don't think I do."

"I think more than just my life depends on you doing what you want to do."

Jimmy laughed low and deep and said, "Yeah."

The preparations were complete in eight days. They set the incursion target date for five days later when there would be no moon, which meant they would leave in four days. Alex crossed town five times during that day wrapping up final arrangements. On her second to last trip she stopped at Raul's bar and went into the bathroom. As arranged, Jonathan was in the second stall sitting on top of the toilet tank so his feet wouldn't show.

Alex went into the stall and sat on the toilet. She hurriedly picked up a scrap of toilet paper and wrote the following on it.

"Tomorrow night at 11:00 PM leave a suicide note in your room, shake your guards and go back to our house in Half Moon Bay. Jimmy will make it possible. Make only one stop on the way at the house we stayed at in Pacifica, but stay only long enough to stack the empty spam cans so I'll know you made it that far, then press on to our house and wait for me there. I will try to join you there, but if I don't arrive at our house by the following evening go to the Sheriff and tell him what we are planning. Please also tell him not to shoot me." She held the paper up to Jonathan, he read it and nodded. Then she stood, threw the paper in the toilet, flushed and looked up at him.

She pulled her waist band down and her shirt up enough for him to see a tiny bulge that hadn't been there before. She took his hand, put it over the bump, and held it there caressing it with her thumb. She looked at him one last time, tucked in her shirt and left the bathroom.

She nearly hit one of her minders with the bathroom door. Alex paused, looked at her, and said, "I'm flattered, but this is unprofessional."

She stopped by Jimmy's office, asked some questions about supplies and coordination, then said, "Let's get some rest tomorrow. I'll check back with you the day after tomorrow for final coordination," and left.

On her way back to her apartment she stopped at the twins and Millie's house, stood on the doorstep and asked for something. Shawna came back with a heavy coat and gave it to Alex. Alex pulled her close, hugged her and whispered in her ear, "All three of you go to Half Moon Bay Five hours after we start the incursion trip. Do not stop anywhere. Use the back roads and report to the Sheriff's Office. Tell him what we are doing. Tell no one here that you are leaving. I'll meet you there."

Then she let her go, wiped a tear that was more real than she meant it to be and went back to her apartment.

She ate dinner, read a book, and when her minders where napping on the couches went into her closet, opened the flap on the inside of the winter coat, and counted eight sticks of sweaty dynamite. She removed them and put them in her hiding place, put some canned goods into the coat and put it back on its hanger.

The next day she slept in. Mid-morning she went to Angela's office and waited while Angela made herself busy just to make her wait.

"We should call this off, Angela," Alex said.

Angela sighed. "We've already been through this."

Alex gave up and said, "Well then, we should have a party tonight. Tomorrow everyone will need to get their gear together and rest up."

"Will you read another poem?" Angela asked.

"No. This isn't for me. This is for morale. I won't say a thing."

Angela shook her head. "No. Let everyone have their time their own way tonight."

Alex shrugged, "Do you mind if I throw a party tonight for whoever wants to come?"

"I don't care," Angela said, "I doubt many will come."

Angela made sure no one did. When the party started at 8:00 it was just Alex and her minders. Alex started pouring the alcohol at 8:30. They resisted at first, but when Alex started getting silly they joined in. At 10:45 Alex said, "Let's go get some more people."

The minders shook their heads. "Let's just stay here," one of them said.

"No. I want to have a party," Alex said, and went out the door. The minders sluggishly followed her. Just outside the door, were two fresh minders. When the first two saw them, they went back inside. The fresh minders followed her to several houses nearby and watched her pound on doors loudly demanding that the occupants come out and party. No one came out. She kept at it noisily until 11:30 then wandered back towards her house, wandered in, and crashed on her bed. She started breathing loudly almost instantly. Her regular minders closed her door and went back to the couch. At 12:30 Alex put on her winter jacket, came out of her room and walked carefully past her sleeping minders, opened the door to her apartment, came face to face with the fresh minders, and vomited on their shoes before going back inside. She went to the closet removed the canned goods and water from the coat, and put the dynamite back in.

She slept in until 11:00 the next morning. When she woke up, Angela was sitting on her couch instead of the minders.

"You're a little late for the party," Alex said squinting.

Angela waited for her to sit down and said, "I have some bad news. Jonathan went missing last night. Jimmy found his jacket and shoes folded in a neat pile next to the old bridge ramp on the headlands, and they found this in his room." Angela handed her a note.

"There is nothing left for me here. I am going home to mother Earth. I give all of my possessions to Jimmy. Tell Alex I 'll always love her, and I forgive her."

Angela watched Alex carefully as she read the note. Alex was thoughtful. "Have they found a body?"

"No. Nor are they likely too. The current there once made a whole sunken mail ship disappear without a trace overnight."

"Well. I will miss him," Alex said and went about her business.

Angela slowly rose and went out. The minders came in. Alex went to the bathroom, closed the door, and wept for joy.

In the afternoon she met with the leader of the Amazonian forces, with Team A, with Angela and with Jimmy finalizing arrangements.

The following morning she put on her hiking shoes, her tactical holster, her heavy winter coat, and her back pack. She assembled with Team A and fell in behind the leader of Amazonian forces who fell in behind Angela. Jimmy walked beside the leader of the Amazonian forces with his forces behind him. Once they'd passed Sam's grave, Angela called Alex up next to her to guide the way.

A little before they entered the Daly City dead zone, Angela smiled and said, "Your coat is very heavy. Alex shrugged and said, "I learned on the road that having a personal stash is a good idea."

The trudge through the dead zone was more arduous than before. It took a while for the group to decide traveling single file was best, and the extra equipment they were carrying took a toll.

They spent the night in Pacifica and feasted on abandoned food. Angela and Alex spent the night in a house with a stack of empty spam cans and ate canned peaches. When they left mid-morning, Angela left first and Alex softly brushed the spam cans with her fingers on the way out.

They rested in Linda Vista and explored the city until mid-afternoon, then arrived at the tunnels an hour before dark.

Angela inspected the entrances, then turned to Alex and asked, "What do you recommend?"

"The road around has been blocked by landslides in several places. Going through the tunnels will be easier with the extra people and equipment than going around, but the tunnels are unstable in places. If I were you, I would split the team, send the Republic through the tunnels with the extra equipment, and march Amazonia around the tunnels," Alex said.

Angela paused for dramatic effect then said, "...And yet you are not me."

Alex imagined she could feel the dynamite sweating in her coat.

"The Republic will not go through the tunnels..." Angela said, and

Alex began to hope. "And neither will Amazonia. We will march together around the tunnels," Angela proclaimed.

Alex nodded grimly.

They marched in formation until they came to the first land slide, then marched in single file up the steep scree slope slipping and cursing under the loads of their equipment. Angela went first with Alex at her side, then came Amazonia, then the Republic. By the time they reached the other end of the tunnels it was dark, and Alex was relieved that no one suggested going back to check the exits. With no moon it was difficult to see even three steps ahead. They traveled slower. An hour and a half later Alex called a halt just short of Martini Creek. They grouped up at the trail head where Alex and Jonathan had met Sam, and Alex explained:

"This is the rally point I showed you on the maps. We are about two miles from the Marina, but from beyond this bridge everything is inhabited. It will be difficult to go through undetected this early. I suggest we wait a couple of hours to move the main force. While we are waiting, we can send through a small group to make sure the fleet is where I last saw it and scout for any changes in the defenses since I was here last."

"Who do you recommend for the advance team?" Angela asked.

Alex controlled the beating of her heart and said, "I know the way, so I should go. I will need someone who can help me if I get into a scrape. Jimmy and I work well together. We could take one more if you like, maybe the Amazonian lead."

Angela chuckled to herself, a low throaty sound that was oddly disconcerting in the darkness. "No. I think the team needs to be different. We do need you on the team and you will walk in front of us, but I and all of Team A will accompany you."

Alex closed her eyes.

"That's seven people," Alex observed. "It will be difficult to pass with so many," she finished flatly, nearly emotionlessly.

"Then we'll wait another hour before sending the advance team," Angela said.

The force waited anxiously. As many as could huddled in an abandoned car trying to stay out of the cutting wind kicking up off the ocean. Fingers grew numb. Courage drained, but all waited stoically. An owl hooted a long mournful song somewhere in the river valley below. When the hour was up, Angela and team A raised their weapons and walked behind Alex.

They moved onto the bridge. The sound of the creek began to compete with the sounds of the ocean and the wind. The owl called out, closer now, and was silent. The wind died down and Alex could smell the creek. They crossed over it and the dark mildew smell of fallow fields beyond began to take over. Just before they reached the foot of the bridge they heard a sound. Team A scattered left and right on the road to take up defensive positions. Angela held her ground, let her M16 swing free, un-holstered her side arm, put her left arm around Alex's neck and held the gun to her head.

A slight twinkle of light bounced off polished metal ahead and a man's voice called out of the darkness. "I'm Sheriff Jimenez. Who is entering my city?"

Angela tightened her grip on Alex and said hoarsely, "Tell him."

"Sheriff, Its Alex, but I'm not alone. I'm here with Angela Steel and her troops, and right now she has a gun to my head."

"I see," said the sheriff. "Ms. Steel, may I ask what your intentions are?"

Angela thought for a second then said, "My intentions are to provide for my people."

"I can understand that. What can we do for you?"

Angela hesitated, then said forcefully, "We need fishing boats. We need supplies."

Amazonian forces began streaming down the sides of the bridge. Jimmy watched through a night vision scope and marveled. Angela now had 15 soldiers lining the sides of the bridge behind her, but they were poorly placed. The bridge constrained them so they couldn't fan out enough. The sheriff had over a dozen men of his own, but positioned much better, spread wide behind defensive barriers.

"Take up protected covering positions, but hold your fire until I give the word," Jimmy said to his lieutenant.

The sheriff said, "How many boats are we talking about?"

"Fifteen," Angela said.

"That's a tall order, Ma'am."

"We could make due with ten," Angela offered.

"I can arrange to transfer one boat now, and we can provide you with fish and vegetables until we can come to an understanding," the sheriff said.

"Well, sheriff," Angela said.

After a moment of silence the sheriff said, "Yes, Ms. Steel?"

Angela shot him.

The rest of the Amazonians opened fire.

The sheriff rolled off the roadway behind a concrete highway barrier they had set up. He swore mildly as he loosened his armor and asked, "Do you have the shot?"

"Not on the leader," his lieutenant said. "The girl's in the way, but we've got the shot on the rest."

The sheriff swore mildly again and said, "We did our best. Take the shot. We'll see if that changes the equation."

The lieutenant gave the signal, 15 shots rang out at once, and the gunfire ceased.

"We got 'em," the lieutenant said.

Jimmy surveyed the scene. Their accuracy was impressive. "They've got night vision," he grunted to himself, and tucked his head lower.

Angela listened carefully. She couldn't hear any of her troops moving. She let out a sound Alex had never heard her make before.

"Ms. Steel, I think that's enough. If you'll withdraw and let the girl go, we won't pursue you," the sheriff said.

Angela shook slightly, she tensed her right forearm, then a single shot rang out and what was left of Angela fell forward on top of Alex.

"Did you hit your target?" Jimmy's lieutenant asked.

"Yes, I believe I did," Jimmy said with satisfaction, "Get ready to fall back."

The sheriff scanned the horizon with his goggles trying to find the shooter.

"Sheriff!" Jimmy called out.

"Yes."

"My men and I would like to take you up on your offer to not pursue us."

"We'll hold our position for five minutes while you melt away, but if we ever find any of you south of Linda Vista, all deals are off."

"Understood, Sheriff," Jimmy said and gave the signal to retreat.

Jonathan sat in misery behind the barrier waiting.

Alex didn't seem to be moving.

"We have to help her!" he said to the sheriff.

"I think she's OK. Whoever fired that shot cleanly took off the top of Ms. Steel's head, and your wife is at least five inches shorter than she was."

"I'm going out there," Jonathan said.

"You're sitting still for another four minutes. I won't have any more people getting shot tonight," the sheriff responded.

Time stopped. The wind came back. The sheriff glanced back and forth between his watch and his goggles.

"Looks like they're pulling out," one of the sheriff's men said.

Jonathan could hear the creek running. He heard the owl take flight and move to safer ground. The sound of the ocean came back to him.

The sheriff stood up. Jonathan stood up beside him. They moved carefully toward the bridge, the rest of the men following close behind. The sheriff kicked Angela's body off of Alex. She was breathing.

"Alex..." Jonathan said, then collapsed, a cross-bow bolt protruding from his chest. The posse opened fire on the Amazonian force leader and she was dead before she dropped the cross bow.

Jonathan saw Alex's face looking down at him. He heard the waves. He wavered between realities.

He was on a stretcher. He could see the stars, then Alex's face again, then the faces of other people he didn't know. They carried him to an ambulance they had towed to the edge of town ahead of time in case of casualties. He heard the sound of a generator. They were sticking him with needles. He felt Alex's hand in his. He slept.

When he awoke, the sky was early morning gray. The cross-bow bolt was gone from his chest. He felt weak. He was still in the ambulance, the doors open to the northern sky. He supposed they had been afraid to move him. He saw Alex asleep on the ground under a tree by the ambulance. He saw the worry lines around her face, that belonged to a much older woman and wanted to reach out and smooth them away. He saw the twins and Millie sitting in chairs to the left of the ambulance, talking to what he supposed was the doctor. He saw the hills catching the growing light of the sunrise and reflecting it back toward him. A winter bird sang. He saw two large slow moving turbo-prop bombers with red, white and green stripes painted on their tails moving serenely northward. He looked at Alex. The wind was ruffling her hair. She would wake up soon. She would wake up and be OK. She would be loved. He felt his pulse run thin. She would be loved, and that was enough.

Farallon
22nd-Century

One

Jonas was dying. He knew that. It didn't particularly worry him. There was still time to do what he needed to do and after months of observation, contemplation, and tests, he was finally sure what that was.

It was a clean, blue sky, Monday morning and he had just left his small home on the edge of the town square to begin his weekly walk to the top of the "mountain." The mountain blocked the harsh ocean wind from constantly buffeting his town, but also blocked the sunsets half the year. Few of the younger generation new what a real mountain was. They would point to the bench and the old coastal mountains 30 miles to the east and claim those were the real mountains. Some of the younger ones would even point to the sand dunes in the middle of the valley and call those mountains. He chuckled at how they might react to the Sierra Nevada, Siskiyou, Cascade, Teton, or heaven forbid, the Rocky Mountains. He had seen them all.

The town of Farallon was prosperous without being wealthy. They had all the food, clothing and building materials they needed. They had the luxury of time for contemplation and play after work was done. The land was fertile, and the sea generous. The distance to the trading routes, the lack of good roads, the strong one way currents of the San Francisco River, and the lack of a decent port made it difficult to transport goods to market. Their fish, crabs, cheese, goat, rabbit, chicken, barley, wheat, lettuce, celery, broccoli, spinach, cauliflower, and strawberries were often too expensive to sell profitably.

It was still early when he set out so there were few people on the streets. Those that were out greeted him as he passed. He liked to start earlier than the first students because it added to his myth, and that myth was important for teaching his strong headed students.

His pack was getting harder to carry than in younger years, but he always brought enough food to feed himself until Friday evening when he and the students returned to town. Halfway up the hill Cody caught up with him. He took his pack from him, almost by force. Jonas let him. Cody was the oldest son of Errol and Flora Shelton. The Shelton family formed the core of the Herdsmen clan, which was already important and growing. Cody thought he was currying favor with the old man, but Jonas hoped that something more subtle was taking root.

Jonas stoked the old stove in the tight little house that served as their school. The other children began struggling in out of the wind that perpetually blew on the ocean facing side of the mountain. It was not a convenient spot for the school, but Jonas had his reasons for choosing it. Partly its views of the endless ocean helped his students to see beyond the petty squabbles of their parents. Partly because the old light at the top of the mountain made a good observatory for his astronomy, but mostly because here they were apart. Here they were in no one's territory, and no one interfered. It was a privilege to send a child to this school, one only afforded to the leaders of clans, and to the occasional rare soul that Jonas simply took an interest in. Going to the top of the mountain for school five days a week throughout the summer, and on Saturdays the rest of the year, was simply part of the tuition.

Luz, the oldest daughter of Miguel and Flor Ochoa of the vegetable growers, another powerful family, was next through the door. She came in directly and sat in her spot on the carpet in front of the stove. Then came Henry Kennegy of the fruit growers, followed quickly by Mark Campton of the grain growers, Jennifer Kai of the fishermen, Anna Smith from the technicians, and Eddie Cooper whose family owned the general store and was studiously unallied with any group and all of them. They sat in their places on the rug, looking up at him expectantly. He took his time tending to the fire then turned to face them.

He looked at their faces, each individually, with great weight and almost ceremony. As he did each child sat up straighter and returned his gaze. This was not all theater. He had taught some of their siblings, most of their parents. In the darker months after the harvests were mostly done and the seas cooperated less with the fishermen and there was more time to deliberate, he met with their parents. He presided over their deliberations for the town. On those winter nights he mostly listened. He was occasionally called upon to break ties, or was asked to settle disputes, but mostly it was his presence that kept the peace. Each faction was ashamed of their more petty ambitions in his presence and usually abandoned them before they even started to exercise them.

Soon enough most of these children would begin to take their parents' places in the council. They had been with him five years now. This was the last year, and it was almost over. As he looked at them, he remembered the four classes that had gone before them and a wave of nostalgia swept over him. He dismissed it.

"Good morning," he said.

"Good morning," they repeated back.

"I hope you had a good weekend with your families. Luz, do you have any good stories from the weekend to share with us?"

Luz thought for a moment, and then brightened. "Yes. After mass on Sunday my Father and I went on a picnic to the beach just the two of us, and we spent two hours talking, and throwing bread at the seagulls and looking for shells."

Jonas nodded appreciatively. He looked at Cody and could read his hard expression. Cody had progressed a great deal. They all had. Five years ago, Cody would have mocked Luz openly for sharing such a story. He would have made kissing sounds, and implied all sorts of nasty things, not because he believed them, but because hearing her story made him want to punish her. It was not even the content of the story that mattered, though the fact that his father, Errol, was not the cuddliest man in town may have made the story uncomfortable for him. It was simply that Luz had spoken anything boldly at all. But he had grown. He would not mock her, openly anyway.

After greetings, Jonas organized them and set them to the individual and team review projects they typically did the first two days of each week. The projects required them to use all of the skills they studied during the previous week and they often produced something useful that students could take home. After the first few assigned projects most of the students made up their own and only needed to have them approved by Jonas before they started. Jonas had an e-book full of possible projects, and general knowledge resources they could look through if they got stumped, but that didn't happen much by the fifth year.

One student project fifteen years before had made an intercom system using old telephones, wire and a battery. The class became interested in it and Jonas let them spend extra days on it until it worked perfectly. They took it home and strung it up between two houses. Three years later some of those same children were on their first scavenging trip to San Francisco and among the rotting buildings, bombed out ruins, and picked over streets they found long runs of telephone wire and old telephones, which, with the help of the whole community, became Farallon's phone system. When the representative from Deseret saw it, he placed an order and a technician from Monterey came and added a satellite uplink to join it to the national phone system.

Jonas floated from group to group observing. Cody had teamed up with Jennifer, Luz with Henry and Mark, and Anna with Eddie. This wasn't an uncommon grouping. He noted, not for the first time, that it roughly mirrored the alliances of their parents. He also noticed that Cody was interested in Jennifer and that she was aware and didn't mind the attention.

When it came time the next day to present their projects, Cody and Jennifer shared an analysis of fishing yields by boat across time. It was fairly sophisticated and was able to strip away several complicating factors to make it clear that the larger boats were getting more fish per person than the smaller ones, and also that any boat with Jennifer's brother on it brought in fewer fish than normal. Luz watched impassively only showing an interest when Cody knocked his papers off the table and got momentarily flustered when he couldn't find his place immediately.

Luz, Henry and Mark were next reviewing crop yields for different fields against fertilizer types and crop rotation patterns. Again, the analysis was sophisticated and able to factor out differences in soil type and water availability. It concluded that fishmeal and goat dung fertilizers were equally effective, and that only one of the crop rotation schemes in use was yielding a significant benefit.

Anna and Eddie analyzed sales of different items against weather. It wasn't very convincing and when they were done presenting the other two teams shredded it mercilessly. When they were done, Jonas asked, "How could this analysis be improved?"

Each member of the class made a recommendation then it was lunch time. While the others ate on the porch, Anna and Eddie worked to salvage their report, snatching bites to eat as they went.

Outside, the wind had died down and the sun was baking the students with its welcome heat. After eating, the boys forgot their alliances, grabbed a ball and ran off to play two-on-one soccer by the old water collection pad.

Luz and Jennifer stretched out next to each other by a tree, put their hats over their faces and dozed, feeling the warmth.

The boys came back sweaty twenty minutes later, and tried to goad one or both of the girls to join them so the teams would be more equal. "Leave us alone," Jennifer said.

"Come on," Cody said.

"You heard the woman," Luz said.

"Who's talking to you?" Cody said, and the other boys agreed.

The girls ignored them. Henry came closer and shook his head vigorously so big drops of sweat came flying out of his curly hair and sprayed the girls.

"OK, that's just gross," Luz said. The girls picked up their stuff and moved to the far side of the tree. The boys sat down in the chairs on the porch and picked through the remains of lunch. Cody picked up a piece of bread and threw it to the seagulls. They attacked it in a mob, fighting over the scrap. He smiled, threw another piece and watched them fight over that, then he tore off a big piece and threw it onto Luz.

Clouds of birds descended on Luz and Jennifer. They both jumped up at first alarmed, then confused, then angry when they saw the boys laughing. They didn't know what they had done, but they knew they'd done something. Jennifer said words Cody didn't know she knew. Some of them Cody didn't know, but silent Luz was scarier. They advanced on the boys, who ran into the school house. When the girls came in the boys ran behind Jonas for protection. Anna, sizing up the situation, joined the girls just in case they needed reinforcement. Eddie sensibly stayed out of it.

The girls maneuvered to get past Jonas, making some very specific threats as they went. Jonas let it play out for a moment then ordered everyone to their seats. When everyone was breathing normally again, Jonas turned to Luz and said, "Miss Ochoa, please use the pattern."

Luz unconsciously rolled her eyes, stood up and said, "Mr. Shelton, Mr. Kennegy, and Mr. Campton, I feel angry and humiliated when you cause birds to swarm us and possibly poop all over us, because I think it shows that you don't care about our well-being and only see us as sources of amusement. My hope outside of my control is that you will apologize for your crappy behavior and never do it again. My hope within my control is that I will refrain from burning each of your houses down while you sleep." She sat down.

Jonas looked at Jennifer, "Did Miss Ochoa's statement cover your feelings?"

Jennifer said, "Yes, but I had a nastier revenge in mind."

Jonas looked at Cody. "Mr. Shelton, what is your response?"

Cody stood up, looked at the girls and said, "We understand that by causing birds to land on you we created a situation where you felt angry and humiliated, because you thought we were careless with your safety and because you thought we saw you only as sources of amusement. We apologize for our behavior, and promise never to repeat it. We hope this will help you to feel better and that you won't burn down our houses." Cody looked at Jennifer and added, "Also, we don't really see you only as sources of amusement. I mean, you can be amusing, but you are more than that."

Jonas looked at the other boys. "Do you agree with your spokesperson?"

They nodded.

"Miss Ochoa, Miss Kai: is that acceptable?" Jonas asked.

Luz and Jennifer looked at each other, then nodded.

Jonas suppressed a laugh, and then was lost in thought. He remembered the first time he had taught that pattern to Luz and Cody. It had been almost five years ago to the day. The weather had been the same, sunny and warm. They had taken a trip to the beach and walked along the shore. It was meant to be fun as well as to learn about the ocean.

Luz had spent less time at the beach before than most of the others, but this day she was feeling adventurous and waded out thigh-high into the water in search of better shells. She was reaching for one when a sneaker wave caught her from behind and knocked her face first into the surf. Cody was the closest to her and instinctively pulled her up out of the water, but Luz's thin white shirt became almost transparent showing her training bra bright against her tan twelve year-old body.

Cody started laughing. Luz tried to make a quick escape, but the water made it a slow awkward retreat. Cody didn't stop laughing until Jonas told him to be quiet.

Jonas covered Luz with his coat. Anna and Jennifer circled around her. Cody had met up with the other boys by then on the beach and was telling them all about it until Jonas commanded silence again.

When Luz had stopped shaking from cold and anger, Jonas pulled Cody aside and asked him to imagine how embarrassed he would have been if the situation had been reversed.

Cody put on a cocky face and said, "I'd have nothing to be embarrassed about!" Jonas looked at him until his face softened. Then Cody looked down and said, "I guess it wasn't very nice of me."

Jonas nodded agreement and added, "... and it wasn't very manly. Any boy can tease a girl when she's in a bad situation. It takes a man to show kindness in a way that builds her up."

They proceeded down the coast to a higher place where they could look down on the ocean and see the straight line of deep blue-green where the continental shelf gave way to the deep sea shelf. It was only about fifteen feet from the beach, close enough to gaze into and imagine sea monsters.

They discussed how that location had formed, then watched it in silence for a while. Jonas let them wander a little and pursue their own thoughts. Cody went to the cliff edge and looked down into the water. It was a good place to observe. This piece of land ran almost to the edge of the shelf so by looking straight down he could see into the deep.

There was a blur of motion, and before anyone could stop her, Luz had shoved Cody off the cliff. The girls restrained Luz. The boys peered over the edge at Cody. He was surfacing. Two of the boys had their shirts off before Jonas stopped them, pulled a rope out of his pack and tossed one end down to Cody, who caught it. He pulled Cody down the shore line away from the rocks and towards a sandy place. The boys ran down to him and Jonas followed. Jonas checked him over.

"Are you OK?" Jonas asked.

Cody nodded, teeth chattering.

They helped him pull his shirt off, and one of the other boys gave him his dry one. He put it on, then lay down behind a rock in the warm sand.

Jonas watched until he was sure he would be OK, charged the boys with watching him and went back up the hill to Luz. Jonas remained expressionless. Luz, fists still clenched in rage, suddenly melted and started to cry.

"Did I kill him?" she asked, her voice breaking, looking up at him.

Jonas hesitated, then shook his head. "No, but you might have."

"Is he all right?" she asked.

Jonas again hesitated, then nodded, "He'll be fine."

As soon as Cody was warm enough, they cancelled the field trip and went back to the school house. That's when he taught them that pattern and made them all promise to use it when there was a serious offense. When they had all promised, Jonas said, "Then this is over. I'll not mention it again."

They all kept that promise. Sometimes they found ways to embed little barbs in it, or to try to make it funny, but Jonas let them. Over the years he also taught them to reach out to each other afterward and do what they could to make up for each offense, but it all took time to learn. Cody and Luz were still learning it.

He came back to the present, looked at Anna and Eddie and asked, "Is your revised presentation ready?"

They nodded confidently and stood up to present. The analysis was much better and at the end of the presentation the class applauded.

Afterward, Jonas stood and thanked Anna and Eddie. He then began resetting for the next topic by saying,

"What can the skies teach us?"

Mark said, "That if you take your shirt off in the fields before noon, your skin is no match for the sun."

Jonas glanced at the ceiling, nodded approvingly, and wrote "Humility" on the chalk board.

The class chuckled. This was an old game they played. They would try to give the worst answer they possibly could, then Jonas would twist that answer into something usable.

"Anything else?" Jonas asked.

"They can tell us when to plant and when to harvest," Luz said.

"Interesting," Jonas said. "How do they tell us when to plant or when to harvest?"

Luz seemed to shrink back a little, "Well, I don't know. I just know that some of the farmers watch the skies to tell them when to do it."

Jonas seemed thoughtful, then wrote "Helps us time events" on the board. "Anything else?" he asked.

"Things in the sky can be used for navigation," Jennifer said.

Jonas nodded, and wrote that on the board.

"The skies tell us when it's time to get up and when it's time to go to sleep," Henry said.

Jonas nodded and wrote "Tell time" on the board.

"They can tell us if it's going to storm or be clear?" Cody said.

Jonas nodded and wrote "weather" on the board.

"They can tell us that there is beauty in the world," Anna said.

Jonas wrote it.

"They can tell us that there is more to existence than this little town," Eddie said.

Jonas wrote "Perspective" on the board.

"Anything else?" Jonas asked, and waited patiently as the silence lengthened.

"They tell us that we are never alone," Luz said.

"How so?" Jonas asked.

"No matter how far you go from home, if you look up at the sun or the moon or the stars you know for sure that somewhere, someone else is looking up at them too," Luz said.

Jonas thought, then underlined perspective.

Cody said, "Yeah, but it's more than that too. It's like an analogy. There are constellations of stars and constellations of people."

"Continue," Jonas said.

"The constellations that we see are really randomly distributed stars that only have meaning from this one position and even then only because we read meaning into them. Constellations of people only have significance from a particular perspective and only because we give meaning to them," Cody concluded.

Mark disagreed. "There are so many problems with what you just said. First, the stars aren't arranged randomly, they follow the concentrations of dark matter and when viewed from really far away would have a pattern almost like a sponge. Second, the arrangements of people aren't random. They clump together because of shared traits, shared biology, threads of DNA."

Cody defended. "The stars may not be random, but neither are the stars arranged to make pictures. We make the pictures. Also there are plenty of towns that do not share much DNA but are grouped by circumstance, or need, or belief."

"What were we talking about again?" Anna asked.

The class laughed. Jonas shrugged theatrically and they laughed again. While they quieted, Jonas sat down on a chair in front of the class and considered the point.

"I think what Cody and Luz might be saying is that just as there are relationships between the stars there are relationships between people and that those relationships have a pattern, though not always the pattern that we think they have. Is that close?" Jonas asked.

Cody nodded coolly and the class laughed again. Jonas waved it off. He turned on the holographic projector and began displaying old Magellan, James Webb, and Hubble based images. The class had seen many of them before. After an hour going through the material and animations of the Earth and the planets orbiting the sun, and the sun going around the galactic core, Jonas said, "We'll break a little early today, because tonight we are going up to the observatory after dinner."

Jonas watched them separate then put his things away. The images from the lesson reminded him of the first time he had seen them.

He was 16 years old and had been away from home four years already. He had just finished at the academy and taken the train to the new capital in Kansas City for advanced studies. It was his second day at his after school job in the new library when a dusty outrider appeared at the door near his work space. One of the older students met him, signed for the delivery, and directed him to the dormitory to rest up.

The older student brought the package to the work space next to his and opened the hard box to see what they had. Other workers gathered around. In the box was a new memory pod like the ones he had seen on his first day in the basement. It was labeled "MAST - Johns Hopkins." They pulled the memory pod out, hooked it up to a local system, ran a quick archive test, then started opening files, and all of these amazing images started spilling out.

He cleared the memory from his head and watched his students. Many of them were rivals, but sometimes they forgot to be that. Sometimes, they just talked, or played or worked together with all the delight of life-long friends and those moments were what fueled Jonas' hope.

An hour later they broke off what they were doing without being prompted and moved to the kitchen to prepare dinner. They organized themselves, checked the supplies and went to work. When they were done, Jonas joined them. Henry said the prayer and they ate.

After the dishes were done, they gathered coats and hats and hiked up the hill on the east side of the mountain to the old lighthouse on its peak. They spread out blankets, huddled up as the night wind dropped the temperature, and watched the sun go down. Then they lay back and watched the stars pop out of the sky one by one.

When it was dark enough, Jonas pulled out a laser pointer and handed it to Cody.

"Show us the constellations?" he said.

"Egyptian or Greek?" Cody asked.

"Mayan," Jonas answered.

"OOOhhh!" the class said, giving Cody a hard time.

Cody looked stumped and Jonas laughed and said, "Just show us the stars."

Cody played it safe and went with the Greek based constellations.

When he was done, he gave the pointer back to Jonas.

"Good," Jonas said. He pointed out Orion's belt and Sirius and the Mayan hearth stones below the belt and they discussed what they all meant to various cultures. Then Jonas grew quiet for a moment and pointed to Polaris.

"They say that Polaris is the diamond in an engagement ring," he said, sketching it out with the laser light. "When my grandfather was a boy, Polaris was still a single man and all the stars danced around him all night. But then he grew up and when the ice came back to the mountains and plains, the nights got colder. So he decided to get married. Now he's joined hands with Kochab his wife and they dance all night in a circle with the center somewhere between them." He turned off the laser pointer and put it away.

He let them lie there looking at the stars another half an hour and then said, "OK. Let's go get some sleep." The students groaned a little, got up, folded up their things and descended to the school house.

That night Jonas lay awake in bed. The cancer that was eating at his guts hurt, but it was the memories that kept him awake. His thoughts touched on Cody and Luz's seaside battle when they were 12, then went further back remembering their parents. Luz's mother Flor and Cody's Father Errol had been in his second class in the school house.

They had started out sparring too. It was natural. The herdsmen's animals worked the soil first, adding organic matter to the sand. As the population increased and the soil improved, the council always allowed the growers to move into what had formerly been the range of the herdsmen. There was no danger of them running out of range, but it meant that the trips to and from town got longer and at a more instinctual level the herdsman felt as if they were the rightful owners of the land and were being generous to allow the growers to use it. The herds themselves, creatures of habit, often tried to return to their former range, doing damage and causing conflict.

But when they were both 14 they had stopped sparring, and started staring at each other. Jonas noticed. He called them to order when their mutual infatuation got in the way of performance, emphasized the importance of maintaining high standards of conduct to the whole class, and left the door to his room open at night so he would hear it if Errol decided to slip out, but otherwise did nothing to discourage the attachment. His faith was rewarded. Neither of them ever did anything at school that would break the rules. He began to wonder if this might be the start of something better in the town.

Then early one Monday morning shortly after Flor's 15th birthday he found her alone on the porch of the school house, weeping. He tried to speak to her but she just shook her head. Errol did not come to school that day, or the next. He skipped the whole week. His father sent a note saying he was needed at the ranch.

In town the weekend following Errol's absence, the regular council meeting was tense, terse and stuck strictly to business. After the meeting, Jonas commented on the atmosphere to one of the growers after everyone else had left. The man glanced around the room to make sure they were alone, closed the door and confided to Jonas, "The Shelton boy, Errol, took liberties with Flor Santos and has discarded her."

"Are you sure?" Jonas asked.

"He denies it. He says they are just friends and were just having harmless fun. But Flor told her mother different. Do you think Flor would make that up?"

Jonas thought for a second, then shook his head and the conversation was over.

That next day Errol went the Protestant church down the street from the Catholic church with his father, something they rarely did. He looked somewhat subdued. After church he went to the post office for his father. On the way back he wandered slowly by the Catholic church, perhaps looking to catch a glimpse of Flor. What he caught instead was a well-aimed right hook to the jaw from Flor's slightly younger neighbor Miguel.

Errol was a good six inches taller than Miguel, but Miguel had surprised him. Errol was on the ground with Miguel on top of him beating his face before he had time to react. Mass let out. A crowd of men hurried over to break up the fight, but when they saw who the combatants were, they let Miguel land two or three extra punches before pulling him off. Errol stood up slowly, spit blood into the dirt not far from Miguel's boots and walked away without saying a word.

When Errol came back to school, Flor would not even look at him. She finished out the year avoiding him, collected her three year certificate and did not come back the next year. Errol finished the whole course. Once after Flor had quit school Errol lingered on the porch, in the same seat where Flor had cried, until Jonas came out and locked the door for the weekend. They walked toward town together, Errol thoughtful.

"I know you think I lied to everyone," Errol said to Jonas.

"About Flor?"

Errol nodded.

"Did you?" Jonas asked.

Errol seemed to study the thing in his mind. "I didn't say anything that wasn't true."

"Nothing you said was untrue?"

Errol reviewed then said, "I downplayed how far things went, but I didn't deny we did things. Everything else I said was true."

"Then no, I don't think you lied to everyone," Jonas said, "I think you lied to yourself and you deceived Flor, and I think that's worse."

"How can I lie to myself?" Errol said heatedly.

Jonas waited until he was calmer, and said, "Think back to before you ever did anything with Flor. Do you remember how you felt around her then?"

"No," Errol said a little too quickly.

Jonas waited, but Errol was stubborn. Finally Jonas said, "You couldn't take your eyes off of her and she couldn't take her eyes off of you."

"So?" Errol said.

"So I never saw you look at Richard that way."

"Of course not, what do you think I am?"

"I think you're a person who is willfully forgetting that you felt something more than friendship for Flor and that she knew you felt that way."

"OK, so I downplayed how interested I was in her, that doesn't mean I wanted to marry her or be her boyfriend or something."

"You knew she thought you two would be together."

"I never told her I wanted to marry her."

"If you had told her you weren't interested in her, would she have done the things she did with you?"

"How should I know?"

"If you didn't know, why didn't you tell her where you stood before taking liberties?"

"I thought she knew," Errol said too quickly.

"Stop and think before you answer," Jonas said.

Errol thought. "I guess I thought if I said something, she might not want to keep going. So, I guess I kind of knew. But I don't see what the big deal is."

"There are three big deals. First, you took something she intended for the man who would stand by her and protect her and you took it by fraud since you knew you weren't that man. Second, you lied to yourself so you could do it and not feel like a creep. Third, you lied to the town and made Flor look bad to half the community. The way you've portrayed things, half the town has to conclude that she is either morally loose or a fool. Do you think she is either of those things?"

Errol didn't answer.

Jonas waited.

"Maybe I didn't do this right," Errol finally conceded, "but why does everyone make such a big deal about it? Why do they have to think less of Flor? We were just fooling around. The goats and cows do this stuff every day in front of everyone and no one cares. Why should anyone care if we do it and move on?"

"What happens if the bull or the billy goat abandons the mother and the baby?" Jonas asked.

"Nothing happens. They always do that and it's fine," Errol said.

"What happens to a woman and her child if the child's father abandons them?" Jonas asked.

"Then she has to stay with her parents until the child is big enough for her to work," Errol said.

"Then what?"

"Then she works and the kid has to stay with grandma or mom's younger sister or something."

"When does she get to have her own home?"

"I don't know."

"What happens when her parents get old?"

"Maybe by then the kid is old enough to work."

"What does the child feel knowing his or her own father doesn't care enough to take care of him?"

"Not good."

"Would you want that for your wife or your son or your daughter?"

"No."

"Should Flor want that for her son or her daughter?"

"No."

"What if most young men and young women thought fooling around and moving on was fine? What would happen to the town?"

Errol tried to imagine that, finally shook his head and said, "I don't know."

"Would it make things better or worse?" Jonas prompted.

Errol thought, "Worse, I guess."

"It would leave women and their children in poverty and create a generation of children who were uncertain of themselves or uncertain of how to relate to people of the opposite sex, and that would ripple into the next generation, and the next."

"Maybe," Errol conceded.

"There is nothing new in the world," Jonas said, "Do you think I'm guessing at that?"

Errol looked at him, studying his face, then looked down.

When he looked back up he said, "It's done. I can't undo it. I'll be more careful in the future and at least we didn't make a kid."

Jonas softened a little but persisted, "What about Flor?"

"What can I do? It's done."

"You could be a man and take responsibility for your actions. You could apologize. You could tell the whole truth, so people would blame your callousness instead of looking down on her. Maybe, if you can actually love her, and she can forgive you, you could be the man she thought you were and then there would be no fraud."

Errol shook his head, "I can't be that man."

"Then at least be *a* man, apologize and take the blame," Jonas said.

Errol shook his head, "It's too late for that to do any good."

"No, it isn't," Jonas said.

Errol just shook his head and walked faster than Jonas, so they parted company.

When Flor was 17 she married Miguel.

Jonas groaned a little remembering it. He turned on his side to ease the pain in his bowels, closed his eyes and dreamed of better things.

Two

The next day the class got up on time, ate, and studied the math of orbital mechanics.

The following day, they studied astronomical calendar systems, then cleaned up and secured the schoolhouse. Before going down the mountain, Jonas asked,

"Cody, do you have a poem for us before we go home?"

Cody nodded, remembering. He pulled a worn piece of paper out of his pocket and read:

Córdoba.
Distant and alone.

Black pony, big moon,
and olives in my saddlebags.
Even though I may know the roads
I will never arrive at Cordoba.

Through the plain, through the wind
Black pony, red moon.
Death is watching me
from the towers of Cordoba.

Oh, what a long road!
Oh, my valiant pony!
Oh that death awaits me,
before I arrive at Cordoba!

Córdoba.
Distant and alone.

Luz shuddered involuntarily. The rest of the group was quiet. Jonas nodded but said nothing.

After an awkward silence Cody said defensively, "What? I like horses!" and there was a small murmur of laughter.

Jonas gave his things to Luz and Mark to carry and they started down the hill.

Half way down the mountain, they heard the unfamiliar buzz of a sea plane approaching the river. They saw it landing on the river and all the students but Mark and Luz began running to see what had happened. Mark and Luz were careful not to look at Jonas or give any sign of impatience, but they moved as quickly as they could double loaded until Jonas took pity on them and released them.

As soon as they were out of sight he regretted it. His back spasmed under the load. He controlled his reaction and stood hunched over until it passed, then proceeded slowly the rest of the way to his house. He shrugged off the pack just inside his door and went to see what was happening.

By the time he reached the dock, the plane was taking off again. He looked around. Cody and his family were getting on a boat. Luz was walking away from the dock rapidly. He saw a member of the council, John Cooper, standing nearby and asked what happened.

"The younger Ochoa boy gutted the younger Shelton boy with a pruning knife," he said.

"Miguelito and Troy?"

The man nodded.

"Is Troy going to make it?"

The man shrugged, "It's more than what our doctor can handle…"

"What happened?" Jonas asked.

"The goats got into the crops and Troy wasn't moving fast enough to suit Miguelito. Words were exchanged. Things got out of hand. There's always been bad blood between the families."

Jonas nodded thanks, turned, and teared up.

They cancelled Saturday's council meeting mostly because Errol was in Monterey.

Saturday evening word came back that Troy wasn't doing well. He was in intensive care and the doctor didn't expect him to make it through the night.

On Sunday morning, some of Troy's buddies pulled down a section of fence on the Ochoa's property and let the goats eat all they wanted. When the Ochoa's hired hand objected, they spit on him. He sized up the situation and withdrew to their disappointment. When Miguel heard about it he was livid but Flor restrained him. "Be glad they didn't do worse," she said. When he had settled down, he announced that he was going to meet with the other growers and left the house.

On Monday morning, the students waited for Jonas half an hour before deciding that something was wrong. They moved down the mountain in near silence together. They knocked on Jonas' door and listened. After a while they heard him say, "Come in."

They found him still in bed, pale and sweating, and sent for the doctor. While they waited, Jonas looked at Luz and asked, "How are you?"

Luz nodded and said, "I'm OK."

"How is your brother?"

Luz frowned, "He's angry one moment, sad the next, and quiet most of the time."

Jonas nodded.

When the doctor came he sent the students out onto the porch and examined Jonas. When he was done, he said, "I think it's just reached that stage Jonas. I can send you for tests if you want, but the last set of tests was pretty conclusive. I can get you some pain relievers."

Jonas shook his head. "I have to stay clear headed a little longer."

"If you change your mind, send for me," the doctor said.

Jonas held his hand and wouldn't let him leave. "How is Troy doing today?"

The doctor shook his head. "Jonas, you know I can't discuss that with you."

"Sure you can. I won't tell anyone," Jonas said.

"Jonas, don't take this the wrong way. You've done a lot of good for a long time. You don't have much time left. Maybe you should let go, review your own life and let other people do the worrying."

Jonas laughed softly. "I'm not worrying. I'm meddling. I'll keep meddling until I can't. Now tell me how Troy is."

The doctor relaxed a little, paused, and said, "He's doing better this morning and usually with trauma like this in a young person once they start getting better, they keep getting better. He could still get an out of control infection, he could get a bowel blockage, a lot of things could still kill him, but I think he will make it."

Jonas nodded in satisfaction then asked, "When will Errol get back?"

"Tomorrow, but just for the day, then he's going back."

Jonas nodded again, said, "Thank you," and let go of the doctor's hand. "Will you do one more thing for me?"

"What is it?"

"Please call a council meeting here in my room for tonight. If anyone resists, tell them I'm dying. That's true enough, isn't it?"

"I'll do that," the doctor said, and left.

The students gathered back inside.

"I think we'll have to have a short lesson today," Jonas said.

The students waited.

Jonas collected his thoughts. "When I was a boy younger than you were when you first came to my school, I had to leave my home because there wasn't enough food for all of us. An outrider passing through saw the situation, saw that I was quick-witted, and talked to my parents.

After they talked, my father sat down with me on the steps of our house and explained it to me. I didn't want to go. When I left the next day I didn't cry because I didn't want to upset my mother or my little brother, but I cried every night after that until we reached the Academy. I never saw my father again. I didn't see my home again for ten years. When I did see it, my mother was old and hard and my brother was grown and barely remembered me. My town made a mistake. When the ice came back to the mountain and the crops failed, they didn't adapt. They fought amongst themselves. In a world of unlimited opportunity, they found a way to starve."

The students were quiet. This was a new story. If they made any sound Jonas might not finish it.

"This town is finding a way to make its own mistake. I prayed a long time that God would turn the town from it, and he has given me a way to provide the town another chance. Whether they will make good on that chance or not I can't tell you, but whether they do or don't I want you all to promise me two things.

First, don't let anger and bitterness into you. Even if you must destroy an enemy to protect your lives, do not hate him. If you hate him you will dim the part of you that must love when the war is over.

If you love him, maybe you can find a way not to destroy him, but even if not, honor what was good in your enemy.

Second, I want the seven of you to stick together. If the town falls apart, go somewhere together with as many as will follow you and try again. Will you do that?"

Concern spread over the faces of the students and they would not speak. Henry finally gave voice for what they were all thinking. "I am willing to do what you say, but I don't think Cody will join with us. All he knows is that Luz's brother cut his brother."

The others nodded.

"Will you, will all of you, make sure that Cody knows you didn't want his brother cut, and will you always make sure that he is part of your discussions and your decisions and that he always has a place with you if he chooses to take it? Will you really do that?"

They were quiet for a while and then each in turn nodded yes.

"Good. You have put my mind at rest. Luz, you more than all the others will have to make an effort. I want you to speak for the group when you tell him about today. I want you to be the one to tell him that all of you, and yourself specifically, want his companionship and his happiness. Will you do that?"

Luz nodded yes. They filed by him one by one, each saying goodbye, then they left him alone and he slept.

In the afternoon, the council met without Errol, but with several of the other herdsman present. They stood around Jonas' bed.

Jonas spoke. "The doctor, and my body, tell me that I don't have long to live. I have been going over my time with you and I am not sure I have done everything I should have for you. I am troubled that there are bad feelings between some of you."

He paused and looked around the room. Many of the men in the room would not look at him.

"If you feel that my life is worthy of your honor, I will ask two things of you. May I ask?"

"Of course," several men said instantly while others nodded or grunted their assent.

"First, I would like my bones prepared and buried beside my wife at my birth place in the mountains. I would like them carried there by two people that I will select from the leading families of the town. Do I ask too much?"

"No," several answered and the others agreed.

"Second, in memory of what I tried to teach you, I ask that there be a truce between all of you until I am buried and my honor guard returns and gives a full report to the council. Then I would like the council to vote on whether or not to extend the truce. During the truce, there is to be no violence or malicious words used against each other, and all business dealings must be honorable and fair to all. The proper justice for Miguelito's attack on Troy and for the destruction of the Ochoa's crops is also to be postponed until that council meeting. Now do I ask too much?"

There were pained expressions on many of the men's faces. Finally one of the herdsmen said, "What you ask is difficult, and it is impossible without Errol."

"I'll speak with Errol tomorrow. If he agrees, will all of you agree?" Jonas asked.

The men looked at each other, at Jonas, into themselves, and finally agreed. They left, uncertain about the future.

Jonas slept again. When he awoke he saw Errol's face looking at him. For a moment he forgot that time had passed and was surprised that his student's face had thickened and formed creases.

"How are you feeling, Jonas?" Errol asked with more tenderness than Jonas had expected.

"I hurt, but I can handle it," Jonas said. "How are you feeling?"

"Like you, I suppose, but I have hope," Errol said.

"Did they tell you why I want to talk to you?"

"Yes. They explained your request, and I will agree to it."

Jonas smiled. "Thank you," he said. Then he wrinkled his brow and said, "I have one other thing that I would like to ask of you. It will be even harder. May I ask?"

"You may," Errol said.

"I once told you that you should apologize to Flor for your treatment of her many years ago," Jonas began.

The muscles in Errol's back, neck and jaw tightened slightly, but he said nothing.

"I know that her boy hurt your boy terribly. I know what I am asking is hard. If you will do it, and do it well, I promise you that a wave of healing will cover this town. If you refuse, many will suffer."

"They owe me an apology!" Errol said.

"I agree," Jonas said. "But whether or not they free themselves of that debt has no bearing on whether or not you should free yourself from yours. Let go of the burden, and give them an easier path to do the same."

Errol slumped into a chair. "Don't ask this, Jonas," he said. "Don't ask me to humiliate myself at the very time my family and my friends need me to stand up for them."

"Errol, you don't understand. I am asking you to stand up for them by humiliating yourself. That is what will bring peace, safety, and in time love to all of them. If you stand up for them in the way you have been planning, you will bring only more hurt."

Errol covered his face with his hands and held that position for a long time. When he looked at Jonas again he said, "I know you think that apologizing will help. I know you are only trying to help and I love you for that. But I think it will only weaken me at a time when I must seem, and be, strong." Errol paused. His eyebrows bunched forward and then he said, "And... I am tired of being wrong. I will do as you ask and I will do it well."

Jonas smiled and wept, and slept.

When he woke up in the afternoon, Henry was reading a book in a chair beside his bed. Henry heard the change in his breathing and looked at him. Jonas smiled. "I need some paper and a pen and an envelope," Jonas said.

Henry went to Jonas' desk and brought the items to him. Jonas worked carefully on a letter to be read to the town after he died. It was not long. He signed it, put it in an envelope and gave it to Henry. "The council should read this to the town when I am gone," Jonas said. Then he lay back in his bed, smiling, grateful.

The next day, true to his word, Errol apologized to Flor. His first apology was in private and after Flor accepted it, the second apology was just public enough that rumor spread it throughout the community.

That afternoon, Errol stood at the dock waiting to board a boat back to Monterey. Miguel approached him. Errol tensed slightly, and adjusted his feet to face him more squarely. Miguel was anxious. There was a hint of perspiration on his forehead. He looked Errol in the eyes and said, "Flor, Luz, Miguelito, and I want you to know that we are sorry that Miguelito cut Troy. Miguelito struck in passion and he regrets it every day. I think I may bear some of the blame for not teaching him to contain his temper better. I have not been the best example of that. I hope that you can forgive us."

An unexpected thrill shot through Errol. He shivered slightly, embraced Miguel and said, "With all my heart."

In the night, Jonas died.

His letter was read the next day but the council held back the names of the honor guard listed in it, telling the town only that they would be named later.

Jonas' body was burned. The bones were collected, sewn into a canvas pouch, and placed in a cedar box for the journey.

When Errol came back from Monterey, Troy was out of danger and he brought Cody with him. After he'd had a chance to settle in, the council sent John Cooper to show him the letter. He read it, shook his head and looked out the window. "Jonas..." he said softly. He called his wife in Monterey.

"Why Cody?" his wife asked. "I can see the honor in it, but we are going to need Cody more than ever. How long would they be gone?"

"I don't know. No one's gone back there since I was a child... a month, maybe longer," Errol said.

"Is it dangerous?"

"Yes," was all Errol said.

"I don't like it," his wife said, "but do what you have to do."

Errol hung up and looked at John. "What does the council say?"

"The council feels that we gave our word and should keep it. We are willing to help with labor while both of your boys are out of action. But we've held back the names of the honor guard in case this is something you can't do. We can substitute another name and few will know," John said.

Errol leaned both hands on the window sill and gazed out at nothing. "What have the Ochoas said?"

"Luz will go if asked," John said.

Errol exhaled, and said, "I hope Jonas knew what he was playing at. Cody will go."

John left, and Errol picked up the phone.

Three

The day after Troy came home, Luz and Cody left. Most of the town followed them out of town to wave goodbye. They followed the San Francisco River, keeping it to their right as they walked.

Luz was carrying the special pack that had been sewn to fit the bone box and still be able to carry supplies and personal items. Cody was carrying a regular pack filled with supplies. They each had new clothes for the trip, leather field jackets, leggings, and new knives. Cody's knife was his father's, and he rested his hand on it absent-mindedly as he surveyed the sand dunes ahead.

They did not speak to each other for the first few miles, because neither knew what to say. The sounds of the river filled the gap. It was the first week of September but the air was unseasonably warm. When the morning sun reached a comfortable height, they paused and drank water from their canteens, then moved on. By noon they reached the first of the dunes and by the time they stopped to eat lunch, they were surrounded by dunes.

When they'd finished eating, Luz ventured, "How is your brother feeling?"

"How is your brother feeling?" Cody shot back.

Luz blinked, then answered, "Guilty."

"Good," Cody said.

Luz let it drop.

In the late afternoon they found a place to camp on the far edge of the dunes out of the wind. They didn't bother with the tent, but spread canvas on the warm sand, rolled out their bed rolls and started a fire with drift wood they found along the river. They only had two weeks' worth of food so they tried fishing. Cody had more luck. He caught two large fish before Luz even got a nibble. He carried them over to Luz and threw them at her feet. "If you clean them, you can have half," he said, and walked away.

Luz continued fishing. When she was about to give up and swallow her pride, she caught a little fish, cleaned it and carried it back to camp. When she arrived, Cody asked, "Where are my fish?"

"Where you left them," Luz said, and began roasting her fish over the fire.

Cody sat with his mouth open for a while, then went and got his fish. When he came back, Luz was already eating hers. He set his roasting. When he had finished eating he had some fish left over that he didn't know what to do with. Luz looked at it, still slightly hungry, but said nothing. Cody threw the fish into the sand on the edge of camp and leaned back on his bed roll. Luz ate some of the fresh fruit from her pack that wouldn't keep long. Cody watched her, but said nothing. Then she climbed into her roll and went to sleep.

In the morning a full moon rose two hours before sunrise and lit the dune field with an eerie glow. It was bright enough that it woke them up, but they stayed in their bed rolls. The moonlight glittered off the dead cities at the tops of the bluffs. They watched as the light shifted and was replaced by the warmer glow of a young sun just slipping up the horizon, then they both fell asleep until it was hot on their faces.

They woke up hungry and irritable. Not willing to lose any more time, they ate the remaining fresh food from their packs, packed up and began following the river again. When they got closer to the bluffs, they began to find things.

"Look," Cody said excitedly when he found a huge ship's anchor eroding out of the river bank.

Luz admired it.

They found chunks of concrete and huge rusted lumps of metal and small things like marbles, glass bottles, aluminum cans, even a plastic doll. There were signs of more recent activity. A case of rusty cans someone had carried this far and decided weren't worth it, a box of bolts that had fallen off a scavenging wagon. In the end they only kept some of the small things that wouldn't be too heavy to carry.

By afternoon they reached where the San Francisco River flowed through the Golden Gate. They said nothing as they walked, gazing up at the bluffs and cliffs they were passing. The presence of the dead city just out of view weighed on their spirits.

An hour later, they emerged into the San Francisco Valley and cut cross country away from the river towards Angel Mountain. They camped for the night along Raccoon Creek between Angel Mountain and Tiburon. They tried fishing again, and again Cody caught two large fish before Luz had caught any. He looked at them, considering what he should do, then cleaned them, took them to camp and set them to roasting.

Luz came back a little after sunset with nothing. She began rummaging through one of the packs.

"You can have some of my fish. We need to save our storable food and I have more than enough."

Luz accepted and ate. That night they set up the tent even though it was warm and there was no threat of rain. The tent was tiny. Really it was nothing more than some poles, a small sheet of canvas, a ground cloth and stakes, but it had to be small so they could carry more supplies. They lay next to each other, each trying to pretend the other wasn't there until they fell asleep. Their dreams were haunted. The millions of anonymous dead walked through their dreamscapes until a little before dawn when the more familiar dead came. They awoke as tired as they had gone to sleep.

"Let's get out of here," Cody said in the morning, and they left as soon as they could. An hour later they came to the San Pablo River and followed it north.

Finding things sticking up out of the ground became so common that they lost interest in it. They crossed several creeks and then about sunset they came to the confluence of the San Pablo and Napa rivers.

They set up the tent again, but the dead were done with them and they woke up strangely happy.

The next morning they packed up. Cody winced when he put his pack on.

"What's the matter?" Luz said.

"Nothing," he said.

They followed the Napa River north. Dill weed grew lush along the banks. As the river valley grew shallower they began to see ruins on the bench above. They came to a collapsed bridge. It had been intended to cross a much wider body of water. Its fragments now easily spanned the modest river. Luz impulsively climbed up the span and stood on top of it. Cody shook his head but followed. Instead of climbing down the other side she walked along the bridge towards the bluffs.

"Where are you going?" Cody said with disgust.

"I want to see what's up there," Luz said casually and kept walking.

Cody considered his options and grudgingly followed. They worked their way up an embankment. Dill weed gave way to fields of mustard greens. They continued north, paralleling the river for fifteen minutes and came to a turn in the deer trail they had been following. They followed it east and saw the outlines of a street with buildings beyond.

When they reached the street, they saw that the buildings were collapsed houses. They were too dangerous to enter. They wandered the streets, looking at faded cars and failed roofs. They found a garage with the door wide open that was still mostly standing. Cody handled the tools at the work bench.

They looked into the backyard and found an orange tree heavy with oranges. They picked some, sat down in the tall grass around the tree and tried them. They were not quite sweet yet. They ate them anyway and filled the empty pockets in their packs before moving on.

They followed the road north. There were signs that others had been in there. Copper wiring had been stripped off the power poles and out of the light poles. In one place a whole light pole had been taken down and the light itself hauled off.

They came to a turn in the road that led them away from the river.

"Which way?" Luz asked.

Cody looked around and said, "the river." They descended to it and toiled along in the midmorning sun.

By early afternoon they arrived at the collapsed railway bridge that was their signal to turn east. They followed the tracks until they reached the airport, then followed the fence until they found a hole in it. They walked down the runway in silence and past the old terminal building. Beyond the airport there was a creek and they paused to refill their water bottles, then moved out of town along Highway 12. At sunset they camped in a field, sleeping in their bed rolls under the stars.

In the morning they ate oranges and packed. Cody winced again when he put his pack on.

"What's the matter?" Luz asked.

"Nothing," Cody said annoyed.

Luz put her pack down. "Take it off," she said.

"No," Cody said.

"Take it off," Luz repeated.

"I said its nothing!" Cody shouted.

"Take it off now!" Luz insisted.

Cody didn't move. Luz marched towards him double-time and started pulling the strap off one shoulder.

Cody took a sharp breath and pushed her away hard. Luz fell on the ground, looked at him, got up and rushed him again.

Cody pulled his knife and angled it towards Luz.

Luz stopped short. The knife sparkled as Cody adjusted it in his hand.

"Seriously Cody?" Luz accused.

Cody lowered his eyes, then put the knife away.

"What were you thinking?" Luz asked.

Cody shrugged defiantly. "Does it matter?"

"Yes Cody, It matters," Luz said evenly.

Cody exhaled. "You were pushing me around. Nobody pushes me around."

"Nobody pulls a knife on me," Luz retorted.

Cody looked away. When he looked back she was still looking at him.

"Maybe you should have thought of that before you pulled a knife on my brother," Cody said.

"I never pulled a knife on your brother," Luz said.

"Your family did," Cody said.

"My brother did," Luz corrected.

Cody stared at her. Luz stared back. Cody shifted his weight and finally looked away.

"You should take the pack off," Luz said.

Cody slowly took the pack off. Luz pulled the collar of his shirt over to where she could see the skin on one shoulder. It had a nasty blue-green bruise where the straps cut across his shoulder. She pulled the shirt the other way and saw the other shoulder had the same bruising.

"Satisfied?" Cody asked.

"No," Luz responded. She hefted his pack. It was three times as heavy as hers. "Your pack is overweight, and I don't think your using the belt correctly."

"I can take it," Cody said.

"Until you can't..." Luz said. Luz dumped the pack out and put it back on Cody. The belt was completely loose.

"Why didn't you tighten this?" she asked.

"I always wear my belts loose," he said.

She pulled the belt as tight as it would go, but it was still too loose on his skinny waist. Luz got out an awl and punched a new hole in the belt, then tightened it up so the pack balanced on his hips and the straps barely touched his shoulders. Then she took the pack off and swapped the thin shoulder straps on his pack with the fat ones on hers and tried it again. "That's better," she said.

Next she reloaded his pack with the large but lighter objects and put the denser small objects into her own pack.

Cody pretended to be disgusted by the whole affair. When she was done rearranging the packs, he said, "Are you through?"

"No," Luz said and went back along the road picking yellow flowers as she went.

"Luz, I don't want flowers," Cody protested.

"Be quiet," Luz said. She brought the flowers back, mashed them into a paste and smeared it on the bruises. Then she helped Cody put the pack on, put her own on and said, "Now we can go."

They walked in silence. Luz watched the country side. Cody watched the ground. After fifteen minutes Cody started looking around too. It was pretty country, a little brown this time of year, but open and clean in a way the San Francisco valley wasn't. He began playing with his pack using his thumbs. The way Luz had arranged things it sat balanced on his hips and he could rock it back and forth. The pain in his shoulders had subsided too. He watched her walking in front of him. She was moving just as fast as before but there was a little less spring to her step due to the extra weight in her pack.

"Where did you learn to adjust a pack?" he asked.

"My mother. We use similar frames during the harvest."

"It's better... the shoulders, too," he said.

"Good," Luz responded.

There was an awkward silence.

"Why do you hate me?" Cody asked.

Luz looked at him funny and said, "Why would you think I hate you?"

"You pushed me off a cliff once."

"I was 12. You had just humiliated me, and once I realized what I'd done I was horrified."

"You always tried to make me look like a fool in school," Cody said.

"No. I just did my best to keep you from making me look like a fool," Luz replied.

"Why do you always take our land just when the grass gets good? " Cody insisted.

"That's just the way land is supposed to work. The herders are supposed to graze their cattle on the marginal land and the growers are supposed to plant things on the fertile land. You know that."

"Your family always look down their noses at us and talk bad about us," Cody said.

"Do I ever look down on you or talk bad about you?"

"I think so."

"Do I ever say it?"

Cody thought and said, "No, but you think it all the time."

"How do you know what I think?"

"If your family doesn't hate us, why did your brother nearly kill my brother!" Cody said.

"Maybe because your brother let your goats eat four months' worth of our labor and when my brother called him on it he laughed, and called our mother a whore."

"Well maybe she is a whore," Cody said.

"Well if she is, your father would be a whore maker, or did you miss that part?" Luz responded.

"So you do hate me, admit it!" Cody said.

Luz held her breath for a second then said, "I can't hate you!"

"Why not!?"

"Because I've got what's left of Jonas strapped to my back and he loved you, so I have to too."

"He didn't love me. He was my teacher, that's all."

"No Cody, he loved you. He made us promise, he made *me* promise, that we would never push you away, that if the town fell apart, we'd bring you with us if you'd come."

"I don't need the pity of a dead man and I don't need your pity!"

"Yes Cody, you do. You are rude, opinionated, selfish, proud, and you have a stubborn streak that keeps you from getting out of trouble when you easily could. You need his pity so you won't end up angry and alone, and I'll give it to you because despite everything I just said, Jonas was right about you."

"What do you mean Jonas was right about me?"

"Everyone thinks Jonas is a genius, a supernatural teacher, but what he was good at was picking the right students. He picked you because he saw what you could become if you'd just drop the crap."

Cody glanced at her and looked away. He opened his mouth, closed it, then exhaled. Finally he said, "I can still hate you if I want to."

They walked in silence for a quarter mile.

Crossing over a hill they slowed their pace until they stopped completely. An intact house had come into view, but more interestingly there were crops planted in the small field beside it. They watched the house carefully for a minute.

"Do you want to talk to them?" Luz asked.

Cody shook his head.

Luz shrugged and they walked carefully past the house. Further down the road they saw horses in a pasture. Cody was all attention. He took his pack off and leaned against the fence, then leaned on the fence and watched the horses.

Luz sighed, took off her pack, climbed up on the fence and watched them with him. The horses were young and spirited. They tore up the ground running for the sheer joy of it. After a while Cody rummaged in his pack and pulled out their last apple. He held it in the flat of his hand and whistled to the horses. The horses slowed their pace and watched them without turning to face to them. Cody whistled again.

"You may end up calling the owners instead of the horses, if you don't stop whistling," Luz said.

Cody chuckled, "That's fine. They can't be all bad if they're horse people," he said, but he stopped whistling.

The horses moved towards them obliquely, the large gray male in the lead, the brown mare keeping pace. They tossed their heads and paced. They knew what Cody had in his hand, but they didn't know Cody. After two or three passes they finally trotted up just out of arms reach and looked at them directly with large brown eyes.

Cody smiled. He glanced at Luz to see if she was seeing this.

The horses inched forward, smelling the apple. The closest one peeled back his lips showing his teeth and leaning his chin ever closer to the apple. When he finally got it he turned so quickly to run that he hit Luz in the face with his tail. Luz moved her arms to her face quickly which startled the other horse into colliding with the fence and before she could react Luz was sprawled on the ground inside the pasture with two horses dancing around her.

Cody was over the fence faster than thought. He pushed at the closest horse and got him moving away from them but not before the horse gave him a parting kick to the thigh. He held his breath and held on to the fence until the words he wasn't saying left his head, then he reached a hand out to Luz and helped her up. When they were both over the fence they rested for a minute.

"How's your leg?" Luz asked.

"Bruised, but not broken," Cody answered.

Luz nodded. They waited another few minutes then put their packs on and started walking down the road in silence.

After a quarter mile Luz observed, "You can move pretty quickly when you want to."

Cody looked at her, suspicious. He was limping.

"Back there I mean," Luz said nodding her head towards the pasture.

Cody nodded comprehension.

"Thanks," she said.

Cody shrugged.

After three hours they reached the big road labeled "80" on their maps. They walked in the grass beside it. Luz picked yellow flowers whenever she found them until she had a handful, then she put them in her pack. The kept walking until they encountered a creek with a tree and sat in its shade while they ate lunch and topped off their water supply. When they were done, they discussed the inventory. They had done well. They still had almost eleven days' worth of food. They decided not to forage until the next town.

They moved on. Around them another ruined city came into view, but there were signs of life. In the distance they could see a column of smoke from someone's fire. Occasionally they would find some sort of litter that was recent. After 45 minutes they hit another creek and topped off again. Beyond the creek the land opened up into a vast meadow with deer grazing in it. They walked through it for an hour before coming to another creek.

Beyond the creek another dead city greeted them. They walked through its concrete gloom for two hours before the country started opening up again. Then the road began to rise.

Luz groaned looking at it.

Cody looked at her and said, "Let's stop here for the night."

Luz nodded.

There were places near the road where it looked like others had camped, but Cody set his sights on a grove of oaks a couple of hundred feet off the road. They set up camp in a clearing. Remembering the smoke they had seen, they skipped the fire. They skipped the tent, too, electing to sleep in the open.

Luz gently set her pack against a tree, rolled out her bed roll and flopped on it. The sun was still up so she covered her face with her jacket. She had her hands behind her head and her shirt had pulled up enough that Cody could see her navel. He glanced at her and went back to fixing biscuits and jam to eat. When he was done he went to bring her some but hesitated. He rarely saw her idle. Lying there like that she was suddenly just a pretty young woman lying out in the late summer sun. He stared for a minute then shook it off and brought her the biscuits. They ate. The jam was from Henry's orchard, and tasted like the fruit had bottled up all the rain water and sun light of the early summer for them to enjoy now. The biscuits were probably from grain grown on Mark's farm.

"What do you think everyone is doing right now?" Luz asked.

"Getting done with work and starting home for dinner, and wondering how far we've gotten," Cody guessed.

"I miss school," Luz said.

Cody nodded.

Luz pulled the flowers out her pack, ground them into a paste and handed it to Cody. He went off into the trees and rubbed it on his bruised leg.

When he came back he sat down next to her. They watched the sun go down, then slept.

Four

In the morning they tackled the big hill, but they were tired and sore and moving slowly. It was two hours before they began descending into another dead city. Just before it, at another creek, they stopped and ate. After eating they walked for another hour and a half. Just as they were leaving town they suddenly stopped. 100 feet ahead there was a man herding a cow across the road. He hadn't seen them yet. Before they could decide what to do, he looked up, saw them and waved.

They approached him.

"Traveling?" the man asked.

"Yes," Cody said, "We're coming from the coast."

The man nodded. "Heading east?"

"Yes," Cody said. "We're going to Five Mile Terrace."

The man looked thoughtful, scratched his chin then shook his head, "Sorry, I don't know it. I only know as far as the train station in Sacramento. But the road is good all the way there. Don't buy supplies in Davis, they'll gouge you. Wait till you get to Sacramento."

"Thanks for the tip," Cody said.

"You're welcome," the man said.

"Do you live around here?" Luz asked.

"Yeah, we have a little town going next to the meadows over there," he said gesturing with his head. "We farm the fields on one side of the road and run the cows on the other side."

"I'm a farmer too," Luz said. "Are growing conditions good out here?"

"The best," the man said.

"Do you mind if we look at your fields on our way through?" Luz asked.

"That's fine. If you want to sample anything, that's OK too. Just don't carry anything off."

"We won't, and thanks again," Luz said.

"Good luck," the man said.

They continued down the road five minutes and it opened up just as the man had said. Luz set down her pack and scrambled into the fields. She sampled tomatoes and carrots and brought some back to Cody.

When they got going again, Cody mused, "He was nice."

"Yeah," Luz agreed, "Why wouldn't he be?"

"I don't know. You can never tell with people," Cody said.

Forty minutes out of town the farmland gave way to open prairie again with tall grass swaying in the light breeze and birds singing. The afternoon sun on their backs with a cool breeze starting to blow in their faces felt good.

"What will you do now that school's over?" Cody asked.

Luz looked at him surprised, then said, "I don't know. Things have been so crazy the last few weeks I haven't really thought about it."

Cody hesitated then asked, "What did you think before everything happened?"

Luz looked at him to see if he was sincere then looked at the sky, squinted and tried to remember. "I had a vague idea that I would save up for another year, then maybe try to find work in Monterey and then maybe try that teacher school Jonas told us about."

Cody shook his head and chuckled.

"What's funny?" Luz asked defensively.

"Nothing. It's just really different than what I thought you would say."

"What did you think I was planning?"

"I thought you'd get Henry to marry you and set up your own place."

Luz shrugged, "That wouldn't be a bad plan except I'm not interested in Henry. It would be like marrying my brother or something."

"But you could get him to do it, right?" Cody prompted.

Luz thought it over, "Probably. I don't know. I never really considered it."

"If not Henry then you could find someone else," Cody suggested.

"Farallon is a tiny town. There's no one there I'd ever be interested in," Luz said.

Cody got quiet, thinking.

After a while Luz asked, "What about you. What are your plans?"

Cody looked at the sky then shook his head. "My dad's talking about expanding the ranching operation to include more actual cows in addition to the goats, but everything seems different now. I like Jennifer, but I don't know if I'd want to marry her."

"Do you think Jennifer would marry you?"

"Sure. Why not," Cody said.

Luz laughed and Cody looked at her warily.

They walked silently for a while, then Cody said, "The more I think about it though, I kind of like your plan. Despite everything Jonas taught us, I didn't realize how small our town is until we took this walk. I kind of like seeing new places."

In the late afternoon they started seeing fields again and farmers working them. The harvest was on. Luz suddenly teared up looking at them.

Cody looked at her.

She shook her head and said, "I'm just being silly. This will be the first harvest I've missed since I was five years old."

An hour later they were standing on the edge of a small town.

Cody was ambivalent.

"Let's see if there's a place we can stay in town. I could use a real shower," Luz said.

"We should camp out another night and save money for supplies," Cody said.

"I seriously stink," Luz said and started moving towards town.

Cody groaned and followed her. There was a little bank, a hardware store, a feed store, two or three restaurants, and just beyond the restaurants a house with a sign saying "Inn" on it. They went inside and waited. A slightly out of breath heavy set woman of about 50 came in from the street a few minutes later and stood behind the counter.

"Are you looking for rooms?"

"Yes," Cody nodded.

"Are you two married?"

"No!" they said in unison.

"Then I have to charge you for two rooms even if you only use one. That's the law."

"Two rooms would be fine," Cody said glaring at Luz.

"That's $10 each for the night."

Cody looked at Luz. Neither of them knew if that was a good rate, but based on what other things cost it seemed reasonable. Luz nodded indistinctly.

"OK," Cody said.

They paid and checked in. The woman led them to their rooms which were across the hall from each other. They stashed their things.

"The bathroom is down the hall. If you want hot water you can come down to the desk and get the key for that, it's an extra $2. There's a phone in the lobby as well, calls are $1 plus long distance charges. You can use the laundry in back. If you need detergent, we have it at the desk. If you get hungry the restaurants are open until 9:00 PM and open again at 6:00 in the morning. Guests get a 5% discount at 'El Pato' next door."

Luz looked a little deflated when she heard that hot water was extra. Cody looked at her and said, "We'll take that hot water key."

By the time Luz got her shower they'd also shelled out an extra $1.50 for shampoo and soap, and Luz was beginning to feel guilty about it, but Cody just shook his head when she started to say something. Standing in the shower she kind of forgot about all of it. At least the water really was hot. She watched the dirt spiraling down the drain as she rinsed her hair. She stayed in the shower until the hot water started to run out, then put on her last set of clean clothes. On the way to her room she knocked on Cody's door and gave him the soap, shampoo, and key.

"You'd probably better wait a half an hour, I think I used all the hot water," she said.

"I usually take cold showers anyway," Cody said.

Luz shook her head, "Trust me. You'll want the hot water."

When they were both clean they checked out the restaurants. "El Pato" was the most expensive. They settled on the smallest of the three at the end of the street, mostly because it seemed alive. There were kids there getting ice cream and a few other groups of people sitting around.

Luz closed her eyes and chewed. "Warm food is soooo much better!" she said.

Cody nodded but didn't say much. He was busy navigating a piece of slow cooked beef brisket.

When their appetite was somewhat satisfied, they continued sitting at the table and listened to the conversations going on around them. A couple of old men in the corner were discussing this year's yields and the town election. A mixed group of 13 or 14 year olds were awkwardly flirting. A young mother was talking softly to her baby and swaying back and forth while her toddler finished his food. Luz closed her eyes again, pulling it all in until she heard Cody saying,

"Yes, we're on our way from the coast to a town beyond Sacramento."

She opened her eyes. Cody was talking to a middle-aged couple who were standing next to their table waiting for a takeout order.

"We're short-handed on the harvest," the husband was saying, "If you put in a day's labor with us we could give you a ride as far as Sacramento in the evening."

Cody ran the math in his head and looked at Luz.

Luz nodded.

"You've got a deal," Cody said. "When and where do we meet you?"

"We're close in. We'll send a kid over to this restaurant at 6:30 AM to bring you over."

"Great," Luz said.

After dinner they each called home to let everyone know where they were and what their plans were. Then they went out to the open air laundry behind the hotel. It was after dark when they got started under a single feeble light on the wall. Cody washed. Luz rinsed and wrung out.

The conversation lagged a little when they got to the underwear, but neither said anything about it.

They lugged the wet clothes up to their rooms. Cody ran a piece of cord across his room and they hung his clothes up on it to dry. There was room left on the line for Luz's clothes, but they took them across the hall to her room anyway. When they entered the room they found Jonas' bone box out of Luz's pack, open, and a seam on the canvas bag inside ripped.

Cody muttered something regrettable under his breath and checked the bag. The bones were still there. They looked around. The pack had been rifled through, and it looked like someone had gone through the drawers.

"Did they get anything?" Cody asked.

"I don't think so," Luz said. "The food and equipment are still here. We had the clothes with us and I keep my wallet on me all the time."

Cody went and got the manager.

"Looks like you got off easy," she said. "You need to keep your doors locked."

"The doors lock automatically, and I made sure the door was shut," Luz said.

"You must have left it open," the manager said and left.

Luz was pale with anger but she said nothing. Instead she got out her sewing kit and fixed the seam on the canvas bag.

Cody examined the box. The latch had been bent but he was able to bend it back. There was a large envelope ripped open on the floor next to the box.

"What's that?" Cody said.

Luz looked up and shook her head. "I've never seen it before."

Cody picked it up, looked at the papers sticking out and immediately recognized Jonas' handwriting. He quickly put the papers back in the envelope and put that in the box.

"What was it?" Luz asked.

"Something from Jonas," Cody said.

Luz didn't ask any more questions.

It was after 10:00 PM by the time they got everything put back together and went to bed.

Luz put a chair under her door knob before going to sleep.

In the morning the clothes were still damp, but they packed them anyway.

They got some food to go at the restaurant and the kid came as promised right after they got their order. They walked east into a field of lettuce and one of the farmers they'd seen at the restaurant the night before greeted them. They stashed their gear in a shed and joined the other harvesters.

They were assigned adjacent rows of lettuce and Luz said, "Race you to the end of the row!"

Cody sprang into action, but Luz was cutting almost twice as fast as he was and her heads were cleaner in the box. He watched her work the cruel pruning knife with a mixture of admiration and nagging sense of disdain. He puzzled over the feelings as he worked until while standing to stretch his back in the morning sun he closed his eyes and saws his brother's line of stitches. He recoiled from the thought, shook it off and continued working, feeling the weight of the knife in his hands.

When it was clear he could not keep up with her he settled into a more sustainable rate, and mused on what must have happened that day. He tried to put himself in his brother's place. His brother was bigger than Miguelito, perhaps he was counting on that, but that didn't make sense either. Miguelito must have been holding the knife in his hand as they spoke. The hooked blade looked menacing. He shook his head at the thought again, and realized his brother must of have felt safe because he had always been safe before doing things like that, even when someone was holding a knife. He didn't like the implications of that thought.

He looked at Luz who was already a quarter of the way through her row and showing no signs of slowing down. She was moving smoothly, joyfully. He thought back to quiet moments with the herd when the sun was at just the right angle, the temperature mild, and the herd content. Luz was looking back at him, grinning. The knife in her hand a tool, not a weapon. She looked away, and he found himself wishing she would look back again.

They worked until noon, then took refuge under a cottonwood on the canal with the others for lunch. Luz had finally started to slow down, but she was keeping up with the fastest harvesters and it had been noticed.

"Dang girl, you're quick!" a sixteen year old boy said a little too admiringly.

Luz flexed her bicep and said, "I'm strong, 'cause I eat my vegetables."

They laughed. One of the other workers said, "What's with your boyfriend there? How come he's so slow?"

"He's a herder. They only eat meat so they get big but not strong," Luz said glancing at Cody with a glint of steel in her eye.

"Well I guess your girlfriend is earning your ride for you," the worker said to Cody.

He opened his mouth to correct him, then changed his mind and said, "Guess so."

Luz looked at him for a split second then turned her attention back to the group.

The afternoon got surprisingly warm and Cody's shirt was soaked with perspiration by the time they stopped for dinner break. After dinner, they switched to packing the containers into the trucks and by the time they were done he was shivering.

"You should change your shirt if you're going to ride in the truck," the farmer said.

By the time he'd finished changing, Luz was already up on the truck snuggled into a nest of packing materials she had made in the back. Cody joined her and the trucks pulled out a minute later.

The sun had set and a few lights could be seen blinking in and out of sight as the truck rolled down the big road dodging some potholes and plowing right through others. They had their field jackets on but it was still chilly in the moving night air. They were both tired. Luz leaned up against him and fell asleep. Cody didn't sleep at first. He watched the lights go by, smelled the crops in the fields cooling down around him, and felt Luz breathing. He drifted into sleep by degrees so that he didn't even know he was asleep until he woke up. The truck's motors were humming a deeper tune. The wind slowed and the cargo was straining at the tie-downs.

The truck took a couple of turns, went down some smaller roads, then backed into a loading dock and stopped. The driver climbed out and plugged the truck in while the farmer and one of the hands opened up the tail gates. The farmer smiled briefly when he saw Cody and Luz nestled together. They gathered their gear and scrambled down.

"Thanks for the help, and good luck," the farmer said.

"Thanks for the ride," Luz answered.

"If you need a ride on the way back, check here. This is our usual loading dock," the farmer said.

"Thanks," Cody said.

They passed through some doors into the enclosed space of the market. There were stalls set up all along the brick wall perimeter and in rows down the middle. A metal roof above kept out the sun and rain, but not the cold. Even as late as it was producers were busy restocking for the next day. Cody and Luz wandered down the rows of mostly closed stalls.

"This makes our general store look like a storage closet," Cody said.

"Don't tell Eddie," Luz said.

Even though they had eaten, the site of so much food made them hungry.

"I wonder if we could find another ride." Luz said.

Henry started looking at crates hunting for place names in the right direction. Luz watched him, amused. After 10 minutes she said, "Any luck?"

Cody shook his head dejectedly.

"Let me try," Luz said.

Cody shrugged.

Luz walked up to one of the farmer's and said, "Are there any producers here that are based out of Placerville or anywhere else up highway 50?"

The man said, "Yeah, most of them have their stalls in the northeast corner."

"Thanks," she said sweetly.

Cody looked at her but said nothing.

Luz smirked at him.

They found stalls for grape growers in the north-east corner and Cody verified they were from Placerville by checking the crates. They were all closed. Cody asked someone passing by what time they opened and if there were any good places to stay the night.

"Six AM," the woman told him. She looked at the two of them and suggested, "If you're looking to save money, there's a fenced camp with showers near the rail yard that some of us use for $2.50 a night."

They got directions. Cody thanked her and they camped for the night. They were both asleep the minute they got into their rolls.

The next morning they arranged for travel in exchange for a day's labor harvesting grapes. They resupplied then got breakfast while they waited until the trucks came back from taking a load to the train station.

Luz built another nest in the back of that truck and they settled in. It took ten minutes for the truck to get clear of the city and then the land on either side of the highway opened up into cattle country. They saw several herds of cows grazing. Cody pointed at one of them and said, "That's where food comes from, lettuce girl!"

"Funny," Luz said. "Those goats seem a little bigger than yours."

"Hey! We have some cows too," Cody objected.

Luz laughed at him.

After half an hour on the highway they were freezing. When the truck finally left the highway and turned so the mid-morning sun was on them, they began to relax again. At the edge of town there was a scaffold with a dummy hanging from a noose and a placard that said, "Hangtown We meant it then. We mean it now. Behave yourself." Luz and Cody exchanged glances.

When they arrived, they started work immediately.

Luz was less familiar with grapes than she was with lettuce, but she watched the others and caught on in less than ten minutes. Cody lagged behind. He nearly cut himself on one cluster so Luz left what she was doing and taught him. When he had it down, she went back to her own work and he was nearly able to keep up.

The harvest was running late, so they ate lunch in the rows. Cody poked at the ground next to him with a knife.

"The soil here is different," he mused. He dug up a little and showed it to Luz.

"Yeah, more iron under the organic matter layer," Luz said.

Cody spread it out in his palm with the knife saying, "... and more quartz grit and decomposed granite."

"Come on professors, let's get back to work," the foreman said.

They put away their lunch and went back to work. In the late afternoon during the water break Cody tried talking to one of the boys working on the next row.

"Why do you have a dummy hanging from a noose at the entrance to town?" he asked.

The boy rolled his eyes. "Because real bodies stink after a couple of days," he said.

Cody didn't ask any more questions.

They worked until dark, turned in their harvest knives and found a place under an oak tree to camp for the night. Luz slid into her bed roll and listened to Cody doing the same. When he had been quiet for a while she asked, "Still hate me?"

"Not really," Cody said, and they went to sleep.

Five

They woke up in a somber mood, ate, packed and hit the road a little after sun up. They didn't talk much. The bones in Luz's pack seemed to rattle more than usual.

They took the back road because it cut off an hour of walking. It was a smaller road and more pleasant anyway. Despite being tired they walked quickly. They passed vineyards and a few orchards and barns, but as they got higher into the hills, pine forest began to take over. Between the trees they could see tumbled down buildings, rusted tractors, and collapsed trellises. Around a couple of bends they saw untended orchards with gnarled limbs and few leaves. They checked one to see if there might be some apples left, but found only a rusty scale covering the bark. They moved on, not touching anything.

After two hours of walking they arrived in Five Mile Terrace. There was no one to be seen. They sat down in a grassy place under a tree and looked at each other.

"Now what do we do?" Luz asked.

"I guess we read Jonas' letter," Cody said.

They took the box out of Luz' pack, carefully opened it, and removed the envelope. There were two hand printed sheets with a hand drawn map. They looked at the map. Jonas had written a compass on it, which helped to orient it, but the land marks had changed.

"That is this orchard," Cody said confidently pointing.

Luz squinted at the map, looked at the orchard and the streets and nodded. They followed the road 30 feet then turned left. After a quarter mile, they came to a pond. They left the road, walked past the pond and found a tumbled down fence surrounding a square of flat ground 50 feet wide on each side. They stepped over the remains of the fence, walked to the middle of the plot and began searching in the deep grass.

After a minute Luz called out, "I think I've got it. What is the name?"

Cody looked at the map and said, "It doesn't say."

"What do you mean it doesn't say? It has to say!"

"It doesn't," Cody reiterated.

They trampled down the grass around the stone and sat down to read the rest of the letter.

"Dear Luz and Cody:

Thank you for carrying my old bones home. I have made a map to guide you to my burial place. Please bury my bones as close as possible to the grave of my wife Olivia and our daughter Atalia. I suppose that by the time you read this, I will be with them, but I would like us to rise together in the resurrection so I appreciate the trouble you are going to."

There was more but they stopped reading and checked the stone. There were markings on it but they weren't deep. They wet the stone, looked at it from an angle and could make out the words "Olivia" and "Atalia." They went back to the letter.

"I met Olivia on my way back from school. She was living in Placerville with her parents and I stopped at their restaurant on my way up the hill from the train station. There weren't many customers in the restaurant so she sat next to me at the counter and asked about my travels. She was good looking, so I didn't mind.

I told her about all the things I had seen, but that didn't satisfy her. She wanted to know all the things I'd learned. She had only gone to school for three years because the only school close enough wasn't open every year, and her parents needed her help at the restaurant and on the farm. But she had taught herself all sorts of topics. We hit it off.

I came to see her every week, some weeks every day, and I didn't mind the long walk.

Eventually she stopped charging me for my meals and one day I said I felt bad about taking money from her parents so I thought maybe I should make that right by marrying her. I thought it was a clever thing, but she didn't like it and told me not to come back anymore. I missed her and I guess she missed me too because just when I was about to go see her, even if it would make her mad, she knocked on my door.

She asked why I hadn't come by and I told her 'because you told me not to,' and she said,

'Well, I wish you wouldn't be so obedient.'

I moved to Placerville and opened up that old school house, and worked until I could buy her a ring and one day I took her on a picnic and asked her to marry me. We stayed in Placerville for a few years and she kept helping her parents and I'd help too sometimes when I wasn't teaching. The third year her parents got sick and died within a few weeks of each other. About that time things were getting worse at Five Mile Terrace so we moved there temporarily to see if we could help.

By that time we knew we couldn't have babies, but within a month of moving she was pregnant. It was a hard pregnancy from the start. When the baby died an hour after being born, Olivia just got worse and worse and died holding that baby two hours later. After that the only thing I could do for them was bury them and miss them. So I did.

Maybe by the time you read this letter you two will be able to understand. If not, I know that someday you will.

Take care of each other.

Love, Jonas."

They sat in silence for a long time. The breeze stirred the trees. A bird called out somewhere and was answered. The sun warmed up the grass and the insects came out and hurried on their way.

Cody put the letter back in its envelope and handed it to Luz. She tucked it away in a pocket of her pack.

They stood up and looked around.

"Let's get this done," Luz said.

"We should clear the grass and figure what other graves are in here. I don't want to dig in the wrong spot," Cody said.

Luz nodded. They got out their hunting knives and cut the grass away a clump at a time until they had cleared a ring around the grave ten feet in diameter, then they examined the ground. The soil over the graves had sunken enough to make their outlines clear and the space to the right of Olivia and Atalia's grave was clear.

Cody put on his kid skin gloves and got out the collapsible shovel. Taking turns, they were able to dig a hole three by three by three feet deep after two hours of work.

"It's not deep enough," Cody said.

"We need a better shovel," Luz said.

Cody agreed.

They walked along the road looking for any sheds or outbuildings that still had roofs on them. After checking five of them they found a shovel and a pick axe still in working order. They took them back to the cemetery and finished the hole in less than an hour. They stopped to eat. A breeze was starting again, but it had shifted direction and was coming down the mountain, cold, with the smell of ice in it. They shivered.

They cleaned themselves up, took Jonas' box out of Luz's pack and put it in the bottom of the grave.

Cody said, "Jonas: We will always remember the things you taught us and try to live up to them. You were the best teacher and a true friend."

Luz said, "Jonas: We will share what you taught us. Take care of your wife and little girl."

They said a prayer, then took turns filling in the hole. It was getting dark by the time they finished so they camped in the field next to the cemetery.

In the morning they decided Jonas needed his own stone so they found one and practiced carving until they could chisel "Jonas" on it.

When it was done the letters were a little uneven but they decided it was good enough and planted it over his grave next to his wife and daughter's stone. When that was done, they still had supplies and they still had time so they decided to fix up the cemetery. They rummaged through buildings until they found a push mower. They found some grease and got it turning and mowed the grass in the cemetery. Then they propped the fence back up and wired the cross bars into place.

They stood back and admired their work.

"Good?" Cody asked.

"Good," Luz answered.

They started gathering the tools to put them back when they heard the sound of a shotgun pump and froze.

Six

"What are you doing in my grave yard?" an old man's voice said.

Cody and Luz turned to face him.

"Fulfilling a last request," Cody said.

"Step to one side," the man said.

Cody and Luz moved towards their packs.

"Not too fast," the man said.

They stopped. He squinted at the plot.

"What did you bury there?"

"Not what, who," Cody corrected.

"Who?"

"Our teacher, Jonas," Cody said.

"Did you stop to think that being found in a graveyard with a shovel is a bad idea?" the man asked as he lowered his shotgun.

"Didn't look like anyone would mind," Luz said.

The man looked her over carefully.

"You have to admit, no one has cared for this plot in years," Cody said.

 The man shrugged. Something in the shrug struck Luz as familiar.

"I'm Barnabas," the man said. "I'm Jonas' brother."

Luz broke into a smile and came at him so quickly he took a step back.

"Jonas said he had a brother!" she said.

"What else did he say?" Barnabas asked.

Luz was taken aback. "Just that he was gone so long that when he came back you hardly knew him."

Barnabas hesitated, then said, "Sounds about right. Come on. I should feed you."

They gathered their things and followed him.

His home was only a few streets over. It looked as abandoned as all the others.

"I'm glad we didn't rummage through his garage on accident," Cody whispered to Luz.

Luz suppressed a laugh.

They went inside and set their packs down. A cheap plastic clock ticked loudly on the mantle of the fireplace. Barnabas stoked the fire and went into the kitchen, leaving Luz and Cody standing in the living room. Luz went to the door of the kitchen and asked if he needed any help.

"No! No, I'll call you when it's ready," Barnabas said.

They hesitantly sat down. The couch was dusty. They waited in silence, occasionally looking at each other but saying nothing.

Cody scanned his surroundings. The room was mostly unremarkable; assorted old furniture, faded drapes, a fireplace, and hanging on the wall between the fireplace and the kitchen door a two foot long hollow tube with a leather carrying strap. He puzzled on the tube.

After a few minutes Barnabas called them to dinner saying, "Come on in, it's ready."

The kitchen was orderly, but not especially clean. Barnabas sat Luz to his right and Cody to his left and served the food. It was a stew, and it was good.

"What is it?" Luz asked.

"Squirrel," Barnabas said.

"Picking the shot out of them must be a hassle," Cody said.

"I use the blow gun for squirrel," Barnabas said gesturing to the tube by the fireplace. "I've got these darts that makes it so the squirrels can't run once they've been hit, but it don't kill them. Then I put them in a cage and I have fresh squirrel whenever I want."

Cody nodded.

When they had eaten, Barnabas brought out a bottle of wine and showed it to them.

"No thanks," Luz said.

He looked at Cody. Cody shook his head.

"What? Don't you two drink?" Barnabas asked.

"My father does, at dinner," Luz offered.

"We're 17," Cody said.

"Law has no reach up here," Barnabas said. Seeing that they weren't going to bite he added, "Suit yourselves. I couldn't get through a day without it." He drank a third of his glass in the first gulp.

"Could you tell us about when Jonas was young?" Luz asked.

"You kind of liked him didn't you?" Barnabas said.

"Yes. He was a great teacher," Luz said.

"I don't remember much from before he went away," Barnabas said. "I remember once he pushed me down for taking his toy... I don't know. But I do remember when he got back."

"Tell us about that," Cody said.

Barnabas looked at him and said, "Well he came back full of book smarts and had all kinds of ideas about how to change things. I didn't think much of it because I had been here the whole time working the land and experience counts for a lot. We had a couple of years of bad luck, and then things got a bit ugly and he ran down the hill to Placerville with his tail between his legs. When things settled down he came back up here with a wife in tow, and that was the smartest thing he done because she was easy to look at. It didn't work out, though. She died and he moped around here until he couldn't take it, then he left and took some of the best people in town off with him somewhere and left me here pretty much alone."

"Why didn't you go with them?" Luz asked.

"This is where my mom and dad are buried. Maybe Jonas can run off whenever it suits him but I can't. Besides, they didn't exactly ask me to come," Barnabas said.

"Have you been alone here ever since?" Cody asked.

"Not exactly. People come through sometimes. The surveyors come through every year and usually they stop by. Sometimes I go down to Placerville, get supplies, see some of the people that used to live up here."

Cody and Luz looked at each other but couldn't think of what to say next.

"So are you two a couple?" Barnabas asked.

"No, just schoolmates," Cody said.

"Yeah, I'll bet," Barnabas said.

There was an awkward silence that Barnabas didn't seem to notice. Then he finally spoke.

"I remember when... what was her name... Olivia first came up here. I asked if she had a sister, but she didn't. She was cute though, and she made Jonas seem almost normal..."

There was another silence. He put his hand on Luz's thigh under the table and asked, "So, is there anything else you want to know about Jonas?'

Luz didn't answer him.

 Cody said, "Yes. Did he say why he was leaving?" Barnabas lifted his hand off Luz's thigh and rubbed his head thinking.

After a minute, he said, "He had this idea that the foothills were getting too cold and that we should move someplace warmer. I said if he was going to do that he should just go down in the valley, but he had this idea that new land was opening up along the ocean and he sold everyone on it." Barnabas stopped talking and finished his wine.

After a few minutes, Cody asked, "Would you like to know where they went and what happened to Jonas?"

Barnabas put his hand back on Luz's thigh, considered the question for a second and said, "Sure. You can tell me about that."

Luz asked to use the bathroom. Barnabas got up, showed her where it was and stood by the door for a few seconds before coming back to the table.

Cody told him about Farallon and the school Jonas taught and how everyone respected Jonas, and how he died. When he was through, Barnabas said, "So, he did well for himself then. That's good."

There was silence. After a while Barnabas got up and started clearing the dishes. "Can I help you with that?" Cody asked.

"No. I've got it," Barnabas said.

Cody went to check on Luz who hadn't come back from the bathroom. He waited outside the door for a minute before knocking. "Are you OK?" he asked through the door.

"Yeah," Luz said. "I'll be out in a few minutes."

"Best leave her alone," Barnabas said to Cody so close that it made him jump. "Come on. Let's get you set up for the night."

"Oh, you don't have to put us up," Cody said. "We've got good gear."

"Don't be crazy. It's after dark and the night wind has a bite to it."

"We'll be fine," Cody said.

"Don't be so proud," Barnabas said, and made up a bed for Cody on the couch. "We'll give the guest room to your girlfriend." Barnabas checked the guest room and was apparently satisfied because he made no changes to it.

Luz came out of the bathroom. "What's going on?"

"He wants us to stay tonight," Cody said sheepishly.

Barnabas looked at her for her answer. She smiled. He turned back to Cody. As soon as his back was turned, Luz mouthed the word "No" to Cody. But he was looking at Barnabas.

"It's settled then," Barnabas said.

Neither of them slept well. Luz slept with her knife under the pillow.

In the morning, things seemed different. With the room lit up by morning sun, Luz noticed a picture of a young woman on the wall with Olivia's name under it. She studied the face. It was strong, but not stern. There was a hint of playfulness around the eyes and mouth that reminded Luz of Jonas. She relaxed and realized there was a difference between a lonely old man and a dangerous one.

Barnabas invited them to breakfast. He'd made pancakes and poured some canned orange juice for them. "You two go ahead and eat, I already ate. I built a fire in the water heater this morning so if you want to clean up before you go, you can. Just leave the dishes in the sink. I've got to pick up a delivery in town first thing, so we'll just say goodbye now." It was the most he had said in one turn since they met him.

Cody and Luz thanked him and he left.

"That must be some package he's expecting," Cody mused.

"Maybe he just slows down in the evening. Old people do that," Luz said.

They had breakfast. The pancakes were good. The orange juice was bitter like canned orange juice often is, but they drank it anyway.

"No way we're just leaving the dishes in the sink," Luz said.

"I'll do them. You get packed up," Cody said.

"You do them and I'll get a shower!" Luz corrected.

Cody nodded and set to work.

Luz washed her hair but tried not to use too much hot water in case Cody wanted a shower, which was hard because the water felt good. When she was almost done she felt a sting in her left buttock. She felt the place with her hand and there was something protruding, but it came loose and went down the drain before she got a look at it. She looked at the shower enclosure. It was missing tiles and a rusty metal mesh poked through in several places. "Better check my tetanus booster," she thought.

She got out, started to towel off and heard a noise coming from behind the wall of the shower. She looked in that direction and noticed a hole where the drywall had rotted away. She bent down, looked into the hole and saw an eye looking back at her for a split second, then motion and then nothing. She jumped back, clutched her towel, ran out of the bathroom and into her room calling "Cody!" as she ran.

He came around the corner from the kitchen in time to see her door close. He went to the door and said, "What's the matter?"

"Leave the dishes. Get your stuff, we have to go!" she said.

"What happened?"

"I think Barnabas was peeping on me!"

"OK," Cody said.

He went back to the sofa, strapped his knife on, and stuffed everything into his pack.

"Ready to go!" Cody said.

"Cody, come in here and help me," Luz said.

He went into the room. Luz had most of her clothes on but was struggling with her socks and shoes.

"Calm down," he said. "I'm sure he's no match for the two of us."

"I am calm. I just can't seem to get my socks on," Luz said.

Cody put them on her feet then helped her with her boots. He started stuffing her things into her pack, then heard her slump over onto the bed. Just as he looked at her he felt a sharp sting. His hand went to it reflexively and came back with a small featherless dart. He looked at it puzzled for a second, then looked at the doorway and saw someone moving. He pulled his knife out and charged through the doorway. Barnabas was standing by the outer door, watching him, gauging his reactions.

Cody advanced on him. He retreated to the front porch. Cody followed him, but when he got to the front door he found it difficult to work the doorknob. He kept trying to grasp it but his hand kept slipping. He tried to turn to look out the window for Barnabas but found it impossible. "Think," he said to himself, but he couldn't think of what to do. His knees buckled and he found himself staring at the dusty floor, conscious but unable to move. Several minutes passed.

He heard the front door open and footsteps. He heard someone breathing. The breathing person went away, set something down and came back. A man's hands grabbed him by the arm and flipped him onto his back. Barnabas' flush face looked at him. Barnabas dragged him into the middle of the living room. He aligned him so he could see the bedroom, even put a pillow under his head. Then he took Cody's knife and rammed it through his shin between the tibia and the fibula and into the floor, pinning his leg. Tears dripped silently down Cody's cheeks as Barnabas turned and went to the bathroom, humming to himself. Cody could see Luz slumped over on the bed. She was breathing, but the breathing was ragged.

When Barnabas came out of the bathroom he looked at Cody, then went into the bedroom. He pulled Luz up from her face down position, laid her flat on the bed and started carefully unlacing her boots.

"You can't be wearing boots in bed," he said to Luz.

Luz sent useless commands to her hand to grab the knife from its sheath on her hip, but her hand did not respond. She tried to close her eyes, but could not.

He pulled each boot off. Then he pulled each sock off, taking his time. He unbuttoned her jacket and the top two buttons on her shirt. He stood back and admired his work, then went into the bathroom, came back with a brush and started brushing her hair. When he was done he stood back, looked at her and said, "That's better." After a moment he seemed agitated and said, "Why do you want to leave? Why does everyone always want to leave? It doesn't make any sense."

He paced around the room for a while then said, "Well, it doesn't matter. You're here now." He sat on the edge of the bed and unbuttoned the rest of the buttons on her shirt and opened it. "You sure are pretty," he said. He paced some more, breathing deep, then returned to the bed and unbuttoned the top button of her pants. His fingers trembled. He heard a sound in the living room and stood to get a better look. Cody fired the shotgun into Barnabas' chest, but he didn't have a firm grip on it when he fired. The recoil knocked it out of his hands and into his face, bloodying his nose, breaking two fingers, and knocking him to the ground.

Barnabas looked at the front of his shirt and watched it turn red. He seemed more curious than anything else. He looked at Cody and a flash of anger crossed his eyes. He stood unsteadily and walked towards Cody and the shotgun. Cody tried to get up. Barnabas reached for the shotgun. Cody kicked the legs out from under him with his good leg and Barnabas fell on top of the shotgun. Cody grabbed his knife and stabbed at Barnabas repeatedly. Barnabas parried the first two blows with his arm and crawled forward trying to get control of the shot gun. Cody slashed repeatedly hitting Barnabas on the inner thigh until he saw blood spurt and Barnabas slowly stopped struggling. Cody rested, still clinging to the knife.

The house became quiet. The cheap clock ticked on the mantle. A spider ran up the wall. The morning wind blew outside the house. Twenty minutes passed, and Luz began to sob. Cody sat up. He pulled himself to his feet and hobbled over to her.

"It's OK," he said. "We're OK."

She looked at him with her eyes, but still couldn't move or speak. She cried more loudly, her eyes darting. He put his hand on her cheek and stroked her hair until his leg hurt so bad he couldn't stand anymore and he slumped to the floor by the bed, leaving his hand on her arm so she would know he was still there.

The next thing he was aware of was that Luz was sitting up. Her shirt was still hanging open exposing her bra and stomach, but she didn't seem to care. She pulled her knees up in front of her and held on to them. She looked at him.

Her left leg was bleeding slightly in four places where stray pellets had lodged in her leg.

They sat that way for a long time. Sunlight came through a south facing window and moved slowly along the floor. They stood up and Cody cried out briefly then got control of himself. Luz helped him and they limped across the room, past Barnabas' body and into the bathroom. They washed their faces. Luz set his broken fingers, made a splint and taped the broken ones together. She tried to pull his pant leg up to look at the wound on his leg, but the blood had dried enough that it pulled at the scab whenever she tried.

"I can't see very well, but I think this is going to need stitches," Luz said.

"It will definitely need stitches," Cody said decidedly.

"What did he do?" Luz asked.

"He..." Cody turned pale remembering it, and shook his head.

Luz got quiet.

They sat on the bathroom floor for a few minutes.

"We'll have to just stitch it up as best we can," Cody said.

"I think we should get you to a doctor. Placerville is only five or six miles. I could go for help," Luz said.

Cody shook his head. "If you get a doctor from Placerville, they're going to want to know how I got hurt and what I was doing up here, and then we'll have to explain the mess in the living room."

"So we'll do that. He needed shooting. Any jury could see that," Luz said.

"We're outsiders. He was one of them. Placerville has a hanging judge. I don't like our chances and I don't want to see you stand in front of a room full of angry strangers and tell them what he did... what he tried to do... He's dead. There's nothing more that needs doing. We've done nothing that needs punishing. I say we just go."

"No," Luz said. "We need to be cleared of this. I need to be cleared of it."

"Luz, do you have any doubt that I did the right thing?"

"No. I know what he would have done to me, and I don't want to think about what he would have done to you."

"Then what do we need to be cleared of?"

"I don't want to have to hide this. I want to know that everyone knows this wasn't our fault."

"If it were any other town I would agree with you," Cody said. "But not in this town."

"You don't get to decide this," Luz said.

"So you're just going no matter what I say, even if it gets me killed?" Cody asked.

Luz bristled, but she paused and thought. After a long time she said, "No. I won't go unless you agree."

"Tell me again why you have to go," Cody said.

Luz rethought the whole thing and said, "I need to know this wasn't somehow my fault. I can't live with myself if I somehow caused this."

"You didn't cause this!" Cody said. "How can you think you could have caused this?"

"Maybe I didn't cause it but maybe I could have avoided it. What if I hadn't taken a shower? What if I had insisted that we not stay?"

"That's nuts Luz. No one can live like that."

"I need someone to say we did right," Luz said.

"What if they say you or I caused this? Would you believe them?"

"No."

"Then why would you believe them if they tell you you're innocent?"

"Because then their worthless opinion would match what my head already knows."

"You would really suffer if you didn't report this?"

"Yes."

Cody looked at her a long time then closed his eyes. "There's nothing I could say, or that people back home could say that would take that doubt away?"

Luz shook her head slightly.

"Then go. I'll take my chances," he said.

Luz looked around town and found another house that was in reasonable condition. She moved their stuff, then helped Cody move there. She gathered food and water from Barnabas' kitchen and brought it to him.

"I should be back with help in a few hours or morning at the latest," Luz said. She gave him a quick one armed hug, started to let go, held on for a split second longer, then left.

Luz went down the same road they had come by, but without her pack and much quicker.

Her leg hurt from the shot in it. In an hour she was back at the farm where they'd worked, but after hesitating near the gate, she moved on. The scaffold loomed over Main Street. She walked to the sheriff's station and stood outside the doors, bracing herself.

She went in. No one was at the front desk. There was a bell she could ring, but she sat down in the chairs by the front desk, suddenly uncertain. She closed her eyes. A fly buzzed against the window by the door trying to find a way out. A couple of deputies were chatting idly over coffee in the room behind the front desk. After a while her heart beat quieted enough that she could hear what they were saying.

"Do you have any leads on that break in on Washington Street?"

"No. They got away clean."

"That's the third one this month."

"I know."

"So what are you going to do?"

"I'll keep looking. If I don't find anything in a week I'll round up the Davis kid or the Gonzalez kid. They're always breaking one law or another. If I don't find anyone better we'll hang one of them."

"Hell, one of them probably did it!"

Luz's stomach lurched. She stood up, slipped quietly out the door and went back the way she had come. Once she was well past the farm, she ducked into an old orchard and hid behind a collapsed barn. She waited. No one came. When an hour had passed she hurried back to where she'd left Cody. She opened the door and he wasn't there. She collapsed on the floor.

Seven

When Luz woke up Cody was lying on his side next her, watching her, concerned.

She looked at him and he smiled, "I think you needed that sleep," he said.

"Where were you?" Luz said, starting to remember.

"I was out back taking a leak. When I came back you were lying on the floor and wouldn't wake up. So, I put you in your bedroll," he said.

Other than the moon shining on them through a window, the house was dark. "How long was I asleep?" Luz asked.

"About four hours."

Cody dug into the pack and got her some food.

They talked into the night.

Luz told him what she heard in town and they decided to dispose of the body and leave. They worked out the details of what they would do and then they talked randomly of anything that came to mind. They talked as if it were their only night to talk and when their minds were too tired to form words they fell asleep again leaving some of the most important words unsaid.

In the morning Cody hobbled to Barnabas' house and gathered a bottle of whiskey, some scissors, and bandages. When he got back to Luz he sat down stiffly and sharpened his knife.

Luz took her pants off and sat on top of them. Cody cleaned the blade of his knife with the alcohol and then handed her a piece of bandage soaked in it to clean her wounds. When she was done he deftly picked at the oozing red spots with the tip of his knife. Even with two broken fingers he was more accurate than she would have been. In a few minutes he had three of the balls out. He struggled with the fourth.

"It's too deep. I can't get it," he said. He handed her another piece of bandage to clean the wounds again. When she was done, he taped bandages over the wounds. Luz got up and carefully put on her clean pair of pants.

When she was ready she said, "OK. Your turn."

Cody took his shoes and socks off, unbuttoned his pants and braced himself. Luz used the knife to separate the fabric from the wound. Cody stiffened and breathed heavy several times. When she finally got it separated, they rested a moment, then yanked the pants off in one continuous move.

Luz examined the entry and exit wounds, looked at the knife in her hand, and looked at Cody. Cody just shook his head. Luz cleaned the puffy wound and soaked it with alcohol. Cody groaned but held still. She sterilized a needle and thread and said, "Are you ready?" Cody nodded. She stuck him with the needle but he didn't seem to feel it much. As she sewed he actually seemed to relax slightly. When she was done with the front, he carefully turned over and she sewed up the back.

When he was dressed again they ate a little and napped. Luz twitched and mumbled in her sleep. Once Cody tried to calm her by stroking her hair, but she had him at knife point before either of them knew it would happen. She lowered the knife, blinking and breathing heavily before wordlessly handing him the knife and going back to sleep.

In the late afternoon they went to Barnabas' house. They pulled the bedspread off the bed, put it on the floor and put the body on it, then drug it out of the house. Cody was useless at dragging the body. Every time he tried to pull his calf muscle exploded in pain. He went back to the house, got the shotgun and followed. They positioned the body halfway down a slope and put the shotgun on the ground in front of it pointing back at it.

They went back to the house, cleaned it, scrubbed the floors and locked it up. Out back they found two caged squirrels wild with hunger. Luz impulsively let them go.

By the time they finished, it was dark. They washed and changed into clean clothes, putting the dirty ones into a bag in Cody's pack. Cody couldn't carry any weight. He reluctantly switched the fat shoulder straps back onto Luz's pack and they put what food they could in her pack and the lightest things in his.

They tried to sleep. Cody was wide awake. Luz twisted and muttered only quieting when she woke up enough to be able to think. Finally an hour past midnight they gave up, loaded their bed rolls and walked down the road. They stopped at Jonas' grave.

"We had to kill your brother," Cody said, his voice catching unexpectedly. "We're sorry."

Luz just kissed her hand and touched the stone with it.

They went down highway 50 walking along its broad expanse under the bright moonlight. The road was utterly empty, built for another time with different imperatives. After half a mile, Cody's pace slowed. Luz slowed to match. After another half mile Cody said, "I have to stop."

Luz nodded. They found a place under some oak trees and made camp. Luz found some cool stones and propped his hurt leg on top of them. They were both asleep in minutes.

They woke up after noon. They ate breakfast then Luz examined Cody's leg. It was swollen, tender to the touch and the wound was weeping slightly. They decided to wait until night to travel again. Cody found an oak branch and began carving a crutch. His leg hurt. His hand hurt. His face hurt. But feeling the early fall sun filtering through the trees onto his tired shoulders, hearing small creatures in the bushes gathering their last supplies for the winter, seeing Luz do normal things like eat food and brush her teeth made him aware of life and the living. During the day they heard the distant whine of trucks on the road, and a few cars closer on the residential streets, but none came near their location.

They packed up and hit the road. Cody had trouble getting up the embankment, so Luz took his pack up then came back for him. The road was as empty as the night before, but now there were points of light spread across the landscape on either side of the road ahead.

Once they saw headlights in the distance but the lights turned off the road before they had to react.

"If we keep acting guilty, someone is going to notice us," Cody observed.

"As beat up as you are, we are likely to get noticed anyway," Luz said.

"Even if they do notice us, it's not likely they even know or will know that Barnabas is dead for months," Cody said.

"You didn't hear those deputies," Luz said. "It was pretty clear they are looking for someone to blame for other crimes and who better than outsiders?"

"Educated outsiders might have friends who can do something. They know those kids you were talking about don't have any friends who can do anything. But suppose you are right. If they are looking for burglars, the worst thing we can do is keep moving at night," Cody said.

Luz considered this. "Maybe you're right. But I still don't want to leave any trace that we've been here. I don't want to present ID to anyone, or withdraw any money, nothing."

"I agree with that," Cody said.

"Should we stop?" Luz asked.

"How far is it to get through Placerville?"

"About five or six miles, seven would be better," Luz said.

Cody sighed. "That should be easy, but what did I manage yesterday, two miles?"

They looked at the map. "Two miles would put us right in the middle of Placerville," Luz said.

"We won't be camping in Placerville," Cody said.

"No," Luz agreed.

"Getting through Placerville isn't really enough anyway," Cody said. "I don't think we want to put our heads up until at least Folsom. Sacramento would be better."

"I don't think you can walk that far," Luz said.

Cody shook his head, "No, probably not."

"How much money do we have left?" Luz asked.

Cody looked in his wallet, "I've got $10."

Luz counted her money, "I've got $14. I think it will be enough. Let's get to the far side of Placerville. Tomorrow afternoon we'll see if we can buy something with wheels for you, then we'll stick to the side roads until we hit Folsom.

"I'm not sure I can make it that far," Cody said doubtfully.

"Give me your pack. As slow as we are going it won't be a problem," Luz said.

Cody, frowned and gave it to her.

They made better time then. By 1:00 in the morning Cody could go no further. They were about a quarter mile beyond the center of Placerville. Cody rested on the side of the road while Luz scouted a camping location. She came back without the packs, took Cody's crutch in her hand, and took its place under his right arm. They made it to a camp site along the banks of a creek to the left of the road. It was surrounded by trees and gave some privacy. They slept fitfully.

Cody shifted positions every few minutes trying to find one that worked for both his leg and his hand. Luz was worse. At first she simply didn't sleep. She looked up at the washed out sky as though she was trying to find some constellation. Later, as she started to drift into sleep she would jerk awake every few minutes. When she finally did sleep a little before sunrise, Cody woke to hear her crying in her sleep, her back turned to him. Cody said her name softly and her crying paused as she listened in her sleep. He turned sideways and reached out his good hand to her, carefully resting it on her upper arm. She reached up and took his hand, pulled it down in front of her, held onto it with both hands, and quieted into a deeper sleep.

They woke up three hours later, the sun shining on their faces and warming them all over. There were sounds of activity both on the highway and on Main Street which ran along the side of the creek now. If their presence was noticed, no one had bothered them.

Luz sat up, rubbed her eyes and looked around. There were three or four old fire pits, and enough trash to show this was a regular camping spot for travelers. She made something for both of them to eat. She was moving slower than usual but there was more life in her face than there had been for the last few days.

Cody was worse. He managed to sit up and eat. His leg was still tender to the touch and it seemed swollen.

"Maybe we should see the doctor here after all," Luz said.

Cody shook his head. "I can make it. Stick to the plan."

She let him go back to sleep and went into town with all their cash.

There was a small restaurant, a general store and a vehicle recharging station not far from their camp. Luz went to the window of the restaurant. A young woman about her age was working there.

"Hi, I'm Maria," Luz said. "I'm getting tired of hiking, do you know where I could find a bicycle for sale?"

"I'm Laura," the woman said. "You could try the bulletin board at the general store over there... If that doesn't work there is a bike shop down the street that way," she said pointing the way Luz had come. "You pass under the highway and it's about five hundred feet down on the right."

"Thanks," Luz said.

The bulletin board had the usual assortment of odd jobs, and odd people looking for jobs. It had a couch, and scooter for sale, but no bike. Luz fantasized about the scooter for a while but it was clearly out of their price range. She was about to go when the hair on the back of her neck stood up.

"Are you looking for work?" a familiar voice said.

She turned. A sheriff's deputy looked her up and down and smiled.

Luz turned pale and shook her head, "No, just traveling. I thought I'd see what was going on in town."

"See anything you like?" the deputy asked, leaning towards her a bit.

Luz's jaw tightened momentarily, then she smiled and said, "Nothing I think my husband would like."

The deputy nodded slightly, then shrugged and said, "He doesn't have to do everything with you."

Luz resisted the impulse to grab her knife. She forced a laugh and said, "Now deputy, some people might misunderstand something like that. You wouldn't want there to be any misunderstanding would you?"

The deputy nodded defeat, shook his head and said, "No ma'am." He took out a card and gave it to her. "If you need anything while you're in town, you give me a call."

"Thank you," Luz said, and put the card in her pocket.

The officer touched the brim of his hat and moved on.

Luz went into the general store and pretended to shop until his car left the parking lot and went east on Main Street.

When he was gone, she left, threw the card in the trash and walked back to camp. Cody was sleeping so she walked to the bike store. She found a used bike with coaster brakes, toe clips, and saddle packs for $18 and rode it back to camp.

Cody was awake and foraging through the pack for food. When he saw Luz come into camp with the bike, he lit up.

"This is going to be great!" he said.

Luz smiled, but it was a brief smile. "I'm glad you like it," she said, distracted.

Cody climbed on. Luz helped him adjust the seat. He clipped the foot of his bad leg in and pushed off with his good leg. He winced as he used his bad leg to help on the first revolution then used his good leg to finish the stroke. He came to an awkward stop. They practiced it again with Luz giving him a push start and he was able to ride in circles around the camp, then carefully time his stop to land on his good leg.

"This will work," he said enthusiastically.

They transferred the heavier contents of Luz's pack into the saddle bags, and the lighter items from Cody's pack into Luz's, then tied Cody's pack to the parcel rack on the back. It stuck out too far and looked funny, but it worked.

By 3:00 PM they were on the road. Luz was amused by Cody's enthusiasm for the bike, but there was also sadness in her face. They moved quicker with Cody on the bike. They covered four miles before exhaustion caught up with him around 5:00. Luz noticed how quickly his strength gave out but said nothing about it.

They set up camp in some trees just off the road. It was a clear evening, but Luz set up the tent anyway and put her jacket over his bedroll when he fell asleep. In the night he shivered even though it wasn't very cold.

In the morning, he moved slowly and wasn't hungry. His eyes were dull. Luz felt his forehead, he was very hot. She sat him down and pulled up his pant leg. His leg was swollen. She felt it and he clenched his teeth and moaned.

"This is really infected," she said. "I think we better drain it."

Cody looked at her, then nodded his head. She cleaned her knife, sharpened the point, held it over the open flame of their small fire until she was fairly certain it was clean, then let it cool.

"Ready?" she asked.

Cody looked away and said, "Just do it."

Luz cut through the bottom two stitches she had made before in the back of his leg, then pushed the point of the blade in a quarter of an inch. White puss and a clear fluid mixed with traces of blood came flooding out of the hole. Cody seemed to relax slightly.

"Feel better?" Luz asked.

Cody nodded.

"Hold on, this is going to hurt," Luz said then she squeezed his calf gently and more puss came out. She had him lie down on his face. She cleaned the wound, then poured the last of the alcohol into it. Cody started to kick, but restrained himself. When it stopped burning she had him sit up again and let it drain. When they were done, she put a stitch in just above the hole she had made to keep the other stitches from pulling loose, then put a bandage over the hole and pulled his pant leg down.

Cody took their last two aspirins, then packed his bedroll. When they were packed, Luz insisted that he drink some water and eat a few crackers.

The road was flat and straight for the first mile. A few farm trucks passed them on their way to Sacramento. Luz considered flagging one of them down. She was pretty sure they'd give an injured person a ride, but she knew Cody wouldn't like it. "Stick to the plan," he'd say. Besides, she wasn't sure what kind of questions would be asked.

Cody was doing better. After the first mile the road started dropping elevation. Luz couldn't keep up with the bike, even though Cody was riding the brake pretty hard. They fell into a pattern where Cody would get 100 feet ahead, stop and wait for her. She caught him smirking a few times, but after a while he said, "Why don't you take the bike for the next section. I bet I could walk a hundred feet."

Luz smiled but said, "Not with this pack you couldn't."

After an hour and a half the road started to level out again. It was still slightly downhill, so Cody didn't have to peddle much and Luz could keep up.

Cody looked thoughtful. "Luz, do you still have nightmares?"

Luz nodded and said, "But they don't last all night anymore. Do you?"

"Yes, but I think yours are worse," Cody said.

Luz didn't say anything for a long time. Then said, "Sometimes when I'm waking up I can't move and I think it's all happening again and I want to scream but I can't. But then I wake up the rest of the way and the relief makes me almost happy."

Cody said, "Sometimes he's hurting my leg again, and sometimes I see the surprise on his face when I shot him, but most of the time I'm fighting him. Sometimes I'm dreaming with my eyes open and I see the tent or the trees that are really around us and suddenly he's standing there in the dark and I have to fight, but I have this busted hand and bad leg and he's got that look on his face..."

"Stop!" Luz said, pale.

"I'm sorry," Cody said.

Luz shook her head. "It's OK... but... I can't, I just can't..."

Cody didn't know what to say.

Luz softened. "I'm sorry. You got the worst of it. He actually hurt you. He just almost hurt me."

"I think he hurt you more," Cody said. "Guys fight. Sometimes it gets pretty bad and people get hurt, but it's not as personal, and we kind of grow up with some idea of what to do with it. What he tried to do to you..."

They continued in silence for a few minutes, then Cody said, "What I can't figure out is why he didn't kill me instead of staking me to the floor. At first I thought he just didn't want to be a murderer, but he couldn't really have let me go after that."

Luz looked at him, deciding something.

"What is it?" Cody prodded.

Luz looked at him a little longer then said, "I don't think he was done with you. Do you remember those squirrels we let loose? Did you notice their feet?" Luz asked.

"No."

"Their toes were cut off," Luz said. "But even before I saw that. When I was lying on that bed listening to him drag you away, I knew he wasn't done with you. My knife was two inches from my hand, Cody. Two inches! And I couldn't reach it." Luz was shaking by the time she stopped talking.

After an hour the landscape opened into cattle country, but Cody wasn't interested. He was fading. They pushed on another fifteen minutes, but he was stopping a lot and Luz had to steady his bike a couple of times.

They camped under an ancient oak and Luz reviewed the map.

"How far did we make it today?" Cody asked.

"About 10 miles," Luz said, lifting her eyebrows.

Cody laughed, "That's pretty good."

They ate and Cody was asleep before the sun went down. Luz cleaned up dinner and sat outside the tent. The evening was warmer here, still pleasant at sun down. She heared cows in the distance.

The first stars came out and she thought of the last lesson with Jonas about stars. She looked at them and wondered what they should be telling her now, but they didn't tell her anything. At least not until she was in her bed roll, listening to Cody breathe and sliding into sleep. Then she knew what they were telling her, that they were very old and had seen it all before and that every moment good or bad passes away and finds its place in our story, and in the quiet place just before un-consciousness she heard them whisper that she was as old as they and would go on and on.

That night she dreamed of being in school, but it looked different. She was standing in front of the students telling them a story they thought was important, but she couldn't quite hear the words she was saying and then she paused and looked to her left and Cody was stand-ing there, older, waiting for his turn to speak. Only later did she realize she hadn't dreamed of Barnabas at all.

They slept until after 9:00 AM. Cody seemed a little better. They packed up camp and while Luz was loading her pack, she came across the bag of bloody clothes. She pulled it out and set it down softly on the ground in front of her.

Cody noticed what she was doing and stood beside her.

"I forgot that was there," he said.

"Me too," Luz said evenly.

"No reason to keep carrying them," Cody said.

They built a fire ring and Cody started a fire on the first try. When it was hot enough they threw the bag in and watched it burn, the paper flashing away quickly, and the clothes wriggling then curling in on themselves, before burning feebly. Cody and Luz stood unblinking until the clothes were entirely consumed.

When it was over, Cody raked out the coals to let them cool, and Luz went to get his bike. After a minute she came back.

"Cody, where did we leave the bike?"

"Leaning against the tree," he said.

They looked at the spot, but all they saw was his pack lying on the ground.

Eight

Luz was angry. Cody wanted to be angry, but he didn't have the energy.

Luz ranted for a while. When she had finished, Cody said, "At least they left the pack."

"That's actually worse, Cody. You can't carry it!"

Cody accepted that. "Let's just leave it here." He stood up, adjusted his crutch and waited.

Luz quieted, shouldered her pack and they began walking.

Cody managed a pretty fast pace, but Luz knew his face well enough to know he was in pain.

When they stopped for lunch she noticed his hand was bruised where it held the crutch. She took his hand, turned it palm side up and ran her fingers lightly over the bruised place, applying no pressure. He closed his eyes.

They moved on. The afternoon turned uncomfortably warm. They slowed their pace. By 3:00 PM Cody couldn't go on. They made camp in the yard of a ruined church and Cody crashed in his bedroll the minute Luz unrolled it for him. She made him drink water, but his eyes were dull again.

She ate cold food straight from the container and crawled into her own bedroll. Just after dark she woke up. Cody was shivering and muttering. She felt his forehead, it was hotter than she had ever felt it and sweaty.

"Cody, how's your leg?" she asked.

He didn't answer.

"Cody wake up."

"I'm tired, Luz," he mumbled.

She cranked up a flashlight and pulled his leg out of the bed roll.

Cody swore then said, "I'm sorry Luz... I'm sorry I said that... I shouldn't have said that... I'm sorry."

"It's OK Cody," Luz said and looked at the leg. It looked more bruised than swollen. She pulled off the bandage. The wound had crusted over.

"Cody, I'm going to drain your wound again. Do you understand?"

"OK."

Luz cleaned the knife and lightly punctured the wound again. Thick puss ran out, but not as much as it seemed like there should be. Cody didn't seem to get much relief from it. She cleaned the wound as best she could and re-bandaged it. She thought for a minute then said, "Come on Cody, we have to go."

"OK," he said, but just sat there.

She got dressed for the road, boots, field jacket, knife in its sheath. She fished her purse out of the pack and strapped it across her shoulders. She helped Cody get dressed and made sure he had his wallet, then she got him out of the tent and onto his good foot. She positioned herself under his right arm and started walking. At first Cody resisted.

"Come on," she said, "We've got to get you to a doctor."

He seemed to understand and they made slow but steady progress to the road. She kept an ear open for any sounds of traffic. She watched for any friendly light, but saw none. The road was theirs alone. They limped along for half an hour. The night was cool. The cricket and frog songs were over but the birds had not begun to sing. Only small things moving in the bushes kept them company. Luz struggled more with Cody's weight. Normally he moved with such agility and confidence that it masked his true mass, but now that she was carrying more of it, it was more obvious. She looked at the stars and said, "I know we don't live very long and a decade here or there probably means nothing to you, but it means something to us. Please don't let him die."

"I'm sorry," Cody said.

"What are you sorry for?" Luz asked.

"I'm sorry. I had to do it. He was going to hurt her. I couldn't let him. You know I couldn't let him," Cody mumbled.

"I know," Luz said.

Ten minutes later she saw some lights to the right of the road and signs of recent activity. As she got closer she saw the backs of stores. She paused, made a decision and led Cody off the highway through the trees and into the parking lot. Her muscles screamed getting him over the little rise and rough terrain. She wanted to put him down, rest, but she wasn't sure she could get him up again.

There was no one in the parking lot. The stores were closed, but she reasoned, at least people came there. They pressed on, more from inertia than knowing where to go, and came to another broad road. It looked like there were more people to the right, so she started steering Cody to the right, but he resisted.

"Come on Cody. We're near help now. Let's walk just a little further."

He still resisted.

"Cody! Come on!" Luz insisted.

"That's the wrong way," Cody said.

"You don't even know where you are," Luz said.

Cody wouldn't move. Luz looked like she might cry for a second, but then shook her head and said, "OK Cody, we'll go the other way."

They walked the other way and Cody cooperated. After five minutes they entered the darkness of trees arching over the old road. The green eyes of a house cat watched them from under a bush. They emerged again to open sky. The house cat followed them. A cluster of newer small buildings pushed up against the sidewalk to the right of the road and beyond that was a broad intersection. Luz got Cody to the corner of the two streets and stood, breathing heavy and trying to decide which way to go. She looked down, catching her breath. She bent forward slightly trying to shift the strain on her back and noticed narrow railroad tracks at her feet. She studied them. They were polished and clean, not rusty. She looked up and down the tracks. To her right she saw a covered area with benches and an illuminated sign.

They limped towards the benches. When they were half way there she could read the sign. "Next train - Downtown -10 minutes." She hurried Cody, then laid him on a bench. She used their remaining cash to buy tickets, and prodded him to stand up. In the distance she heard the train coming.

Cody whispered, "I will. I will."

The train stopped. Luz struggled to get Cody up the steps then they fell into the nearest seats.

Luz tried to remain alert. For the first twenty minutes she saw nothing that looked like a hospital or a doctor's office. A hint of gray light started to light one end of the sky. She fell asleep briefly, then woke up when the train stopped. An old woman was looking at them.

"Is he OK?" she asked Luz.

"No. I need to get him to a doctor. Do you know where we should get off?" Luz asked.

"39th street," the woman said. "It's the stop after next."

When the stop came the old woman helped Luz get Cody off the train, took them to a pay phone and waited with them for the ambulance.

"What happened to him?" the old woman asked.

Luz teared up and when she had control of herself said, "We were running through a field and there was an old steel fence post bent over in the grass. He impaled his leg on it, and it's gotten infected.

Luz had trouble looking at the woman after that. The old woman hugged her. Luz thanked her and climbed into the ambulance after they loaded Cody. She sat in the front because they wouldn't let her ride in back. She watched the tree branches and the houses go by her window and wished she could have told the old woman the truth both because she deserved the truth and so she could tell her what kind of man Cody was. She closed her eyes.

She followed Cody into the Emergency Room and then they took him away from her. She tried to go with him, but they steered her to registration instead. They asked her questions, she gave them the same story she'd given the old woman, only this time she didn't mind lying because she didn't like these people. She didn't like people who would take him away.

After a few minutes they realized she was too tired to deal with them and let her go. They gave her the number of a hotel a mile away with a shuttle and told her they would call her, but she curled up in a chair in the ER, and fell asleep.

She opened her eyes a while later. The light coming through the doors said around an hour had passed. She found a nurse and asked about Cody. They gave her a room number on the third floor.

When she found him he was breathing more normally, but he was very cool to the touch and perspiring. He had an IV in his arm. She lifted up the blanket and saw they had re-bandaged his leg.

A nurse saw what she was doing, "Miss, you can't do that."

A doctor standing by the nurses' station looked up to see what was happening and waved the nurse off.

He looked at a paper in his hand then went into the room.

"Are you Luz Ochoa?" he asked.

Luz nodded.

"I'm Dr. Osbourne," he said. "Was that your stitching we took apart?"

"Yeah," Luz said.

"That was pretty good stitching. You even left a place for it to drain."

"Yeah but he got sick anyway," Luz said, conflicted.

"Sometimes it just happens. We cleaned the wound out but we didn't find any debris. It looks like you gave him excellent field care."

"Is he going to be OK?"

The doctor knit his brow together, "Well, he's got severe sepsis. There's a possibility his kidneys have shut down, but we won't know for at least an hour. We've started him on anti-biotics. He's young and strong. Personally I think he has a good chance. He's going to need you when he wakes up, but that won't be for at least a few hours. Why don't you go get some rest so you'll be ready."

"What if he gets worse?"

"We'll call you," the doctor said.

Luz didn't answer.

"If you need me, the nurse knows how to contact me," the doctor said, and left the room.

Luz pulled her chair closer to the bed and rested her head next to Cody. She held his good hand. After a while the nurse came in and said, "Visiting time is over. He needs his rest. You can come back in the afternoon."

"He's resting just fine with me here," Luz said.

"Unless you're family, those are the rules," the nurse said firmly.

"I'm as close as he has here," Luz insisted.

The nurse sat down across from her and said, "I know you've been taking care of him. The truth is we're worried about you. We will give him excellent care, but if you don't take care of yourself at least a little, you will get sick and then you won't be able to help him at all."

She got into the hotel shuttle, sat down and woke up when they opened the door for her at the hotel. She took a shower, but when she got out she didn't have any clean clothes. She puzzled over what to do for a minute and then just crawled into bed and slept. She slept hard without remembering her dreams. When she woke she lay in bed staring at the phone. It didn't ring. She picked it up and called home.

Her father answered the phone and she blurted out, "Papa it's me, Cody got stabbed... We're telling people it was an accident but it wasn't. He got stabbed and it got infected and I don't know if he's going to live."

"Slow down, Luz. Are you OK?"

"Yes. Mostly. I'm fine, but Cody's not."

"Where is he?"

"He's in the hospital in Sacramento, but you can't tell anybody it wasn't an accident, promise me you won't tell anyone."

"Luz. Calm down. We have time to sort things out. What does the doctor say about Cody?"

Luz repeated what the doctor had said.

"Where was he stabbed?"

"In the leg, below the knee," she reported.

"Luz, I need to know. Did you stab him?"

"No Papa, of course not. Why would I ever stab Cody? I could never, never..." Luz couldn't finish because she was crying.

Her father waited and said, "I'm sorry, Luz. It's just with all the trouble the last few months I had to know. I think he's going to be fine. The Sheltons have always been tough. I'll let everyone here know what's going on, and we'll put some more money in your account. Get whatever you need. Keep us up to date. I love you."

"I love you too, Papa," Luz said.

Luz gave him the contact information for the hospital to pass on to the Sheltons, then added, "Papa, can you have the Sheltons tell the hospital to treat me as family. They won't let me stay with him all the time and I can't take that."

"I will."

"Thank you, Papa." Luz hung up the phone.

She called the hospital and got an update. Cody still wasn't awake, but he was urinating so that was a positive sign.

She looked at her filthy clothes, put them on, went downstairs to the restaurant and ate an early dinner. She went across the street, bought a whole new outfit including underwear, then did the same for Cody so he'd have something to wear when he got out of the hospital. She went upstairs, showered again, and changed into her new outfit.

The shuttle took her back to the hospital. This time they didn't give her any trouble. After a couple of hours she fell asleep again with her head resting on his bed. She woke up because something was touching her hair. No, not touching, stroking it. She looked up. Cody was looking at her. She grabbed his hand and held it to her cheek, smiling. He smiled back, then closed his eyes and fell asleep again.

In the morning he was out of danger. They had breakfast together in his room. They were both tired. They didn't say much, just sat together. In the afternoon she ventured out to find some decent food she could smuggle back into the hospital for them. She stood in line at a fast food place like a normal person; got her food like a normal person;

walked back to the hospital like a normal person. It was all too much normal for a person like her.

She told Cody about it while he ate and they laughed. Then she told him about how worried she'd been and he looked at her thoughtfully.

"I wish I'd said something so you wouldn't worry," he said.

"What could you have said? Not even the doctors knew you'd be OK until this morning," Luz said.

"I saw Jonas," Cody said. "...at the train station."

Luz looked at him.

"He said we'd be OK, and he was sorry for what his brother did, and to tell you he's proud of you."

Luz asked looked him, worried.

"I'm OK," he said. "I'm really OK," he said again, and laughed softly.

Nine

They kept Cody in the hospital for a week. He talked with his family several times. They were relieved to hear him sounding well. Everyone in town insisted they take the train to Monterey and come back to Farallon by boat. As the time got closer for Cody to be released neither of them felt right about it. Jonas' instructions had been clear. They were to go overland and come back the same way.

"Surely Jonas didn't mean for you to do this injured!" Cody's father said.

Still they resisted.

When they couldn't be budged, Cody's father said, "Jonas didn't say when you had to start back. If you're going to do this we have some business in town you can take care of while your leg heals. You can be our agent."

The nurse taught him to change his own dressings, gave him a bunch of pills, got him a local doctor to check in with once a week, and discharged him from the hospital. Cody wore the clothes Luz bought for him.

"These fit." Cody observed surprised. "How did you know my size?"

Luz shook her head.

Cody moved into the room next to Luz's in the hotel for the first few days. After that they moved to a cheaper place at the Cattlemen's Association downtown. Since she was there, Luz decided to serve as an agent for the growers, hand picking new seed varieties for next season's planting. Errol sent word that Cody should buy two horses and two male and six female Hereford calves to bring home. When Cody saw the price of the horses, he called his father back and told him he would be perfectly capable of walking in a few weeks, but Errol insisted the horses would be needed for the expanded herd.

After three weeks, Cody's leg was good enough that he could join Luz in the pasture behind the stables during her riding practice. He watched her handle her horse for an hour and then walked with her to the stables.

"You're really good with your horse," Cody said.

"Thanks," she said.

"No. I mean it. I think you must be a natural horse woman."

By the fifth week he joined her for some gentle riding each day.

In the evenings, they studied to see if there was a way to make back the cost of the horses. Towards the end of the fifth week Cody asked, "What do you remember about the commodities market?"

"Just that it's a place where current and future harvests can be bought and sold, and that it helps stabilize prices and supply levels," Luz recalled.

"Turns out the cattlemen have a seat on the exchange," Cody said mysteriously.

"And..." Luz prompted.

"...And the guy next door to me is the guy who makes the trades for the cattlemen, right here in this building."

"So..."

"So, he's going to let us go to work with him and watch," Cody said raising his eyebrows.

"When?" Luz asked.

"Tomorrow. He'll teach us the basics, but we can't interrupt him too much," Cody said.

"I'm there," Luz said.

In the morning they met at Cody's room and waited until his neighbor, Tim, came out then followed him to a room on the first floor. They watched him trade all morning. At intervals and when things were slow Tim would explain what he was doing and what he was watching for. In the afternoon he set up a couple of mock trading accounts running against real data and let them practice. Luz concentrated on crops she knew best, mostly things they grew at home. She did OK, coming out ahead about as often as she lost money. Later in the day she began to explore crops she was unfamiliar with. She sorted the display by most to least expensive ground crops and discovered several that were getting outrageous prices. Cody seemed to have a knack for trading. By the time they had been practicing two hours he was up $10,000 in paper money. When Tim saw it he was impressed.

"Do you actually know what you're doing, or did you just get lucky?" Tim asked.

"Yes," Cody said.

"Have you got any money?" Tim asked.

Cody looked at Luz then said, "We've got about $300."

"I'm about done for the day. If you want to try trading with real money, I can let you do it on my account, but once your losses get to $300 I'm going to step in and liquidate whatever position you have. That will make it harder to make money, and you could easily lose everything you put in, but I'm game if you are," Tim said.

"What do you think?" Cody said looking at Luz.

"I think that if you lose we're going to get sick of eating beans and rice long before we get it paid back. Do you think you will lose?"

"Maybe," Cody said.

"I don't think you will," Luz said. "Just do it."

Cody started with the smallest contract he could. It lost money immediately and he almost sold it to start over, but just as he was about to, the price leveled out. He waited. It moved along sideways for twenty minutes then moved up slightly just enough to get back to break even. He waited. It dipped again, then came back up to break even, then shot up 20% and Cody sold it. He lost money on the next contract, but then the whole market seemed to come alive and he made money on the next four trades. During the next lull he took stock of his situation. He decided to switch to a different commodity and he bought a larger contract on the next up swing. It rose 10% then started falling. He sold as fast as he could and lost 4% only to watch the commodity rally.

"I should have stayed in!" he said mildly disappointed in himself.

On the next round he used a smaller contract. It too rose then fell abrudptly. He decided to ride it out. After 15 minutes all of their gains for the night had been erased and they were eating into their $300.

"I should have gotten out!" he said seriously disappointed.

Just as Tim was preparing to step in, it turned around and rallied again. By the time Cody sold they were slightly ahead of where they had been before the trade. He made two more trades before turning to Tim and saying, "I think I better stop. Thank you so much." Cody's shirt was soaked with perspiration.

Tim wired their earnings to Errol's account.

They took Tim out to dinner, and talked about farming and ranching and markets.

Cody walked Luz back to her room.

"We made back the money we spent on the horses," Cody said looking at Luz.

"I thought you would," Luz said.

When they reached her door she went in, and Cody found himself standing awkwardly by it for a second before going back to his own room.

In the morning they reviewed what had happened over breakfast.

"There's money to be made in the market," Cody observed.

"That's for sure," Luz said, "but I noticed something else. The crops we grow are selling for low prices compared to other crops. I wrote down the highest priced ones and assuming they don't cost a lot more to raise, we might be able to sell them for a profit even with our shipping costs."

Cody listened with interest. "We should check and make sure that those prices aren't just a blip."

"Yeah, and we have to see if we can grow them at all and what it takes to grow them," Luz added.

"OK, I'll get the market data and you check out the crops themselves," Cody suggested.

By evening Luz had identified three crops she thought they could grow at a profit and Cody had confirmed the prices Luz had seen were fairly normal.

"Not only that," Cody said, "I got a copy of the prices we've been getting for our leather, meat, cheese, and wool, and compared them to the market prices the same days. It turns out that our agent in Monterey has been taking an eight percent spread on our transactions. A membership in the Cattlemen's Association plus trading commissions would still only work out to about four percent of our transactions, so we could improve things four percent by dumping our agent."

The next day they switched places and went over each other's notes to make sure the conclusions were sound. Then they forwarded the information home to the council.

By the beginning of November, Cody was strong enough and Luz experienced enough with horses to start the trip back to Farallon.

They left early on a late fall morning with a blue sky reaching all the way to space. As the sun got higher a golden light played over the brown fields. The cattle moved compliantly. The air was still.

Cody felt himself relax into the saddle. The tension and effort and fears of the preceding weeks melted and almost unreasonably went away.

Luz seemed to feel it too. She moved effortlessly with the horse, smiling slightly, and closing her eyes at intervals.

In the afternoon a light wind came up from the south and clouds moved in. The cattle became restless.

They made camp a little short of Dixon. Cody taught Luz to hobble the calves and horses without getting kicked in the face then left to find the local farmer and get his permission for the cattle to graze. The weather grew worse. Cody was gone longer than expected, and Luz watched for him.

With the horses they could carry slightly more gear, so they'd replaced the tiny tent they lost in Folsom with a larger one. They bedded down.

The wind grew stronger and in the middle of the night there was thunder, lightning and heavy rain. The tent held. Luz curled up next to Cody. He rested his hand on her arm and she took it and pulled it close, but sometime in the night, when the rain had passed, she pulled away.

The next day was fair. They found the cattle and horses huddled under an oak and freed them from their hobbles. They were out a half hour after the farmers were in the fields. Luz waved to them as they rode past, and those that saw waved back without knowing why.

At mid-day, the country widened into grazing land and they took the calves off the road, hobbled them with the horses and let them graze while they leaned against a tree, ate their own lunch and watched puffy white clouds drift across the deep blue sky.

Cody had Luz take the lead with the cattle in the afternoon. The cattle were thirsty and stopped at every creek along the way. At one particular creek several of the calves got bogged down in a mire. They bawled for help even while resisting every effort to help them. Luz and Cody got down into the mud together and managed to pull several of them out, but the last one was stuck so fast they had to get a rope and use a horse to pull it out.

"Be careful," Luz said as Cody pulled with the horse.

Once free, the calves, only slightly wiser, sunned themselves before finding a tree to hide under while Luz and Cody scraped the mud off themselves in the stream.

They pushed past the small farms and ranches on the edge of the first dead city and made camp next to a small lake an hour before sunset. The calves drank all they wanted and lay down in a bunch under some trees.

They set up camp then watched the sky turn iridescent, before starting a fire. After dinner they enjoyed the luxury of slow easy conversation.

The next day was simpler and they reached Napa with two hours of light left and camped. During the night, the calves and horses got spooked. Luz and Cody got their rifles and checked on them. They didn't see anything, but the hair on their arms raised and they could feel something watching them. They moved the herd into camp, built up the fire and spent the night sitting next to it, rifles ready, talking at intervals.

They tried to sleep in the next morning, but couldn't. They hit the trail only an hour later than usual. The day was drudgery. The calves were uncooperative. Luz was cranky. But in the afternoon they stopped at "their" orange tree behind the houses and were rewarded with sweet ripe oranges.

They camped at the confluence of the Napa and San Pablo as before. The dead city around them was more familiar than the first time, but also heavier now that they had experienced a living city.

"What do you think it was like to live here?" Luz asked.

"It's a good climate. It should have been nice, but it looks like it was even more crowded than Sacramento is," Cody speculated.

"I wonder if they all died here or if some of them made it out?" Luz mused.

Cody shrugged. "It didn't burn or blow up, so I guess they had a chance."

"When we talked about those days in school I thought of destroyed cities, but the tools in the shed and the old toys in the yards belonged to individuals like you and me," Luz reflected.

"Everyone dies eventually," Cody said softly.

Luz nodded, "Yes, but I'm glad we get a little more time. I hope some of them had more time, too."

Cody agreed.

They kept the animals in camp again and went to bed early.

The following day they dropped deeper in the river valley and deliberately forgot about the ruins. The weather was cooler so they pushed the cattle a little harder and camped in the golden gate valley that night.

In the morning they got clear of the old cities and suddenly didn't feel in such a hurry.

"Are you looking forward to getting home?" Cody asked.

"Yes," Luz said unconvincingly.

Cody laughed.

"No. I really am," Luz tried again. "I'll be glad to see everyone."

"Let's not go back to how we were," Cody said, suddenly serious.

Luz shook her head, "No, let's keep who we are now."

"If I start acting weird, tell me," Cody said.

"You do the same for me," Luz said.

They traveled on silently for a while, thinking. Then Cody said, "Let's promise to spend time together away from everyone else at least every few days. That way we won't forget."

Luz nodded, "I promise," she said.

"I promise, too," Cody said.

The cattle had gotten disorderly while they talked. Luz struck out on her own and quickly got them back in line while Cody watched, smiling.

Then he laughed.

"What?" Luz said, "I did a good job!"

"You did a great job!" Cody said. "I was just picturing people's faces in town if they saw you doing that. None of them know you can even ride, let alone drive cattle."

They could have made it home that night, but they camped just beyond the sand dunes anyway and sat looking at the big moon over the dunes.

In the morning they packed up for the last time and moved towards town. After an hour they saw kids playing on the outskirts of town. As soon as they saw Cody and Luz they ran back to town to tell everyone.

Luz and Cody looked at each other.

Luz set her hat more firmly on her head and said, "I'll bring them in."

Cody nodded and hung back slightly.

Luz got the cattle in order. When they reached the outskirts of town she made a show of driving and cutting them until she had them in a tight group in the middle of the town square. Excited kids ran or road bicycles alongside as much as they could. Adults stopped what they were doing and tried to make out who was invading their town.

Luz took her hat off, let her hair fly and announced, "We're home!"

Epilogue

Luz and Cody drifted from one thing to another. They were treated like heroes one day, and expected to do chores the next.

They disappeared together regularly and everyone in town assumed they would get married, but Cody didn't propose and Luz didn't want him to.

One day they roamed along the sea shore. When they were done playing with the breakers they stretched out under a tree overlooking the sea.

After a moment she said, "Do you ever wish we hadn't come back?"

"Every day," Cody said.

"Then we should go," she said.

They saved money, applied for school, and six months later they were on the docks waiting for Jennifer to take them to Monterey. From there they caught a train to Kansas City and as the world rolled by they began to comprehend its size.

They studied and worked and dated other people, but the only constant was each other.

One night, after an outing, she closed the door and looked at herself in the mirror. Her face had become more graceful in the last year. The make-up and earrings that made her look like she was trying too hard before, now fell into the background only accenting her.

She was going to bed when she heard music outside. On the third song she realized they were all favorites of hers. She went to the window. Six men playing instruments beneath her window and beyond them a seventh stood in the shadows. She opened the window a crack but stayed hidden behind the sheer curtain, watching. After three more songs, Cody stepped into the moonlight, thanked the men, and they left.

A cool breeze rustled the leaves, then quieted.

"Luz, will you marry me?"

Luz watched him. She knew her answer, but giving it would make the moment pass.

They married in the fall. The morning sun sliced through the air making everything brilliant, the brightness contrasting with a sky so dark blue Luz half expected to see stars popping through.

Their first baby girl, Atalia, was born in late May.

Graduation came and the students scattered.

Luz, Cody, and Atalia followed jobs to Iowa, Colorado and then New Mexico.

Just short of their third anniversary Atalia's little brother, Emer, was born, and later, a little sister named Ruth.

And then as though it just happened, they were on the dock in Farallon.

The council appointed Luz and Cody co-teachers at the school on the mountain. They chose their first class.

They started a homestead on property straddling farm and range land, had more children, and watched them grow.

Class succeeded class. One harvest succeeded another.

Grandchildren came and Luz and Cody began to feel the effects of gravity.

Some days were good, others hard. On the hardest nights, Luz would rub Cody's shin scar with her toes, and hold him tight.

The world toiled on, spinning and swinging in circles while the people on its face and in one small town, grew up, burned bright, and softened into something stronger, and the stars patiently waited.

###

Afterword

BOHEMIA

Bohemia is a work of fiction that tightly follows the real life of Nora May French, a poet and associate of prominent members of the Bohemian club in San Francisco just after the great earthquake.

Nora May said, "I have an idea that all sensible people will be damned," at the Coppa. She also may have said, "I need to polish some silver," when she bought cyanide from a chemist in Carmel. Cyanide was used to polish silver, but this may also have been a reference to polishing George Sterling by killing herself in his house. All the rest of the dialogue is my invention, though I have woven language and imagery from Nora May's poetry into the story.

The story implies Nora wanted to marry Harry. The words and images used to imply that are from a poem she wrote while they were together for the wedding of a mutual friend, but whether or not she wanted to marry is conjecture.

There is no record of the real Nora May French having an abortion or even being pregnant. However, in George Sterling's poem to her he calls her "Evadne" who was the daughter of Poseidon, had a child by Apollo and left that child to die in the woods.

Nora was almost certainly dead before the doctor arrived and there was probably no attempt to save her life.

The poem read at her funeral in this story was written about her and to her by George Sterling after her death. It probably wasn't read at her funeral.

There really was a fight among her lovers about who should scatter her ashes, but who reached for the urn and who finally scattered the ashes is conjecture. One source says it was George Sterling.

The "Prude" Mary Austin was anything but. She was an actress who put her career first and her marriage second. Her husband did not share her passion for acting and although he tried to be supportive eventually came to feel abandoned during her long absences and cheated on her, ultimately choosing his mistress over her.

After her divorce she had a series of affairs and one great tragic love (as she saw it) that ended in that man also choosing another lover over her when she insisted that her career came first. She eventually re-married but her new husband also accused her of abandonment. She was instrumental in getting Nora May noticed by the poets of San Francisco.

Both Mary Austen and Jack London were accepted members of the group at Carmel. They each criticized the extreme promiscuity among the bohemians and predicted ruin would come of it. George and Carrie Sterling divorced. Both Carrie and George later committed suicide by cyanide, decades apart. Allen Hiley's marriage also collapsed. James (Jimmie) Hopper's marriage survived.

Several of the bohemians gained regional prominence as writers. George Sterling has a park named after him in San Francisco. Only Jack London achieved national recognition. The work of the others is largely forgotten and they are remembered mostly for their "free-spiritedness."

AMAZONIA

All of the people exhibited in the "museum" that Angela drags Alex to, including Mary Ellen Pleasant, are real people mostly from various radical feminist movements in the 19th and 20th centuries. Between them, they have attempted, advocated for, applauded, or done most of the things Angela does in this story.

The universe used for Amazonia borrows from Orson Scott Cards "Folk of the Fringe" universe but with significant alterations.

FARALLON

In its original conception the town of Farallon was much more tribal and the Jonas character was more of a chief like Ish at the end of George Stewart's "Earth abides."

About the Author

Adam Kelley lives in the Sierra Nevada foothills of Northern California with his wife of 30 years, Alta. They have four children. He has traveled widely in the U.S., Canada, and Mexico, including an 18 month stay in Central Mexico as a missionary. If he is not working or writing, Adam likes to do home improvement, hike, explore new places, scuba dive, and sleep. He likes dark chocolate and doesn't care for broccoli or asparagus.

Other Books by This Author

RAIN

The story of young people during a time of great upheaval on a mostly terraformed Mars.
Published 2015.

HALF LIGHT

A collection of short stories arranged in a narrative arc.
Published 2020.

Connect with Adam Kelley

I hope you enjoyed my book.

You can review the book on your favorite book retail site and on goodreads.com.

If you'd like to comment or ask a question about the book you can send an email to:
TTBTB@quailsong.com

For general updates on what I'm up to, visit my website:
https://quailsong.com/adam.html